TAKING IT EASY

BOYS OF THE BIG EASY BOOK TWO

ERIN NICHOLAS

ISBN: 978-0-9998907-3-8

Editor: Lindsey Faber

Copy edits: Nanette Sipe

Cover design by Angela Waters

Cover photography Wander Aguiar

To Shannon,

*for choking down the hurricanes and
touching the alligators.
Best research trip ever.*

————

Acknowledgements

*I also want to thank several military wives (and their husbands!) for
their input on aspects of the story!*

*Emily Chuma, Mr. and Mrs. Griebe, Tiffany Franks, Heather D., and
Kristi S.*

*Thank you for your help and for your service to our country. You have
all my respect and my sincere gratitude!*

1

"I'm going to kill you."

Those were absolutely not the words that Logan Trahan had been expecting to hear when Dana Doucet pushed him into his office, shut the door, and backed him up against it. *Take off your pants. I need you. I haven't been able to stop thinking about you. Fuck me. Now.* All of those had been possibilities.

"Well, I—"

"You had *one* job." Her cheeks were pink and her green eyes were flashing.

And Logan realized she really was pissed. And that if he kissed her right now, it wouldn't help.

But he still wanted to.

"What did I do?"

"You got me pregnant."

Okay, *those* were absolutely not the words that Logan had been expecting to hear from Dana Doucet. Ever.

"*What*?"

Dana let out a long breath and paced to the other side of the office. "I'm pregnant."

Holy...

She spun back to face him. "I can't believe you tried to get me to go out with you for *nine months*, and I finally give in—*once*—and now I've got another nine months of not being able to avoid you."

That was *not* funny. But Logan felt his mouth curl anyway. "I do make an impression."

Dana's mouth dropped open. Literally. She stared at him and Logan glanced around, checking for things that she could use as a weapon. Unfortunately, there were several pens, a stapler, and a fork all within her reach.

He put his hands up, the sign of surrender. "Okay, I'm sorry. That was..."

"An asshole thing to say."

"Yes."

"Dammit, Logan!" she suddenly exclaimed. "All you had to do was put the condom on correctly. That's it. Something you've—allegedly—done dozens of times. I was handling everything else."

"*Hey*," he said, breaking into her rant. "I've done that *hundreds* of times."

And right before his eyes, he watched one of the most beautiful women he'd ever met morph into a murderous ball of fury.

She came at him with her fist back, hell-fire in her eyes, and he almost didn't grab her in time to prevent her from breaking his nose.

His fingers circled her tiny wrist and he pulled her up against him, their mouths barely an inch apart. "And by the way," he said, low and gruff, "I was *handling* a lot more than the condom."

"Well, apparently, you're not very good at multitasking," she told him.

She was still clearly pissed, but her voice had a breathlessness to it now that made Logan feel a surge of male satisfaction. Even when she was pissed off at him, he affected her.

Not that he was going to point that out to her. Just like he wasn't going to mention how fucking hot she was when she was all riled up like this.

"I think making you come with my fingers while sucking on your nipples as I planned the next four ways I was going to fuck you could count as multitasking."

He was aware that he was being kind of a jerk, but her little intake of air and the way her pupils dilated made him think nothing but *yes*. This woman was way too uptight. Way too stressed. And yet, he'd wanted her since the first time he'd met her. Men didn't talk to her the way he did. Men didn't pursue her the way he had. Most egos probably couldn't handle her I'm-way-better-than-you attitude. Then again, most egos wouldn't see that she was full of shit and was actually a little wounded and slightly scared and a lot amazing.

She'd lost her army sergeant husband, Chad Doucet, two years ago in the Middle East and was raising her two girls alone now. She was protective of them and of her heart. Understandably. But even with that, Logan couldn't leave her alone. If she'd *really* wanted him to, he would have, of course. He didn't force women to spend time with him. He didn't need to, for one thing. For another, as the co-owner of Trahan's Tavern, he'd stepped in too many times when a guy couldn't take no for an answer to ever *be* that guy.

But no, Dana Doucet didn't want him to leave her alone. She just wanted him to work for it. To earn it. And that was fine with him. Because, as much as it had surprised him at first, the widowed-single-mom thing did it for him. Dana was strong and protective and heartbroken. All of her stress and stick-up-her-ass stuff was because she didn't want to mess things up for her daughters or get hurt again. And he admired the hell out of the way she was doing it all alone.

But if anyone needed to get laid—and laid well—it was this woman, and something Logan did very well was lay women.

And now, she was stuck with him.

That thought seemed to come up out of the blue. While the pregnant stuff was a pretty damned big surprise, he didn't mind at all that it was going to be with this woman. *That* thought made his whole body clench with a feeling of *damn right*.

Was he reeling from the idea of being a dad? No, actually. He hadn't planned it. He'd put that fucking condom on *right,* thank you very much. But this was hardly the end of the world. In fact, it was pretty damned great.

His brother, Gabe, had been a dad for almost six years now and Cooper's mom had been out of the picture for five of those years. Logan had been very involved in helping with Cooper as much as he could. Then Gabe had met Addison and her five-year-old daughter, Stella, and had fallen head over heels for both of them. Gabe had adopted Stella and knocked Addison up within a few months.

Fatherhood, as far as Logan was concerned, was awesome and rewarding and something he'd always wanted. And Dana was an amazing mother.

Yeah, he'd absolutely fucked this up perfectly.

"If you kill me, I won't be able to help change diapers," Logan said to her, the feel of her warm breath on his lips, making it hard to concentrate on what they were discussing. Namely the news of their pending parenthood. Yeah, he really did need to concentrate on that. "And you definitely want me to help with that, right?"

He realized that most men would probably not be quite this laid-back about the news Dana had just dumped on him. But hey, people sometimes got pregnant when they had sex. And with the number of times he'd spun that particular roulette wheel, it was probably past time for his number to come up. He was just grateful it was with this woman. Not only was she already a fantastic mom, but hanging out with her for the next eighteen years was going to be just fine with him.

"Oh, you're definitely helping with diapers," she said, her eyes narrowing slightly.

She had yet to push away from him, Logan noted with some satisfaction.

"I'm also excellent at mixing up formula in the middle of the night," he said. "And Gabe's better at swaddling, but I'm a pro at car seats."

Suddenly all of the starch went out of her and she slumped against him, resting her head on his chest. She drew in a shaky breath. Logan stroked his hand up and down her back. "It's going to be okay, Dana," he said softly.

"I can't believe this," she said. "The first time."

"You don't know that it was the first time," he said, with a grin she couldn't see. Which might have been a good thing. "We did it like six times that night. It could have been any of those."

He probably needed to shut up. But he couldn't. Dana needed a lot less seriousness in her life and he was the perfect guy to provide it.

She sniffed and he felt his chest tighten. Shit. Was she *crying*?

She lifted her head and looked up at him. She wasn't crying. She also wasn't glaring at him anymore. "I meant, it was the first time in two years and, of course, I get pregnant."

"The first time..." Logan trailed off, his eyes widening. "That was the first time you've had sex in *two years*?"

But the next instant, the truth slammed into him. Her husband had died two years ago. Holy. Shit.

Dana arched a brow, watching him process the information and arrive at the obvious conclusion.

"I—" He had no idea what to say. Being with her had been amazing. He'd felt like a king just finally convincing her to go home with him and let him make her laugh and come. But he'd been her first since her husband's death? That was humbling. And yet he could feel his ego ballooning.

Now her eyes narrowed again. "Really?"

"What?" he asked innocently.

"You're feeling like a big stud now?"

A little part of him liked how well she knew him. He lifted a shoulder. "How can I not? You're a conquest, babe, and I not only set foot on your island, but I planted my flag. Deep."

Logan was half bracing for her to slap him across the face for that, but the little snort-laugh she gave had him grinning, and pulling her closer.

"You should have warned me how damned fertile you are," he told her, bringing her hips against his.

She licked her lips. "Maybe I should have."

He laughed lightly. "So this *isn't* my fault?"

"Well, I did get pregnant two other times on the first try."

"You only had sex with Chad two other times?" he joked. He had no problem talking about the other man. Chad was a war hero. He'd died in action. Two years ago. There was nothing there to be jealous of.

"No, but *he* knew how to use a condom."

Logan grinned. "Well, the good news is, I don't have to use one at all now."

Both of her brows went up now. "Oh, really?"

Logan started gathering her skirt in his hand, inching it up her thighs. "Well, I can't really get you *more* pregnant than you are right now." Though the image of her getting bigger with his baby filled his mind, and he actually felt his cock hardening. Good god, he'd had no idea what a caveman he could be deep down.

"Logan—"

He trailed his fingertips up the back of one of her bare thighs and she sighed. He smiled and ran the pads of his fingers to the lower curve of her ass. He put his lips against her neck and just breathed in for a moment as her hands fisted the front of his shirt. He dragged his jaw along the side of her neck, his days' worth of stubble rubbing against her soft skin, and he felt her hands tighten.

He started walking her backward toward the wall behind her.

"Logan—" she tried again.

She bumped into the exposed brick and gave a little sigh. It was part resigned and part turned on.

"Dana," he said softly, opening his lips over the spot where her neck curved into her shoulder, deliciously bare next to the strap of her sundress.

"I came here to yell at you."

"And now you're going to come here," he said gruffly.

She sucked in a quick breath. "The last time we did this, we ended up pregnant."

He kissed his way to her collarbone and then to her shoulder. "It could have been the first time we did this." That's right, *six* times that night. He wasn't going to let her forget that or pretend it had been a lose-her-mind quickie in the front seat of his car. She'd put her hand in his, she'd let him tug her up the stairs to his apartment over the bar, and she'd stayed all night.

Dana's head fell back against the wall behind her and she arched closer. She was definitely not trying to discourage him here. Not really. "You don't think we should learn a lesson? Realize that this is nothing but trouble?"

Logan lifted his head and looked down at her. He waited until she opened her eyes and focused on him. "*This* is nothing but amazing," he told her firmly.

"We're *pregnant*." There was a little waver in her voice now, as if maybe the realization of that was sinking in more and more as she said it. "That's not a sign that this is trouble?"

He gave her a half smile. "That is a sign that I really am the luckiest son of a bitch my brother knows."

She didn't smile as she shook her head. "You barely know me. You have no reason to feel lucky here."

"I get to be a dad." He put his hands on either side of her face as she tried to shake her head again, holding her still. He traced his thumbs over her eyebrows and then smoothed the lines between them. "Dana, I know this isn't something we planned. I realize that we didn't pick this. I understand that you've already done this twice with another guy. But I'm thrilled with this. And I will be there to make sure you are too."

"You barely know me," she said again, softer.

And she barely knew him. He heard that part of her thought as if she'd said it out loud too. He nodded. That was true.

"Arthritis on my mom's side. A little bit of dementia on my dad's." He paused. "Okay, honestly, probably more than a little. You'll see when you meet my aunt Marie. You'll *think* that's what it is when you meet my aunt Cora, but she's just crazy. I'm messy, but I always show up on time. I hate broccoli, but I'll choke it down in front of the kids. I love Cheetos. Like *love* Cheetos. And no, I can't control that. You'll have to just deal with it. I *will* hold the door for you. You'll also just have to deal with that. I love rain. I watch too many YouTube videos. I hate shopping, but love going to the grocery store. And I know every damned word to *Goodnight, Moon* and *It's Not Easy Being a Bunny*." He leaned in and kissed her. "I also come with an amazing grandma, a kickass uncle and aunt, and the best cousins a kid could ever want. As long as the kid is into alligators. At least a little," he finished against her mouth.

She didn't say anything, and when he lifted his head he was startled to find tears in her eyes.

"You okay?"

Dana shook her head. "Cheetos' dust on my furniture is a hard line."

Logan felt a strange rush of relief. "I use wet wipes. I'm not an animal."

She gave a little laugh, and Logan felt his chest tighten again.

"I will be there for this," he said, firmly. "I will be there for *all* of it." Then he realized that maybe he wasn't making her feel better. "If you want me to be. As much as you want me to be." Then he realized that he really couldn't give her full-on permission to leave him out because he *was* going to help raise this baby. And Dana really might think it would be better without him. "As long as you let me in on a lot of it. Most of it. Like 95 percent of it."

He watched her watching him. He knew the wheels were turning in her head, and he was holding his breath. He would insist on being involved. He'd be a regular pain in her ass if she tried to keep him out of this. Then again, he'd probably be a bit of a pain in her ass if she let him in too. They were very different people. She was regimented and organized and in charge. He was laid-back and loved to have a good time and took only a few things seriously—his good times, his bar, and his family.

But she was going to be his family. So she was definitely going to get to see his serious side. Such that it was.

"You can have ninety-seven percent if you keep giving me nights like the one where this all happened," she finally said.

And Logan's knees nearly buckled with the relief that washed over him.

She wanted more. She wanted *him*. At least in her bed and in the baby's life. That was all he needed to know. It had taken him nine months to talk her into this, but it wasn't like they could get into *more* trouble now, right?

"I'll make you want ninety-nine percent," he nearly growled. Then he took her mouth in a deep, hot kiss. One hundred percent was a lot to ask, but he had no doubt that he could make up for the Cheetos' dust and the other things he was going to bring into her very ordered life. Okay, most of it.

She arched against him, her hands letting go of his shirt to slide up to the back of his neck, holding him close. She opened her mouth and he stroked his tongue along hers boldly. She gave a little moan and he palmed her ass, only a thin layer of silk between his hand and bare skin. Then he slid under that thin barrier and squeezed. "Tell me you've got the next thirty minutes free," he said.

"Fifteen."

"Take your dress off."

She reached for the straps of her dress and pulled them down, revealing her skimpy, pale pink bra. "Best I can do."

"That'll work." He reached behind her for the hooks, as she reached for his fly.

He had her bare breasts in his hands a moment later, as he felt his zipper give. He thumbed her nipples, making her arch and moan as she slid a hand into his boxers. He groaned at the contact. She had tiny hands. She had tiny everything—feet, ears, breasts. And he loved it all. He was six-one and had never felt particularly short with women, but Dana made him feel big and dominant and...dammit, manly. Cave-manly to be exact. Because he'd love nothing more than to throw her over his shoulder and carry her upstairs. He might even grunt as he did it.

"Fourteen minutes," she told him breathlessly.

And she was a stickler for schedules. That was another way they were very different.

"I could make you forget about whatever you've got going on," he promised gruffly.

"Nope." She stroked her hand up and down his length, and *he* almost forgot what they were talking about. "Have to pick the girls up from school."

The girls. Right. Her kids. Because she was a mom. He was going to have to get better at schedules and stuff.

"Well, then, we'd better get to it." He reached under her dress, gripped the back of her panties and pulled them down. She kicked them off and he cupped her ass, lifting her. She wrapped her legs around his waist and he turned, walking them to his desk. The bricks of the one office wall not covered with filing cabinets and shelves were too rough for him to pin her against for what was about to happen.

Just then, there was a knock on the door.

Dana froze in his arms. Logan groaned. "What?" he shouted.

It was his brother, Gabe. It had to be. He knew that Logan was in here with Dana. The bastard.

"Logan? It's Reagan."

Okay, it might not be Gabe.

"Uh, just a second, Reagan," he called.

Logan looked down at Dana. Her previously unwrinkled dress was bunched below her breasts and above her thighs, her light brown hair with its perfectly applied gold highlights was wild around her shoulders, and her lips were pink, not from her never-without-it lipstick, but from his lips.

He liked all of that. A lot.

Of course, one of her perfect eyebrows was arched as well.

"Our accountant," he said.

"She sounds pretty."

Reagan was, in fact, very pretty. "People can *sound* pretty?"

Dana was already pushing him back and pulling her dress back into place. Without putting her bra back on first. Which meant she was in a hurry to get covered back up. Dammit.

Okay, so he was a bit of a ladies' man. A flirt. A playboy. But he was monogamous. And for the past nine months—he still thought that was awesomely ironic—the only woman he'd been interested in was Dana.

Plus, Reagan wasn't interested.

He tucked himself back into his boxers and re-zipped, watching Dana run her hand through her hair and then a thumb over her lips. As if to wipe away his kiss.

Yeah, well, she could do that. For now. But she was *pregnant* with his kid. There was no wiping that away.

"She's here for work," he said.

"Okay." Her tone suggested that she didn't care, but the fact that she wasn't looking at him said otherwise.

"Seriously. There's no other reason for her to be here."

Dana snorted at that. "Okay." That was said with a little more sarcasm at least.

He reached out and snagged Dana's elbow, pulling her around, and then up against him. "You have nothing to worry about."

She actually rolled her eyes at that. "I'm having a baby with a man I barely know, who is actually acting *happy* about it, who runs a bar and flirts with tourists like it's his job."

"It is my job," he said, lifting a shoulder. The women who came to New Orleans, particularly those who were checking out the bars in the French Quarter, were generally there for a good time. Part of that good time included delicious drinks and great music. Good-looking bartenders who had a Louisiana drawl and loved to flirt made it all that much better.

Dana frowned. "It doesn't matter."

It did. He could tell. She didn't think he had it in him to take this seriously.

But he was eighty percent sure that he could. At least seriously enough. He'd seen great parenting up close and personal. He wasn't the same guy Gabe was, but Logan had helped out with Cooper a lot and had a great relationship with his nephew. He expected he'd have the same with his kid. "Would you prefer I was upset about the baby?" he asked.

"I just want you to realize that this is a big deal. Huge, actually. Not something that will go away by next weekend."

And then he saw it. The flicker of vulnerability in her eyes. He was shocked by the streak of protectiveness he felt at the sight.

He squeezed her arm. "It's a huge deal," he agreed. "A huge, *happy* deal."

She pressed her lips together and nodded. But she didn't look convinced.

"Look," he said. "We're in this together. I want to be involved, but I'll follow your lead. I will take it seriously." He paused. "For the next *three* weekends. At least."

That got a tiny smile from her. "You really will?" she asked. "You'll really go along with what I think needs done?"

"I will...definitely consider everything you think needs done," he hedged. He dropped his hold on her. He and Dana were different people. They had different styles. That had been clear even in the limited time and circumstances he'd known her—namely at the monthly family get-together held by the single parent support group that she and Gabe were both a part of. Logan had seen her daughters. They played with Cooper and Stella at the get-togethers. He'd even handed one a cupcake once. So he knew who they were. One was named...Katie. No, Cori. No...Chloe. It was Chloe. He was pretty sure. And the other was... shit. He needed to call Addison ASAP.

"You will *consider* everything I think needs done," Dana repeated.

"We'll talk about all of it," he promised. He sat back on the edge of the desk, striving for nonchalant. Something he never really needed to *strive* for, interestingly enough.

"And then you'll do what I think you should do," she said.

"We look at things differently," he said. "I fully intend to help with *everything*, but I might do things my way once in a while."

"Your way?" She crossed her arms. "Do you even *have* a way?"

He absolutely did. It was called "Don't Sweat the Small Stuff." Logan had been watching Dana closely enough to know that she was firm with her daughters, but that she loved them very much. The girls were well-behaved and polite. But Dana was a smoother. She smoothed things over for people. Made things easier. But that also required effort and diligence from her. Logan didn't do a lot of...diligence. He just did his thing and was lucky that people generally liked his way. "I've been around Cooper since he was born. And I'm with Stella a lot. I know what all of this is like." And that a vast majority of things fell into the small-stuff category.

"Being the fun uncle is different than being the father."

He shrugged. "It doesn't have to be."

Her eyes went wide. "It *does* have to be. As the dad, you can't be all fun and games all the time. And it's full-time. It's not just for a few hours here and there. It's through all of it. There has to be rules and routines and—"

"Dana," Logan cut in, calmly but firmly. "*We* are doing this together. That means we both have a say."

She narrowed her eyes. "We can do partial custody," she said.

Logan felt an arrow of alarm go through him. "No. I want more than that."

"I don't—"

"Marry me."

Dana stopped with her mouth open. She stared at him. Yeah, well, he hadn't been expecting to say that either, but the partial custody thing was a no-go. His mom had been a single mom. Gabe had been a single dad. They'd both done an amazing job, but it hadn't been easy. Logan had seen his mom struggle at times. He saw how much happier Gabe was with a partner. This was going to be Dana's *third* child. She wasn't doing that alone.

"Marry me," he said again.

"I'm not marrying you," she said. She swallowed hard. "We barely know each other."

"We'll get to know each other."

"You already pointed out that we're very different. That will be hard enough as we parent together. If we get married, that means my girls too. Shared bank accounts, the same house. And...everything else."

Yes, it did. And he was okay with that. As long as he had full-time with his son or daughter, and Dana was no longer doing this alone. "It does. Let's do it all."

"Logan, I can't. It's too much."

He felt panic welling up. He didn't understand it. He didn't know why he was suddenly feeling the need to get this all decided and her committed right now. Maybe because she *was* firm and rule-oriented. He was going to drive her crazy. Having a ring on her finger might make it harder for her to move and change her phone number after a few weeks outside of the bedroom with him.

"It's a lot," he agreed. "But I can make it better." Yes, there would be Cheetos' dust, but he could make things easier for her. "Let me show you."

She stood, just looking at him.

There was another knock at the door. "Logan?" Reagan called again. "Is everything okay?"

"I'm not sure. I need another minute," he told Reagan. He looked at Dana. Was everything okay?

"How will you show me?" Dana asked.

Logan felt his gut unknot slightly. "Let me be around. Let me...I'll show you with your girls," he said, a sudden lightbulb going on. "I'll show you what kind of dad I can be with them."

"Chloe and Grace will be your guinea pigs?" she asked.

Grace. He grinned. "I have a feeling those girls are pretty well-grounded already," he said. "Surely I can't screw them up too badly by helping you out a bit."

Dana studied him, clearly considering his words. Logan just let her process it.

Finally, she uncrossed her arms. "Okay."

"Really?" Huh, that had been easier than he'd expected.

She nodded. "Yes, really. You can help me out. With the girls. With the house. All that husband and father stuff you think you'll be good at."

Okay, now they were getting somewhere. "That sounds great."

She nodded again. "Yeah. It actually does."

"And then we'll talk about getting married in a couple of weeks."

She laughed. "Oh, it's going to take a little longer than that."

Logan straightened from the desk and moved into her

personal space. "You think so? Because there is some husband stuff I know for a fact you already think I'm good at."

He was gratified to see her cheeks get a little pink.

She took a deep breath and blew it out. "Yeah, well, I'm going to consider *that* a perk of now having *three* children to take care of."

He gave her a slow grin. "One of many perks, babe. One of many."

She didn't look impressed. "You realize I was referring to you as one of those children, right?"

No, he hadn't. "Does that mean you'll be tucking me in every night?" he asked, letting his drawl deepen. She hadn't *said* she liked his southern-boy sound, but her body had. He'd talked dirty to her in that slow, Louisiana, good-old-boy way, and she'd been putty in his hands. It often worked that way. He liked that Dana wasn't an exception to *every* rule he knew about women.

She swallowed but lifted her chin. "We'll see."

She moved toward the door and he followed. "When do I start this audition?" he asked as she reached for the doorknob.

"Dinner. Tomorrow night. Me and the girls. My house," she said.

"What can I bring?" he asked.

"Wine," she said, without hesitation. "A lot of wine."

He chuckled as she pulled the door open. Reagan was on the other side, looking worried and confused. And pretty.

He sighed as Dana shot him a look. Yeah, yeah, okay. So his accountant was pretty. He'd actually been into her when they'd first met—as he was with most pretty women he met— but he'd stumbled over himself whenever she was around. He said stupid things, spilled drinks, dropped paperwork. He hadn't been able to figure it out, until Reagan had told him that she was a lesbian. Suddenly his ineptness around her made sense.

He knew three ways to relate confidently to females—seduce them, let them feed him, or play swamp boat tour captain with them. He was a huge hit with six-year-old Stella because of that last one—especially when he'd come home with three stuffed turtles that joined her congregation of stuffed alligators in her "bayou." And yes, a group of alligators was called a congregation. Just one of the many things he'd learned from Stella and Cooper's latest fascination.

His mom and aunts obviously fell into the second category.

Most other women fell into the first.

Except Reagan. But once he knew *why* he couldn't win her over, he'd stopped saying stupid things and dropping stuff. Now, with Reagan, he'd added one more way to relate to females—give her pep talks when she wanted to buy another woman a drink.

"Turns out, everything is absolutely fine," he told Reagan.

"I see." The sweet redhead was studying Dana with interest.

"Um, mine," he said, tapping Reagan on the top of her head.

She turned back to him, eyes wide. "Oh?"

"Yeah."

"Huh."

Okay, so him staking a claim on a woman was unusual. "Yeah. I even knocked her up just to be sure."

Reagan made a choking sound, but Dana's heavy sigh pulled his attention away from his accountant.

"Really?" Dana asked. "Wouldn't it be easier to just get me a T-shirt to wear around?"

"One that says, *Most fertile woman in NOLA*?" Logan asked, grinning widely. He did love her sass. And she seemed to have adjusted to the whole pregnancy thing pretty quickly.

"I think it would be more accurate if it said, *Drawls make me stupid*," she returned.

That did nothing to lessen his grin. Or his feeling of happiness. "There are a lot of boys around here who might want to test that out," he said, his own drawl thick. "I think *Logan Trahan impregnated me* would be more direct."

Dana rolled her eyes. "Thank you for not saying *Logan Trahan's Baby Mama*."

"Oh, I like that *a lot*," he returned.

"I need to go."

"I'll see you tomorrow night," he said cheerfully, watching her walk away.

Suddenly she stopped and swung around. "*Dammit!*"

"What?"

"I can't have wine tomorrow night."

He started laughing. "Sorry, babe."

"No, you're not." She turned and headed out the door, slamming it behind her.

And no, he wasn't. Not even a little.

2

"So it's okay to give him a trial run?" Dana directed the question mostly at the men in the group.

Caleb, the firefighter who was raising his niece, nodded at her question. "Definitely okay to test things out with him."

"Really?" She didn't know why, but she needed to know that it was okay to not fully trust Logan to be the perfect father right off the bat. And that it was okay to offer her daughters up as trial subjects in his quest to prove to her he could handle it.

The fact that tonight was the night her single parent support group met was not a coincidence. She'd suspected she might be pregnant a few days ago, but she'd waited to take the test until that morning so she could go and tell Logan and then come here for advice right after.

But she hadn't expected to need advice about Logan wanting to be *fully* involved, however. Involved even with her girls. Or that he would have suggested they get *married*. She'd been expecting... well, she didn't know. Even now. That was one of the things about getting pregnant with Logan—she didn't know him very well.

Predictably, however, the group had been supportive when

she told them about the baby and happy for her once she convinced them that she was happy.

And she was.

She'd been anxious up to taking the test. She'd been irritated when the test turned positive—they'd used a condom. Every time. But now she was feeling a little sheepish actually. What grown woman, mother of two, accidentally got pregnant these days? Well, one who hadn't worried about birth control in about eleven years. And one who thought a grown man who was one of the best tourist attractions in the French Quarter would know how to use a condom.

She almost rolled her eyes at that. But then realized that there was no way Logan hadn't used the condom correctly. He was, by all counts, an expert. At least, there were lots of very satisfied women leaving New Orleans because of him, and he had no other children...that she knew of.

It seemed that this baby was meant to be.

And a little bit of her heart had swelled at that thought. Yes, she was happy in general.

She'd wanted more kids. Grace had only been four when Chad had been killed. Dana had assumed when he was home again, they'd get pregnant. So the idea of having three kids wasn't something that worried her. The motherhood thing was nothing new. She'd been doing that for ten years now, pretty much. Alone. Technically, she'd been a *single* mom for only two, but Chad had been deployed on and off for most of their marriage, so she'd never had a full-time partner. She'd been on her own for most of both pregnancies and had even done the delivery thing alone once. She could handle that part.

But this baby wasn't Chad's. It was Logan's. And Logan was very much around and wanted to be involved.

"I think you *need* to try things out. It's the perfect way for you *both* to figure out how he'll do as a dad," Corey said.

Corey was a widower who was raising his four kids on his

own and doing a fantastic job, Dana had to admit. She often hired his oldest daughter, Kylie, as a sitter. He also had a lovely girlfriend, Melissa, who had started coming to the support group family get-togethers. Lindsey thought Corey would propose within the next year. Dana gave it six months.

"I didn't know Chad would be a good dad for sure," Dana pointed out. "I had two kids with him anyway."

"Because you were young and dumb and in love—like most of us," Roxanne said. With her signature eye roll whenever she talked about love. And being young.

She was one of the single parents through divorce in the group. She'd long maintained that her divorce had nothing to do with her ex as a father. He'd been good at that part and they co-parented successfully now. She was one of the people Dana knew she could depend on to help her navigate co-parenting with someone she wasn't married to.

"No reason not to try him out as a dad before you commit to anything. I fully intend to *completely* test my next husband out prior to any commitment," Roxanne said. Then she grinned. "He's going to have to be able to build a deck, fix my car, shop for tampons and sex toys without blushing, and make the best chili I've ever had."

"Chili?" Caleb asked. "That's a prerequisite?"

Roxanne nodded and sighed. "My ex made amazing chili. I miss it."

"But he *is* the baby's dad," Austin said, bringing the conversation back to Logan. "Even if he doesn't do a great job, she has to let him be a dad to their baby." Austin was also a single parent because of divorce.

"But this is her chance to see what he's not good at," Lindsey, Dana's best friend and fellow military wife, piped up. "And what he *is* good at," she added, clearly trying to be fair.

"And she can train him in the stuff he's not good at," Bea said with a chuckle.

Bea was the oldest member of the group and was raising her grandsons while their mom was in jail. She was no-nonsense and practical. Dana loved that about her.

And if Bea thought that hadn't occurred to Dana, she didn't know Dana very well. She was absolutely aware that this could be a chance to mold Logan into the perfect co-parent. He didn't have his own ideas about parenting. Not from experience anyway. He was the fun uncle, of that she had no doubt. But being a dad was something else. And she could handle three kids on her own. If she had to. So if he wanted to be a big part of this—*this* meaning her whole life and not just the baby one day a week and every other weekend—then he was going to have to do things her way.

"Exactly," Lindsey said to Bea. "These are *her* girls. She can tell him exactly what she needs help with and how to do it. Then he'll be well practiced for doing it Dana's way once the baby comes."

Dana gave her friend a grin. Lindsey totally got her. Dana was so grateful for Lindsey. Not that she wasn't grateful for all of her friends in the support group, but Lindsey understood what it was like to have a husband who wasn't really around.

Chad had been excited to have kids, but it had been completely different for him—for them—because he was on another continent for a lot of the girls' lives. He hadn't even been there for Grace's birth. Thanks to Skype, he'd been able to give Dana encouragement and had seen his daughter's first breath, but he hadn't *been there*. He hadn't been there for a lot of things. They'd talked through big decisions, and she'd kept him up-to-date on the girls, of course. He saw videos of Chloe's first steps and her first day of school. He'd been on Skype when Grace had first pushed herself up to crawl. But the girls hadn't taken their steps *to* him. He hadn't been there during Chloe's first meltdown over a dance recital costume. And he hadn't dealt with Grace's ghost fascination. Because that hadn't started until after he'd died.

They'd talked through discipline decisions, but he was never the one to carry them out. When he *was* home, he hated being the bad guy. Probably in part because he had to be a hard-ass at his job. When he was home, it was a break. And he didn't want to spend it being a hard-ass with his daughters. So things had gone off the rails when he was home. Routines were scattered, rules were fudged...or totally forgotten...schedules didn't matter. He'd taken the girls to the zoo one day instead of dropping them off at school, and Dana hadn't known about it until after he was back in the Middle East. And even then, he'd been unapologetic. He wanted the time with the girls to be fun and free and he wanted to make memories and make them laugh.

And Dana got it. She really did. But it took her weeks to get the girls back on schedule and following the rules again after he left. And it broke her heart every time one of them said that it was a lot more fun when dad was around.

Lindsey understood *all* of that. She lived it too. Dana felt a lot less guilty ranting about it to Lindsey than she did other friends or the group.

Lindsey wasn't technically a single mom. Her husband Matt was currently serving in Afghanistan. He and Chad had been with the same unit. Matt was full-time, active Army and that meant Lindsey was here raising their sons without his physical help. She had his emotional support, his help with decision-making, his financial assistance, but she still benefited from time with a group of other parents who understood her challenges.

Lindsey definitely got where Dana was coming from when she said that Logan was tempting because of his two hands, his driver's license, and his credit card. Lindsey had said, "You *deserve* to have all of those things. Take him up on it. For sure. If you don't, I might."

Dana really wanted to. It would be so nice to have another person there to pick the girls up, take Chloe to dance, run to the store for more milk...seemingly little things that some days exhausted her beyond words. She and Lindsey helped each other out with that stuff. They also had all the members of the support group to lean on. She knew that. But the idea of having someone who didn't have his own kids and their activities, or a job where he had set hours or a strict boss, was all just as tempting as Logan's brown eyes and slow drawl. And that was saying something.

"He doesn't get to have a say?" Austin said, still championing Dana's baby daddy.

"Why should he get a say?" Lexi, one of the youngest members of the group, asked. "I agree with Lindsey and Bea. They're Dana's girls. And she's an amazing mom. He should just go right along with whatever she says."

Dana gave her a smile. She'd enjoyed being a bit of a mentor to the younger woman. But Lexi's mom was a single mom too—and had also gotten pregnant young—so Lexi had seen the single-mom-doing-it-all up close and personal. Lexi was more mature than other girls her age, including Ashley, the other young mom in the group, and Dana chalked that up to Lexi having to take care of herself a little growing up. But the girl also had Caleb to lean on. Lexi was a nurse and Caleb was a fire-fighter, so they both worked crazy hours and needed that extra pair of hands and driver's license that Dana was coveting a bit. They'd teamed up shortly after Lexi had started with the group to help each other out.

"But what about the baby? That's *his*," Austin argued.

They all knew this was coming from the fact that he and his ex did not see eye-to-eye on a lot of the things having to do with their girls.

"He might want to do things differently," Austin continued. "That doesn't mean it's wrong."

"I think it could be really good for him to practice doing *any* of it," Gabe said. "His way or Dana's way or a combination—it all sounds like it will be something new for him."

Dana swallowed hard. It was weird to have input from Gabe, considering he had no idea she was talking about testing his brother out as a parent. She hadn't told the group much about the father, and definitely not his name. She was going to let Logan tell Gabe and the rest of his family about the baby. Including Addison, another member of the support group. Gabe and Addison were married now with a baby on the way, but the group had decided that once part of the support group, always part of the support group, so they still came to meetings and the family get-togethers. And honestly, they'd both been single parents for five years. That wasn't something you forgot, and seeing their perspective from both sides—single and married—had been interesting and insightful at times.

"Babies are different than older kids who already have routines and opinions, though," Addison said from across the circle. She and Gabe had always sat across from one another at the meetings and they'd continued that even after they'd married. They were an amazing couple, definitely a team, but they also disagreed at times and they were transparent about that in group meetings. "Getting used to kids Grace and Chloe's ages isn't going to help prepare him much for the baby."

"It will for *parenting*, though," Gabe said. "If he can solve bad dreams and torn tutus and deal with Grace's...quirks...he can handle diapers and colic."

The group laughed and Dana found herself nodding. He had a point.

The whole group knew her girls, of course, and they knew about Chloe's love for dance and all about how important—and dramatic—the costuming and hair could be. They also knew about Grace's obsession with death and ghosts and the supernatural. It obviously came from her father's death and her being too young to really comprehend or fully deal with it. The psychologist had confirmed it, though Dana had figured that out all on her own. But a six-year-old who was into ghosts and zombies could be a little creepy if you didn't know the whole story, Dana couldn't deny.

"You're not worried about bringing a guy into their lives who might not stick around?" Ashley asked.

Dana shook her head. "He'll be the baby's dad no matter what. I think maybe spending some time with him before the baby comes would be good for them?" Yes, she'd ended up making that sound like a question. "That way they're not getting two new people in their lives at the same time. And...they won't be jealous of the baby getting a dad and not them." She hadn't really thought of that last thing until she said it, but it seemed like a legit concern suddenly.

She looked at Bea, the grandmother in the group and the older, wiser member who everyone saw as the voice of reason. Or at least experience.

Bea nodded. "That makes sense."

"Oh, God," Dana said, slumping in her chair. "Do you think they might be jealous of that?"

Bea shrugged. "Sure, maybe."

The thing about Bea's words of wisdom was that they were completely honest and usually a little blunt. She was a tough lady with short-cropped gray hair and a voice that clearly indicated that she'd smoked a pack of cigarettes a day for decades. Her husband had been an over-the-road trucker for years and she'd ridden along with him for about three of those. Up until their daughter stole a car and ended up in prison and Bea had to take her grandkids in. She loved her grandkids, but she was pissed at their mom for interrupting her plan to travel the country and get a T-shirt from every state in the continental US. As it was, she wore her collection of eighteen shirts proudly.

Dana blew out a breath. She really needed Logan to be awesome with her girls. Dammit.

"How are you going to tell them about why this guy is

suddenly hanging around all the time? What if they want you to get married?" Ashley wanted to know.

Dana frowned. Would Chloe and Grace want her to marry Logan? She couldn't imagine that. They were both completely enamored with their father. Chloe remembered him. Grace did too, vaguely. Maybe. She'd only been four when he died, and he'd been deployed for a lot of those four years, so Dana wasn't always sure if Grace truly remembered him, or if she just thought she did because of the stories she'd heard. Chloe though—she'd been eight when he'd died. He'd been deployed for long periods during her life too, but there had been more visits home overall than there had been for Grace. She could actually imagine Chloe *not* wanting Dana to be close to Logan.

What was Logan going to do with a ten-year-old who was into sparkles and dancing and who thought her dad was right up there with Captain America? Or a six-year-old who loved cemeteries and *wanted* to meet ghosts?

She had no idea. But it might be kind of fun to see.

"I'm going to tell them the truth," Dana answered Ashley. "I'm going to tell them that we're having a baby and that I need them to help him learn to be a great dad."

Bea gave her a big grin and Gabe and Caleb chuckled.

Lindsey nodded. "That's perfect."

Yeah, these people knew her girls. Chloe and Grace loved the other kids in the group, and she knew they'd be excited about the baby. And they loved projects. They were very responsible—thank you very much—and if she told them that a grown-up needed their help with something, especially something that had to do with a baby—*their* baby brother or sister—they'd be all over it.

"Okay," Dana said, focusing on Austin specifically. "So what if I let him totally take over some things that I think he'd be good at? He can do those things his way. Any way he wants."

Yes, she'd given this a lot of thought. In fact, she'd been

thinking of nothing *but* Logan and the baby all day. She'd completely blown off the fact that she was supposed to bring the new dance shoes when she picked Chloe up at school today, and she'd taken Grace all the way home before remembering she was supposed to pick Kylie up to stay with the girls tonight because of this very meeting.

Austin gave her a look. He knew she was thinking something sneaky. "Like what?" But the corner of his mouth was curling.

"Like...parties at school. Cupcakes that are supposed to look like hippos for bake sales. Birthday party planning. Slumber parties with the dance team."

Austin's grin was wide now. "I sense a theme. You think he'd be good with parties."

She laughed. She was pretty sure parties were Logan's specialty second only to orgasms. "Oh, yes. *And,*" she added, "just so we throw some responsibility in there too, I'd be happy to share school carpool with him. And he can do dinner two nights a week."

Austin flat-out laughed now. As did most of the rest of the group. Everyone knew that kid parties, specifically school parties, and carpool were Dana's *least* favorite parenting things to do.

But in her defense, she basically kept Miller Brothers Marketing running single-handedly. The two men, Kevin and Dave Miller, were multimillionaire marketing specialists. And they were two of the most scatterbrained people she'd ever met. They could charm a sultan into buying sand, but they couldn't keep track of a lunch meeting. Or a stapler, for that matter. She was their executive assistant and she ran that place like the drill sergeant Chad had hated to his very core. So, routine and schedules and organization were just a natural thing for her and yes, it extended to home too. Kids' parties, hippo cupcakes, and carpool were chaotic and loud and messy and anything but organized. No matter how hard she tried.

"Oh my God, you might never have to turn Nutter Butters into butterflies again!" Lindsey said with a laugh.

Lindsey thought Dana's aversion to making food look like animals was hilarious. Mostly because Lindsey was very artsy. And patient.

Never making Nutter Butter butterflies again sounded awesome to Dana. "I do think he'd be good at that," Dana said. "And enjoy it, actually," she added, lest they think she was just trying to pawn off the stuff she didn't like.

She didn't *mind* the baking activities and craft activities, exactly. She just wasn't good at it. Well, she could bake. It was the decorating that she struggled with. And, okay, hated. Deep down she realized that the cupcakes didn't have to look *exactly* like hippos, but she hated that they'd really looked like gray blobs with pink something-that-could-maybe-be snouts. If you turned them sideways. And squinted. Not that she'd redone them. Who had time for that? But she'd hated sending those to school with Chloe. And now that Grace was in kindergarten, there were even *more* events and parties.

The more she thought about it, the more having a party guy who loved to entertain kids—if his actions at the family get-togethers were any indication—who could get off in the middle of the day to *attend* the parties, sounded pretty damned good. And it would be downright progressive to have a Room Dad instead of a Room Mom, wouldn't it? What a great example that would be to the young men and women in the class. Dana was feeling better and better about this.

"There's nothing wrong with you telling him what you and the girls need help with and letting him handle it," Bea said decisively. "We could all use a break now and then. As long as the girls have what they need, it's absolutely okay for this guy to be the one doing some of it."

Austin nodded. "Yeah. I mean, you're letting him be a part of things and if you think that's something he'd like to take the lead on, then great. Just remember, that if you're co-parenting, that means together."

Yeah, well, they were going to be *practicing* the co-parenting thing with the girls first. Which meant Dana still had final say in how things went. Then they'd see how Logan managed and decide on which baby duties he got.

But Logan did have a car, a credit card, a job that was flexible, no kids of his own—yet—and two capable hands.

Two very capable, very knowing, very *big* hands...

She cleared her throat and smiled at the group. "Thanks, you guys. I feel a lot better about all of it."

"So are you bringing him to the next family get-together?" Roxanne asked.

Oh boy. Dana glanced at Gabe. Everyone in the group already knew Logan. He'd been to every family get-together since Gabe had joined the group. Logan loved the events. He loved the potluck food, the games, playing with the kids. Because they were, after all, parties.

She sighed. Yeah, he really might be fantastic at the party stuff and the carpool stuff, and the art projects. "I think it's safe to say that he'll be there," she said honestly.

He hadn't missed one yet and judging by his reaction to the pregnancy news, she didn't think it would be long before *everyone* knew that she and Logan were having a baby together.

———

Logan set the tray of drinks down in front of his buddies. There were three pink drinks and three blue. He grinned and stepped back.

Owen Moreland looked up at him. "Huh?"

"What?" Logan asked.

"This isn't beer. Or bourbon," Owen pointed out.

"Right. These are new. My own mixtures," Logan said.

"What the hell is in this?" Josh Landry picked one of the pink ones up and peered at it. He was the bartender Logan and Gabe had hired after Gabe got married, so he'd have more time at home. Josh was a master. And he was good-looking, loved to flirt, and was a good old Louisiana boy from down by the bayou. The ladies loved him. He'd been very good for business.

Logan pushed one of the blue ones toward where Josh was, for a change, perched on the other side of the bar. "You tell me."

"I'm not drinking this," Owen, Josh's cousin, decided.

"You have to."

"You said, 'come up for a beer,'" Owen said. "We drove all the way up here and now you give us *this*?"

Owen and Josh had driven up from Autre, the little town along the bayou southeast of New Orleans. It was a suburb of the city, for fuck's sake. A twenty-minute drive. Maybe twenty-five with traffic. Logan made the drive down there to hunt and fish—and yeah, drink beer—on a regular basis.

"I said, 'come up for a *drink*,'" Logan corrected.

"But 'drink' means 'beer,'" Owen said.

Josh chuckled and picked up the nearest glass. It was one of the pink ones. Watermelon flavored. Josh would like it. Then again, Josh just liked liquor in general. He drank everything from cheap beer while fishing, to top-shelf bourbon. He was always up for trying something new and liked to come up with his own concoctions. Owen was a little more traditional. Or simple. He liked beer and whiskey. And that was about it.

Still, this was a celebration.

Josh took a sip of the pink drink and nodded. "Not bad."

"Oh, man," Owen groaned. "We're really not having beer? Come on. I had a kid puke on the airboat today. Before noon. Then a woman lost her sunglasses overboard and you would have thought someone was fucking dying. I had to jump in to get them. Who the fuck spends three hundred dollars on sunglasses?"

Logan rolled his eyes. Owen and Josh ran the Boys of the Bayou Swamp Boat Tour Company with Josh's older brother, Sawyer. They took loads of tourists out on the bayou every day to look at the cypress trees and the gators. And yeah, Owen probably went through a pair of sunglasses every week himself. He didn't worry about things like breaking sunglasses or losing hats or getting muddy. His job wasn't glamorous, but it was fun. He got to be outside, on his beloved bayou, speeding along on his airboat and flirting with female tourists all day long. He could wear shorts and T-shirts and hats to work and didn't have to shave. It was the perfect job for him, and no matter how much he bitched, he loved it.

"And was she pretty?" Logan asked.

Owen gave him a grin. "In a high-maintenance kind of way."

Logan chuckled. "Which meant you made *her* hold the baby gator?"

Owen just shrugged.

Owen had a particular penchant for the women who were clearly way out of place in the swamp. If they showed up with a designer bag or heels on, he made sure they got a little dirty...and saw him without a shirt. He swore it was always a coincidence that he needed to strip his shirt off when the really girly girls were on a tour. But he also admitted that he liked to show the city chicks what a *real* man looked like. And if a girl showed up with a spray tan? *She* was going to end up wet from the swamp. Period. Owen also maintained that if they spent an hour with him on a tour, they weren't just wet from swamp water. And he always wiggled his eyebrows in a really annoying way when he said it.

"You drink half that blue drink and I'll give you a free beer," Logan said.

"You'd give me a free beer anyway," Owen said, picking up one of the blue drinks with his thumb and forefinger, looking at it like it might bite.

And considering the guy messed with alligators every day, that was pretty funny to see. "Quit being a pussy," Logan told him.

Owen flipped him off and then, predictably, tipped the glass back as if it was a shot, drinking the eight ounces down in one swallow. Then shuddered. "Jesus, that's nasty."

"It's fruity," Logan said, but it did look like Owen was feeling a little pukey himself.

"I need a beer chaser," Owen told him.

Logan pulled a bottle from the fridge beneath the bar, popped the top and slid it to his friend. Owen took two long draws, before sighing happily. "What the *hell* was that all about?"

Logan braced his hands on the bar and gave them a big grin. "This is my baby reveal party."

Owen and Josh both just blinked at him.

Before they could respond with what would have likely been "Huh?" the front door of the tavern opened and Gabe and Caleb walked in.

The men all greeted one another as Caleb took a seat and Gabe came around the back of the bar.

Caleb noticed the pink and blue drinks. "What's going on?"

Logan pushed a glass toward him. "Having a little celebration. Have one."

Caleb picked the glass up with caution. Logan rolled his eyes. These guys were acting like he was trying to poison them.

"What kind of celebration has pink and blue drinks?" Caleb asked, lifting the glass toward his mouth.

But he froze partway as his question seemed to hang in the air. His eyes widened and he looked at Gabe.

"A *baby* reveal party?" Josh asked, focusing on Logan. "Isn't that what you said?"

Logan nodded. "Yep. I'm having a baby."

"And *this* is how you tell us?" Owen asked, frowning at the offensive drinks.

"It's the new thing," Logan told them. "It's all over Facebook."

"What is?" Josh asked.

"Using pink and blue stuff to reveal that you're having a baby," Logan said, lifting a shoulder. This seemed pretty obvious to him.

Caleb frowned. "So you're having *two* babies?"

Logan shook his head. "No. I mean..." Well, shit, he supposed there was a chance of that. Not a good chance, but he didn't know for a fact that Dana was pregnant with only one. "I assume just one. It's kind of early to know. I think. Probably." She couldn't be more than three weeks pregnant, after all. Not that he knew when exactly people knew details like how many babies there were.

"So why do you have pink *and* blue stuff?" Caleb asked.

"Because I don't know if it's a girl or a boy," Logan told him.

"Then why are you having a gender reveal party?"

Logan frowned. "What's a gender reveal party?"

"The parties where they reveal if the baby is a boy or girl to the rest of the family and their friends. Sometimes the couple doesn't even know."

"How's that work?" Josh asked. "How can you reveal something you don't know?"

"The doctor writes the sex down on a piece of paper and puts it in an envelope, and then the woman or couple gives it to the bakery or the party people. They make the inside of the cake pink or blue, or put a bunch of colored balloons in a box, or whatever. Then when the couple opens it, they find out at the same time everyone else does," Caleb explained.

Josh and Owen stared at him as if they'd never seen him before. Logan, on the other hand, was thinking that would be a hell of a lot of fun and he intended to tell Dana he wanted to do that with the baby.

"How do you know all of that?" Owen asked Caleb.

"My sister did the cake thing for Shay."

The men all immediately went quiet. They'd known Caleb before his sister and her husband were killed in a drunk driving accident, and Caleb became the guardian to his two-year-old niece, Shay.

"Man, the dead sister thing always brings the room down," Caleb said after a second. "Sorry."

Josh slapped him on the back. Then he said to Logan, "So this isn't a gender reveal party?"

Logan shook his head. "No."

"Then what is this?"

He shrugged. "It's an I'm-gonna-be-a-dad party. Guess I should watch those Facebook videos with the sound on."

Josh started laughing. "You saw a video and thought that's what people were doing?"

"Pregnant woman, guy with her, lots of big smiles, a ton of pink and blue shit everywhere." He frowned. "Why did *they* have pink *and* blue stuff?"

"Uh, twins? One of each?" Caleb suggested.

Huh. Logan nodded. "That makes sense."

Josh and Owen both laughed at that.

"So, damn, Logan," Gabe finally said, settling a hand on Logan's shoulder.

Logan turned to his big brother. "Yeah. Pretty big stuff, huh?"

"Yeah. I'm sorry, man."

"For what?"

"I really thought the condom talk I gave you was a good one. Sorry if you got confused."

"Ha-ha," Logan told him. "Super hilarious."

"How long have you known?" Gabe asked, dropping his hand and any pretense of concern.

Logan appreciated that. Gabe wasn't a guy to judge other people. He'd made his share of mistakes, but Logan knew that Gabe didn't consider his unintended pregnancy with Cooper's mother one of them. Cooper was the light of Gabe's life, and Logan knew Gabe would be there for him as he did this dad thing. "Just found out this morning."

Gabe paused. Then he blew out a breath. "So it *is* Dana."

Logan felt his eyebrows rise. "How did you—" Then it dawned on him. "You had support group tonight."

He'd known that. He hadn't realized that Dana would tell everyone about the baby right away, though. He should have. That group told each other everything.

"We had support group tonight," Gabe said with a nod. "She didn't say your name, if you're wondering. But she told us about the baby."

Logan grabbed beers for Josh and Caleb. "She didn't say anything about me?"

"I didn't say that," Gabe told him. "She just didn't say your name."

"What *did* she say about me?" he asked, trying to act nonchalant.

Caleb chuckled, but he just took a draw of his beer instead of answering.

Logan glanced from him back to Gabe. "What did she say?"

"That you were really happy and had offered to help with whatever she needed," Gabe said.

"I am and I did."

"And she said you're going to be hanging out with her girls some."

Logan nodded. "Of course."

"Of course?" Gabe lifted an eyebrow. "Just like that? You think you're that good?"

"I do." And he really did. They were little *girls*. "I'm totally into snacks and cartoons and playing. I'm a natural."

Gabe laughed and nodded. "I can't argue with that."

"And Dana really just needs someone to be there for *her*."

Gabe nodded slowly. He looked at Caleb. Logan glanced at Caleb too.

"Well?" he said. "No advice?"

"I actually think you might be right on track," Caleb said.

"I agree," Gabe said.

Logan grinned. All right. This was good. Gabe knew him and how he was around kids. His stamp of approval meant a lot. "You willing to put that in writing to Dana?" he asked.

Gabe laughed. "Like a permission slip for you to go over and have playdates with her girls?"

"Something like that."

"You know anything about glitter?" Owen asked.

Logan looked at him. "Glitter?"

"Yeah. Girls like glitter."

Stella wasn't really a glitter girl, but she was definitely into art. Logan knew all about clay and markers and paints. "I think I can hold my own with glitter," he said.

"You need to get some glitter," Owen told him.

"What do *you* know about glitter?" Logan asked. "The girls you hang out with are Kennedy and Ellie and Cora."

Kennedy was Josh's younger sister and Owen's cousin. She ran the office and handled reservations for the tour company. She was sassy and kept the guys in line, but she wasn't the glitter type. She had a pierced nose, several piercings in her ears—and probably other places—and tattoos. And while she wore sundresses to work in the sultry summer weather, she wore tennis shoes or combat boots with them. When she wasn't barefoot. Logan loved to talk to Kennedy because she was whip smart, had a fantastic sense of humor, never took him seriously, and cussed like a sailor.

And then there was Ellie and Cora. Ellie was Owen, Josh, and Sawyer's grandmother. She ran the little bar across the street from the tour company's headquarters where she served tourists beside all of the fishermen who lived and worked in the tiny bayou town. Cora was the cook and her best friend since childhood. Even though Ellie had a boyfriend twenty years her junior, her ex-husband, the guys' grandfather, lived in town too and when they weren't fighting like cats and dogs, they were laughing and drinking together. Ellie and Cora were no-nonsense, tough old girls and they would not only not know what the hell to do with glitter, but they'd laugh their asses off if someone asked them.

"I know some things about glitter," Owen said, scowling.

"Do *not* take advice about girls—little or big—from Owen," Josh said. "His glitter experience all comes from dating strippers from Centerfolds."

Centerfolds was one of the strip clubs down on Bourbon Street. Logan grinned.

"She didn't wear glitter," Owen said.

"She?" Josh said. "Which one? Jenna or Megan?"

Owen flipped him off but muttered, "Either of them."

"I don't think stripper glitter is the same kind of glitter," Logan said, suddenly feeling a little perplexed. At least, he didn't *think* stripper glitter was the same kind of glitter that was used in art projects. But now he was going to have to find that out.

"Jenna took me to her best friend's little girl's birthday party," Owen said. "She had a unicorn-themed birthday party and one of the activities was making unicorn poop. I added glitter to mine and I was a freaking hero."

Logan stared at his friend. He wasn't sure where to start with all of that. "Unicorn poop?" he asked, just picking something.

Owen grinned. "Rainbow colored slime. It was pretty cool."

Logan had to admit, it sounded pretty cool. "And *you* did this activity with them?" That was maybe the hard part to understand. He was picturing Owen crouched in a little kid's chair at a plastic play table surrounded by little girls.

"Well, yeah." Owen shrugged.

"You were really into the unicorn theme?" Josh asked, clearly hearing this story for the first time. "Did you get a headband with a unicorn horn on it too?"

"I did," Owen said. "And I got laid so *good* that night it was all worth it."

There was a beat of silence and then Josh and Logan shared a look and started nodding. "Ah."

"There's nothing like being awesome with little kids to get a woman all hot and bothered." Owen smirked as he lifted his bottle of beer.

Well, that was a universal truth. Logan had seen it work with his brother over and over, as a matter of fact, before Addison came along. He glanced at Caleb. "You concur?"

Caleb just smiled and lifted his bottle. "Shay's not into unicorns."

"That's not a denial," Josh said with a chuckle.

"And Shay's only three," Logan said. "You could so introduce her to unicorns."

"Lexi would kill me."

"Why?" Logan asked. Lexi babysat for Shay a lot, and he knew the younger single mom had a lot of influence with Caleb's niece. Influence Caleb was happy for. But influence over Caleb too. "Lexi is anti-glitter?"

Caleb frowned briefly, then shook his head. "I don't think so. But she just decorated Shay's room in a cat theme. I can't get Shay into something else."

Caleb had no doubt said "whatever you want" to Lexi and handed over his credit card too. Logan was sure the room was amazing. He shook his head. "Those two girls have you wrapped around their little fingers, you know," he said. "Gabe showed me pictures of the bed and bookcase you built for that room."

Caleb sighed, but nodded. "I know."

"Now that you mention it, Jenna did end up covered in glitter later that night," Owen said, clearly still reminiscing about the glitter and unicorn poop...and his stripper girlfriend. "Not for a show, but..." He trailed off with a wicked smile.

"You took glitter home from a little girl's birthday party and used it to do dirty things to her mom's best friend?" Logan asked, trying to sound shocked. He wasn't. At all.

Owen laughed. "Nah. But that shit gets everywhere. It was on my clothes and my hands, no matter how much I washed. It just kind of came home with me. And got all over. *Everything*."

Logan grinned. "I might need the directions for this unicorn poop slime stuff." He wouldn't mind seeing Dana a little sparkly. Or a lot sparkly.

Owen nodded. "I know how to make rainbow painted toast too. And pink tea."

"You drank pink tea?" Josh asked.

"And got laid *well*," Owen reminded him.

Logan picked up one of the pink drinks he'd mixed and toasted the men around him. "Here's to glitter."

They all saluted with him.

Yeah, this was going to be a piece of cake. Or toast. Rainbow toast, even.

3

The doorbell rang and Dana glanced at the clock. Logan was right on time. She actually hadn't been expecting that. But as she wiped her hands on a dishtowel and put the lid over the spaghetti sauce, she had to admit that was unfair. Logan ran a successful business. He helped take care of his nephew and niece. He was not a complete fuck-up. He was just...fun. And fun was not a four-letter word.

"Girls! Logan is here!" She heard the thundering of little feet overhead and smiled as she headed for the door.

The girls were *thrilled* with the idea of having a baby, and they couldn't wait to meet Logan and tell him *everything* they knew about babies and parenthood. She could hardly wait to hear this.

She smiled as she made her way to the door. Fun. This could be fun. And her girls deserved it. Dana wasn't opposed to it—she just wasn't that good at it. But Logan definitely was and honestly, as long as she remembered that *that* was his role here and she didn't start leaning on him too much, she'd be fine.

"We're ready!"

Chloe and Grace ran down the stairs, stopping three steps up from the bottom, gripping the handrail and peering through the spindles at the front door.

Chloe was in blue leggings and a white top with blue flowers. Her blond-brown hair was down, curling around her sweet face with the big eyes that reminded Dana of Chad every time she looked into them. Grace was in a black T-shirt dress with black leggings. Her darker hair, the color of Dana's, was pulled into a ponytail.

"Okay, here we go," Dana told them with a smile. She grabbed the doorknob and pulled the heavy front door open. "Hi, I—"

Her smile died as she took in the small crowd of people gathered on her front steps. Logan was at the front, grinning. Right behind him was Gabe, with Addison's hand in his. His mother, Caroline, stood to the side. Stella and Cooper were right in front of Logan.

"Hi, Dana!" six-year-old Stella said brightly. "We brought balloons!"

And they certainly had. Every single person in the group held at least three large, brightly colored helium balloons. Some were simple, single-colored orbs. But others were shiny mylar and said things like *Congratulations!* and *Party time!* There was also one that said *It's a boy!* and another that read *It's a girl!*

"Wow, I guess you did," Dana said, finally recovering.

"And cupcakes!" Cooper told her, pointing at the container his grandmother held.

Caroline lifted the box slightly with a smile. "Pink and blue."

Dana shook her head. "Wow."

"Cupcakes?" Suddenly Grace was down the stairs, poking her head around the edge of the door.

Dana put her hand on her daughter's head. "After dinner." Which pulled her back to the entire situation. Dinner. Logan coming over for dinner. With her and the girls.

And his entire family.

"Oh geez, come on in," Dana said, stepping back and opening

the door fully. "Sorry."

Logan nudged Stella and Cooper and they hopped forward, clearly eager to be there.

"Hi, Chloe!" Stella said as Chloe came down the stairs more slowly.

"Hi."

The girls knew one another from the family get-togethers. Chloe was four years older than Stella, but they played together well.

Logan followed the kids in, five balloons in one hand and two bottles of wine in the other. But instead of stepping around her and moving further into the foyer, he somehow wrapped an arm around her and pulled her in for a kiss.

His mouth moved over hers for a long, sweet moment. It wasn't a deep, lots-of-tongue kiss, but it was hardly a peck either. He even dipped her back slightly. Impressive with wine and balloons in hand.

When he righted her again and leaned back, he grinned down at her. "Hi."

She was feeling a little flushed. "Well, you do know how to make an entrance."

He seemed pleased by that.

"Give the woman some space," Caroline chided as she came into the foyer next. "Grace, can you show me to the kitchen?" she asked.

The girls knew Caroline—and Gabe and Addison too, of course—from the family get-togethers. Grace nodded and Caroline held out a hand, and they headed down the hall together toward the kitchen.

"Here, give me that." Gabe took the wine bottles from Logan. "We'll take this stuff to the kitchen too."

Dana noticed that Addison and Gabe were each carrying a casserole dish. She watched them go, then turned back to Logan. "I can't drink wine." Though she really, really wanted to.

"Nonalcoholic," he said. "That way the kids can toast with us."

"Toast?" Dana asked. She felt very...befuddled. Not something she was at all familiar with feeling. And he'd been here for about two minutes.

"This is a celebration," he said with a huge smile. "We're having a baby!" He looked over at Chloe, Stella, and Cooper. "That's a pretty big deal, right?"

"Yes!" Stella was nearly bouncing. "I love babies! We're having one too!"

Dana couldn't help but laugh. "I know. That is pretty exciting."

"Stella! Cooper!" Addison called from the kitchen. "Come help!"

The two started in that direction. Dana looked at Chloe. "Honey, go help them find the dishes and silverware. We need to set more places at the table."

Chloe jumped off the steps and followed them, though she seemed to be hanging back. Dana bit her bottom lip. This was supposed to be a dinner with just them and Logan. The girls knew him—or knew who he was, anyway—but they needed a chance to talk with him. She and Logan needed to work out who would be doing what, and she wanted to let the girls in on it. If Logan was going to be doing some pickups and carpool and class activities, obviously the girls had to know to expect that.

"I didn't realize you were bringing everyone over," she said to him as Chloe turned the corner.

He pulled her in close and kissed her again, this time lingering and really tasting her. When he lifted his head, he said, "I got nervous."

Dana wiped her thumb over his bottom lip, removing the smudge of lipstick there. "Nervous?"

"About all of this," he said. "I brought my backups in case I'm not good enough."

He said it with a smile, but there was a flicker of vulnerability in his eyes that made Dana's heart trip. "Good enough for what?"

"Good enough for the girls to be excited about having me around. I thought I'd show off the cool cousins and awesome grandma they were going to get too."

Dana felt a warmth in her chest. This was supposed to be a *trial* to see how involved Logan was really going to be. But in his mind, this all already included his family being involved with her girls. She had to admit, that was nice. She still saw Chad's parents as much as possible. They lived in Texas, but came to visit a couple times a year, and she made sure she and the girls made a trip to Houston during each summer break. She believed firmly in the idea that you could never have too many people loving your kids.

"And cupcakes and balloons?" she asked, not entirely ready to just let him off the hook for blowing in here with extra people and props on what was supposed to be a quiet, introductory evening.

"You can't have a party without cupcakes and balloons," Logan said seriously.

"This is a party?"

"Well, yeah. It's a boy or a girl!" He grinned.

She couldn't deny that even if he did show up with extra people to feed, she appreciated how excited he was about all of this.

"Yeah, usually people buy balloons like that—and bring colored cupcakes—when they know which it is," she commented.

"I apparently got things mixed up with gender reveal parties or something," he said. "But the cupcakes were made and the balloons bought, so what the hell?"

"You know what a gender reveal party is?" Dana asked, admittedly surprised.

He chuckled. "Well, *now* I do. And I've learned to watch Facebook videos with the sound on so I don't miss important details."

She couldn't help but laugh. "Yes, please watch any videos about babies with the sound on. Details are important."

He palmed her butt and pulled her in for another kiss. "Promise," he said against her lips as he pulled back.

She had to admit that she was surprised by his shows of affection in front of his family and her girls. But it didn't bother her. They were having a baby together. It was good for her girls to know that they liked each other and liked to be physically close. It would make future conversations about physical intimacy and reproduction easier. And she supposed it was time for that conversation. She sighed.

"So another detail," she said, pulling back from him and the urge to just let him wrap his arms around her. And maybe tell her that he'd handle the hard conversations *and* the class parties. But she couldn't turn over parenting entirely, of course. No matter how tempting it was at times. And she wasn't great with making leprechaun hats out of construction paper, but she was pretty good about tough conversations. "When you invite five extra people for dinner, it'd be good to give me a heads-up."

"I know. That's why I also brought extra food."

She'd been wondering about those casserole dishes. "You did?"

"Well... I asked Mom to make something."

Dana peered up at him. "Do you cook?" In that moment, she realized she'd been entertaining the idea that she could now potentially stay for later meetings at work. Every once in a blue moon, it was unavoidable and Lindsey stepped in to help out on those nights. But as their executive assistant, Dana oversaw the schedule for the Miller brothers and that meant she could control when meetings happened most of the time. Now, though, if she had Logan, maybe she wouldn't have to be as strict about that.

But he needed to be able to feed her children.

"I can definitely make sure there is food provided," he said, clearly hedging.

She smiled. Well, that was something. "So what did your mom make?"

"Chinese chicken casserole," he said. "And baked mac and cheese."

Dana nodded. "You're good."

"Yeah?"

"Well, you know that you need a backup meal sometimes if you're introducing something new in case the kids don't like it."

"Oh," he said, "the mac and cheese is for me. But I'll share."

She snorted and shook her head. "No casseroles?"

"Just not that one. Water chestnuts," he said with a shudder.

"You don't like water chestnuts?"

"No. Hell no, even."

"You can't just pick them out?"

"I could," he said, looping an arm around her waist and turning her toward the kitchen. "Or I could use your girls as the perfect excuse to get my mom's mac and cheese."

"You could, you know, learn to make the mac and cheese yourself."

"Or I could, you know—" He leaned in and put his mouth against her ear. "Promise to lick your sweet pussy until you come twice in exchange for *you* making it for me."

And that would definitely work. A shiver went through Dana just remembering how good he was at one of her very favorite things.

She didn't respond but Logan clearly read her body language. He chuckled, the sound low and rough. "This whole thing is going to work out so well."

He started toward the kitchen with her hand in his.

Dana swallowed. She hoped so, she realized. She really did.

"Hey, is art glitter the same as body glitter?" Logan asked.

She looked up at him. "Excuse me?"

But they stepped into the kitchen just then. The room was full of activity, voices, laughter and delicious smells.

"We can talk about that later," Logan said. Then he deftly caught Cooper by the back of his pants, swinging the giggling boy up into his arms.

Yeah, they had a lot to talk about later. But Dana had to admit, looking at Chloe and Stella talking as they went around the table, laying out spoons and forks, watching Grace helping Caroline mix up the lettuce salad Dana had left half-prepared, and seeing Gabe catch Addison by the arm and give her a quick kiss on the head, that this was a really good start.

He'd swept into her house with balloons and cupcakes and casseroles and people. He'd toasted their new situation with nonalcoholic wine that the kids thought was "so cool!" He'd made Dana close her eyes to pick a cupcake, then he'd done the same, claiming to the kids that it was a way to figure out if the baby was a boy or a girl.

They'd both picked blue.

Chloe and Grace were extremely excited about the idea of a baby brother.

They'd laughed and chatted around the table for nearly an hour after the meal was over.

Now his family was gone, Chloe and Grace were upstairs in bed, and Dana's feet were in his lap.

This was pretty much perfect in his book. And he knew that the foot massage was getting him even more points than the idea to make green leprechaun poop and use rainbow toast for mini sandwiches for Chloe's St. Patrick's Day party.

He really owed Owen a case of beer.

"So what do you say to *this* every night from now on?" he asked, pressing his point even as he pressed his thumb into the arch of Dana's foot.

She moaned with pleasure.

That sound shot heat to his cock and he had to shift her leg back slightly, lest she think he was just trying to get into her pants. Or her shorts, as the case may be. She'd changed while she'd been upstairs getting the girls ready for bed. She was now in a pair of short cotton shorts and a tank top. And no bra.

She was trying to kill him, he was sure. Or test him at least. And he was going to pass, dammit.

He was a bartender. Sure, he was a successful business owner, a good son, a good friend, all of that. But bottom line, he was a bartender who set his own hours and basically did what he wanted.

He had a chance to be more than that now.

He was going to be a dad and yeah, he wanted a shot at being a husband and step-father too. Something important. Something that was admirable. Something that, frankly, showed he was becoming better. He'd always admired his brother. He'd thought the epitome of that respect had come when Gabe had become a full-time father after Cooper's mom had left them when the kid was only one. They hadn't been together. The pregnancy had been an accident, and she'd left most of the caretaking to Gabe right up until she'd left. And Logan had admired how seriously Gabe had taken fatherhood from day one. But being with Addison and Stella had made Gabe grow and change even more, get even better.

Logan knew he had some room for growth, and the perfect opportunity was right in his lap.

At least, her feet were.

He rubbed up over her arch to her heel. "So, we can do this every night? Right here? Same couch, same time?"

Dana looked at him with soft eyes. "You're making a pretty good case."

He grinned.

"Even though you blew in here with frosting and balloons

and mac and cheese without asking."

"But I came with a mom who does dishes, a niece who makes up the best games, and I fixed the leak in your kitchen faucet."

"So you're saying for every crazy, annoying thing you do, you'll counter it with something great?"

He would like to promise that. The thing was, he wasn't one hundred percent sure what all the crazy, annoying things were. "How about I'll try, and when I don't quite balance it out, I promise foot rubs and orgasms to make up the difference?" He ran one big palm up her smooth calf, watching her pupils dilate.

"I feel like crazy and annoying might be a regular thing," she said, her voice a little huskier.

"You're probably right." He couldn't deny it.

His lifestyle, at least to this point, was that of a teenage boy who had a big allowance. He made good money so could afford bigger, more expensive toys, but that was, admittedly, what he mostly spent his money on. He and Gabe owned the tavern building outright, which meant he had no rent on the apartment. He had a girl come and clean the apartment when she cleaned the bar below. He ate at his mom's at least three nights a week. He was rarely in to work before ten. He did most of the general maintenance on the building because he liked it rather than because he had to. And he spent every night and every weekend in a bar. Sure, it was usually *his* bar—though his off weekends would find him down in Autre with the Landry boys in Ellie's bar—and yeah, he was making money being in the bar, but still, it wasn't a super serious job.

"So that would mean a lot of orgasms," Dana said.

He pressed into her arch. "Yeah. You should probably prepare yourself for that."

She suddenly shifted her legs, leaning forward, and tucking her foot under her. She braced her hands on the cushion next to him. "Well, at least I won't need to replenish my condom supply."

Logan felt his heart kick against his chest wall. He lifted a hand and tucked her hair behind her ear. He'd told himself he was going to be good. Not even making out. Maybe just a hot kiss at the door when he said good night.

She licked her bottom lip. "I think this could really work out well."

"It was the leprechaun poop, wasn't it?"

"Strangely...yes."

He laughed just before she pressed her lips to his. Kissing Dana was always awesome, but having *her* initiate it made hot desire streak through him fast and hard. He moved his hand to the back of her head, pulling her closer. She shifted, sliding onto his lap, straddling him.

He was sure her thin cotton shorts did nothing to hide how hard he was for her. Then she pressed closer and ground against him. Yeah, she knew.

Logan tangled his fingers in her hair, his other hand going to her hip and pressing her more firmly against him. "Am I making up for anything tonight?" he asked against her mouth. "Anything crazy or annoying?"

"Well," she said breathlessly. "There were a few things, but you're picking the girls up tomorrow and you're taking over the St. Pat's party, so I think you're evened up."

"Huh." He slid his hand from her hip to the bottom of her shorts, then underneath the cotton onto silky bare skin. "Well, maybe I should bank a few orgasms. Just in case."

"Yeah, no doubt there will be crazy and annoying coming up. You might as well get ahead."

He grinned as she rubbed against him even as part of his mind thought how much he'd love to *not* have any crazy or annoying coming up.

Then he stopped thinking as Dana stroked her tongue over his lower lip and her hands reached between them for his fly.

"Damn, Dana," he said gruffly. "Right here? Like this?"

"Right here, like this," she confirmed.

He lifted his hips to help her get his jeans open, but just then he heard a soft thud behind the couch. Dana stiffened in his arms and his hands froze.

There was a little sniff. Dana groaned. Logan slumped back onto the cushion as Dana slid off his lap. She peered over the back of the couch.

"Grace? What are you doing?"

Logan tipped his head, pulling in a long breath. Grace was up. And down here. Right behind the couch where he'd been about to…yeah, he couldn't even think about that with the little girl right there.

"I have to move the globe," Grace said in a whisper.

Dana looked at the table at the end of the couch. "I can do it for you."

"No!" Grace said loudly. Then her voice dropped to a whisper again. "*I* have to do it."

Dana sighed. She looked at Logan. "Okay, sweetie, go ahead."

Logan pulled a throw pillow over his lap as Grace came around the corner of the couch. He watched as she picked up the globe from the end table and moved it to the table on the other end of the couch. Then she looked up at the ceiling and said, "'Night, Daddy!"

Logan felt his gut tighten, but then the little girl looked at him and Dana. And gave them both a grin. "'Night!"

Then she ran back upstairs.

"Good night. I love you," Dana called after her.

After Grace had thumped up the steps—and how had they not heard her thumping *down* the steps?—Dana turned to him. She tucked one foot under her butt on the cushion and rested her elbow on the back of the couch.

"So…"

He shrugged as she trailed off. "She's six." Little kids did weird things. It wasn't a big deal.

Dana nodded. "Yeah. She is. She's also into ghosts."

Logan lifted a brow. "Oh?"

Dana sighed. Her eyes went to the couch cushion behind him. "It started last year when her grandma, Chad's mom, told her that her dad would always be with her. Now she's convinced that he's here, living in the house with us."

Logan thought about that as he felt a little shiver go up his spine. Huh. That was out there.

Or was it? What if...

He shook his head. "That doesn't freak her out, though, right?"

"The opposite," Dana said. "It makes her feel good. Safe."

"Well, that's good."

"Yeah. Until she starts talking to him. Or...the globe thing."

Logan glanced at the globe on the table behind Dana. "What's that about?"

"Chad gave the girls the globe so they could always find where he was when he was away. Grace doesn't remember that because she was about one when he gave it to them, but it's, in her words, the best present he ever gave them. Now, she...um..." Dana pulled her bottom lip between her teeth.

Logan leaned in, putting a hand on her thigh. "Now she what?"

"She moves it to that table every night before bed. Then in the morning she comes down and checks it. And it's always moved to the other table. She thinks it's Chad's way of telling her that he's *here* now."

The shiver trickled down Logan's spine again. "The globe really does move from one table to the other?"

Dana looked at his expression and gave a little laugh. "Well, I'm pretty sure Grace is the one that moves it. But yeah, it's always on the other end table when I get up in the morning."

"That doesn't freak *you* out a little?" Logan asked, eyeing the globe.

Dana put her hand over his. "No, tough guy. Because Grace is the one moving it. The psychologist thinks it's Grace's way of telling *me* Chad is still here with us."

Logan didn't look around the room. But only because that was silly. Not because he most certainly did *not* want to see some see-through white image of Dana's dead husband floating by the fireplace watching them.

"That's...nice," Logan finally managed.

Dana snorted. "It's creepy. You can say it."

"It's not." He shook his head, thinking about what Dana had really told him. Not that Chad was floating around the house, watching over his girls, but that Grace took comfort in the idea that he was there and that she was trying to comfort her mom. "It's kind of sweet."

"Yeah, well, wait until she starts talking to you about the undead."

His eyes widened. "The undead?"

"She's very into zombies and vampires. Angels too," Dana added. "Really anything that can't die."

And Logan's heart thudded at that. A six-year-old shouldn't have to be dealing with the idea of death and what that really meant for her dad. "I can handle zombies."

"You sure?"

"Definitely."

"She also...um...wears black a lot," Dana said.

"Okay. Black's great. I have no problem with black."

"And she..." Dana licked her lips and for a second Logan was distracted, "...has a lot of funerals."

That snapped his eyes back to hers. "Excuse me?"

Dana nodded. "She plays funeral. With her dolls and stuffed animals."

Logan slowly nodded, thinking about that. "Okay. She plays funeral. That's a little..."

"Morbid."

"Different."

Dana huffed out a laugh. "Yes, it is. But you might actually get behind it," she said.

"Oh?"

"She thinks funerals are just big parties. Her dad's was like a birthday party but instead of celebrating his birth, it was his death." Dana sighed, this time a heavier sound than before. "The psychologist has done a great job with her. But she hasn't gotten her over any of this fascination."

Logan shook his head. "I don't think she should have to get over it. In fact, she sounds better adjusted about death than most adults I know."

"Really?"

"I know a thing or two about being without a dad," Logan said, taking Dana's hand and linking their fingers. "I was a lot younger than Grace, but dealing with that...I don't think there's a right way or a wrong way."

Dana swallowed hard, her eyes wide. "Oh my God, Logan, I didn't even think of that."

"Think of what?"

"That you lost your dad. I knew that. From Gabe. But I guess...I just didn't connect those dots just now. I'm so sorry."

He gave her a half smile. "No worries, babe. I'm okay."

"Yeah?"

He shrugged. "Well, as okay as you can be when your dad dies when you're only two and you don't remember him."

Dana blew out a soft breath. "I didn't even think about you having that in common with Grace and Chloe."

He nodded. He actually hadn't either. He'd been so young that not having a dad was just how it was. He didn't know life any other way. But he supposed that did give him something in common with the girls. "I can see why the idea of him still being around would be comforting," he said honestly. It seemed reasonable that a little kid would be scared of ghosts, and yet, when he really thought about it, if she thought of ghosts just as people who had died but still wanted to hang around, it wasn't scary at all.

Dana gave him a wobbly smile. "You don't think my baby girl is creepy?"

Logan gave her a grin, suddenly feeling a surge of optimism. He got where Grace was coming from. Maybe he was going to be okay at this dad thing. "Babe, she's growing up in New Orleans. The home of jazz funerals," Logan said. "And there are lots of cultures that celebrate at funerals rather than cry. And as for ghosts...New Orleans is one of the most haunted cities there is. She might be on to something."

Dana nodded. "True."

Logan put his hand on her cheek. "Don't worry, Mama. She's going to be okay."

Something flickered in Dana's eyes. "You think so?"

"I don't think you'll have it any other way."

She leaned in. "You know, I kind of like you."

Logan's heart squeezed at that. "Ditto."

Then she kissed him again. One hand tangled in her hair again as she pushed the pillow off his lap and slid onto his thighs. His hand skimmed up the side of her thigh and underneath her shorts, the pads of his fingers rubbing over the warm silk of her panties. She pressed against his suddenly renewed erection and Logan groaned.

But there were kids right upstairs.

"Hey, babe." He tried to pull back, but her hands went to his face, holding him still. He relished the way her tongue stroked boldly over his for a moment. But then reason returned again and he tugged on her hair as he leaned back.

The tension on her hair made her moan and he grinned even as he bit back a growl. God, he loved that.

"We're not alone," he reminded her.

She frowned slightly. "Don't tell me you believe in ghosts."

Well, he couldn't say he *didn't*. His bar was supposedly

haunted, in fact, and while he'd never *seen* an apparition, things did get moved around inexplicably and there were strange noises at times. Of course, the building was well over a century old, so noises were probably to be expected. Still, Trahan's was a stop along three of the city's most popular ghost tours—and those tourists liked to buy drinks when they stopped in—so he didn't argue the stories.

But that wasn't what he was talking about here. "Your girls," he said.

Her eyes flickered to the staircase behind him. "They're down for the count now," she said.

His cock stirred. "You're sure?"

She nodded. "They don't get up at night much."

"Much."

"Hardly at all."

"But they do sometimes."

Dana wiggled on his lap. "Sometimes. But they won't tonight."

"You sure?"

She studied him a moment. Then she pushed back off of his lap and stood. "Don't move."

Logan watched her cross to one of the cabinets beside the TV. She bent over to rummage in the cupboard. The short shorts rode up, and he suddenly hoped like hell she had a plan here to be sure they wouldn't be interrupted. When she straightened, she was holding a roll of shiny red paper.

She grinned at him. "Cellophane."

"Oooh-kay," he said slowly.

She laughed and unrolled part of the cellophane. Then she wadded it in her fist. It made a nice crackling-crinkling sound. He grinned. "Where's that go?"

"On the landing. They step on it and I'll hear it." She headed for the steps, tearing of a big piece and laying it out over the carpet on the landing above the first set of steps.

It made a lot of noise as she did it, and Logan had to admit that was pretty smart. And that he really liked her too.

Dana was actually giggling as she returned to the couch and slid onto his lap. But she immediately started kissing him again and Logan had no choice but to grip her ass and kiss her back, feeling as if he was starving for her.

Her hands slid up under his shirt, her fingers splaying over his chest. He did the same, running his hands up under the back of her shirt, the smooth expanse of skin uninterrupted by any bra straps. His hands came around to cup her bare breasts, his thumbs flicking over the hard tips, and suddenly Dana was yanking his shirt up and over his head.

The kiss broken, she stared down at him, breathing hard. He watched her gorgeous green eyes darken with desire as he continued to play with her nipples. She reached for the bottom of her shirt and pulled it up. She didn't take it off completely, but he supposed that even with the warning of crinkling cellophane, she had to be ready to hide what they were up to. Didn't matter. Her sweet tits were bared to him. He immediately took one of the tips in his mouth, circling it with his tongue, then sucking. Her back arched and her hand went to his head. "Logan," she breathed softly.

He sucked for a moment, then switched sides, plucking at the wet nipple he'd just left. Dana's hips circled, pressing against his aching cock.

"Need you," he told her gruffly, looking up as he ran a hand down to her ass and then slipped his fingers under the edge of her shorts again. "Need to make you come."

A little shudder went through her body and she shifted, reaching for his fly. It was still unbuttoned and she lowered the zipper quickly, reaching inside his boxers for his hard-as-steel shaft. She squeezed and stroked and Logan's breath hissed out between his teeth.

"Tell me I can be buried deep when I come," he told her,

leaning in again for a taste of her, sucking on her nipple as he slid his finger under the edge of her panties and against the wet heat between her legs.

"Yes, please," she said, raggedly. "I need you."

"Pull them out of the way." He knew she knew he was talking about her shorts and panties.

She let go of him to lean back, reaching down to pull everything to the side.

Logan worked his jeans and boxers down far enough to fully release his cock. He couldn't see as much of her as he wanted to, but he was going to feel it.

"Give me that sweet pussy, Dana," he told her, his voice like gravel.

She sucked in a breath. He knew she loved when he talked about cocks and pussies and fucking.

"Let me have it," he said. "Ride me." He reached for her hips, pulling her close.

Dana leaned in, lifting herself slightly, still holding her clothes out of the way. A moment later, she sunk down on him, taking him deep.

Bare. They didn't need a condom anymore and damn, this was so, so good.

They groaned together. She slumped forward, her mouth against his neck.

"God, you feel good."

He squeezed her hip where he held her. "I will never get tired of driving deep into this sweet body."

She took a deep breath. "Good."

He took her hair in his hand again and pulled her back to look at him. "Now ride me."

She licked her lips and then started moving. She lifted herself, nearly to his tip, then sunk down again, taking him deep. She did it again, slowly, nearly driving him crazy.

He had a suspicion that was her intent.

He growled and lifted his hips. "Dana," he said through gritted teeth.

"Yeah?"

"Either fuck me or lie back and spread your legs and let me do the work."

He saw her eyes flare with heat and her breathing hitch. She didn't move.

"Dana," he said warningly.

"I'm just trying to decide."

Yeah, he was going to decide for her. He flipped her to her back on the cushion beside him, lifted her knee to his shoulder, and thrust deep.

She moaned his name and he did it again. And again. And again. Fast and hard. Until she was gripping his ass with one hand, the back of the couch with the other, and was gasping his name amidst the *yeses* and *oh, gods*.

He felt her pussy squeezing around him and could tell she was climbing toward a hard orgasm. He angled his hips slightly, hit a spot that made her neck arch, and then she was coming apart around him.

He let himself go. He drove deep and hard and let his orgasm thunder through him, grinding out her name between gritted teeth. It went on and on, and he let the pleasure shudder through him for long, delicious moments.

Finally, Logan sucked in air, bracing his hand on the couch beside her, holding his weight up even as he stayed buried deep for nearly two minutes after the shock waves faded away. Eventually, he shifted back, letting her leg slide to the cushion.

She lifted her lids and gave him a slow smile that was the sexiest thing he'd ever seen.

"This is all going to work out *so* well," she told him.

Yeah. It really was. It really, really was.

4

He really would have thought that the ghost fanatic would have been his biggest challenge. A little girl facing the death of her father and all that meant. The idea of an afterlife. The many questions about life and souls and how everything worked.

As it turned out, twisting hair into a bun and securing it with bobby pins had been his downfall.

It had taken seventeen tries, eleven bobby pins, three "Ow!"s and three "You're doing it wrong!"s, not to mention four muttered cuss words. From him. But now Chloe's hair was up and twisted —kind of—and she was wearing the green leotard, which had been the hardest one to find in the laundry room that looked like a tornado had gone through it, and she was on her way to her dance lesson.

Ten minutes late.

"We're going to get better at this," he told her as he shifted his truck into park and turned to look over the seat at the girls. "I promise."

Chloe glared at him as she slid off the seat to the ground. Just as her second foot touched the curb, a long strand of brown hair slipped from the sort of bun on top of her head and curled against her cheek. She blew out a frustrated breath and let her backpack drop to the ground. She reached up and began yanking bobby pins from her hair and throwing them onto the floor of his truck.

"I'll just wear a ponytail," she said. "Even though *everyone else* will have their hair in a twist."

He watched, eyes wide, at a loss. When her hair was all down, she ran her fingers through it, pulled it back into a ponytail and then looked at him.

She was clearly waiting for something. But he was clueless as to what.

"Do you have something I can hold it with?" she asked, as if he was, well, clueless.

"Like a rubber band?" He leaned over to open his glovebox, praying he had a rubber band, but ninety-nine percent sure he did not.

And he was right.

He also didn't have any string or anything else helpful whatsoever. He sat back, frustrated. It was hair. This was *not* going to be his first failure at the helping-Dana-out thing. His gaze landed on his shoe and he had a revelation. He bent, untied the shoe, pulled the shoestring from the holes and handed it over.

Chloe looked like he was trying to hand her a rattlesnake. A shit-covered rattlesnake, to be precise.

Okay, so the shoestring was more gray than white and more than a little ratty, but...he glanced back at Grace's shoes. She had bright blue shoelaces. And they sparkled a little.

"Gracie, can I borrow a shoestring?" he asked, reaching for her little foot before she even responded.

Grace giggled. "But then my shoe will come off."

"I'll give you piggyback rides everywhere we go," he told her, untying the closest shoe.

"Where are we going?" she asked, her eyes round.

He thought fast. "How about a cemetery?"

Until two days ago, when Dana had told him about Grace's ghost fascination, he would have never in a million years thought of taking a six-year-old to a cemetery. But this was no ordinary six-year-old. Her eyes got even bigger and she clasped her hands together as if he'd told her she could have a puppy *and* a pony. "Okay," she said, almost breathless.

He didn't laugh. But he wanted to. She was something. He pulled her shoestring loose and held it up to Chloe. "Best I can do. But I'm buying a whole stash of hair stuff and sticking it in my glove box, I swear."

She rolled her eyes. But she turned her back to him so that he could tie the shoestring around her ponytail. With a big bow drooping over either side, Chloe finally picked up her backpack, gave him another frown, and slammed the truck door.

Logan winced and watched her run up the steps of the school where her dance class met. When the door closed behind her, he looked back at Grace. "So we've got an hour and fifteen minutes. You want to buy new hair stuff before or after the cemetery?"

Grace gave him a big, bright smile and said, "After."

Yeah, he'd seen that coming. He laughed and turned back to the steering wheel. He shifted the truck into drive and headed for the closest cemetery he knew of. The one where the Trahans had been buried for the past hundred years or so. He glanced up into the rearview mirror to find Grace nearly bouncing in her seat.

Well, at least he was winning one of them over. With dead people, but still.

And by God, he was going to learn to do hair if it killed him.

———

By the next afternoon, he was pretty convinced it was going to, in fact, kill him.

What the actual fuck?

He had all of the hair accessories that had been available in aisle eight at Target spread out on the bar at Trahan's.

"This is maybe my favorite phone call ever."

And he had his supposed friend Caleb on the phone. The only single dad he knew with a little girl and the one who Logan had, mistakenly, thought he could call for sympathy.

Actually, he had him on video chat. "Just tell me what the hell all of this is," Logan said, holding up a plastic thing with prongs on one end and flowers on the other.

"That's a comb," Caleb said. "You just...slide it into the hair."

Logan realized that Caleb thought this was hilarious. He also realized that if it was the other way around and Caleb was wondering about little girl hair accessories, Logan would have thought it was hilarious too. And that made him kind of an ass. He sighed. "What's the point of it?" he asked.

"To hold the hair back. Like everything else," Caleb said.

"Show me on Shay," Logan said of Caleb's niece.

"Can't. We don't have any of those," Caleb said.

"This one!" Shay was on Caleb's lap with the phone on the coffee table in front of them. She was holding a crown. Actually, a *tiara* as Logan had been corrected. It was also the only thing Shay wanted in or on her hair at the moment.

Caleb laughed and positioned the shiny tiara on top of the little girl's head. "You sure you can't just talk Chloe into a tiara?"

"I wish," Logan said. Or a headband. Caleb had put one of those on Shay a few minutes ago. That one seemed easy enough.

Caleb had yet to really show Logan anything helpful. Barrettes he understood. The little brightly color clips were clear enough. But Caleb hadn't done a ponytail or a braid or a fucking twist.

"Do you even know how to do this stuff?" Logan asked, spinning a puffy yellow ponytail holder on his finger.

"I'll admit that Lexi does the braiding," Caleb said. "But I can do ponies."

"What about a twist thing?" Logan asked. "Seriously."

Caleb shrugged. "Probably. It's just a ponytail that's twisted and clipped, right?"

"Fuck if I know." Logan shook his head. "I can't believe we're having this conversation."

Caleb didn't laugh at that. He nodded. "I know. Weird right?"

It was definitely that. Logan straightened. "Okay, show me the twist thing."

Caleb reached for the tiara on Shay's head, but the three-year-old clapped her hand down on top of it. "No!"

"Come on, baby," Caleb said. "Let's show Uncle Logan really fast, then you can have your crown back."

Shay frowned at the phone. "No!"

"Come on, honey," Logan tried. "Help me out. Chloe needs pretty hair."

"*No.*"

Caleb rolled his eyes behind Shay's back. "Lex will be here in a little bit. She'll get Shay to do it. She can show you."

Logan was desperate. "Okay, great. Actually, come down here. Bring them all. I'll buy you dinner."

"Sorry, can't. I've got to work tonight and Jack's been sick," he said of Lexi's little boy.

Both single parents with crazy hours, they took turns watching each other's kids. Lexi and Caleb were like the perfect married couple. Without the living together. Or the sex.

"You're ridiculous."

Logan looked up to see Josh unloading a tray of glasses into the bin behind the bar. He was helping out in the restaurant tonight while Gabe was off. He knew that Josh had heard the whole conversation. He'd certainly noticed the blue, pink, green, yellow and purple hair accessories of all shapes and sizes on the bar.

"Dude, give me a break. How would I know how to do hair?" Logan asked him.

"It's not that hard," Josh said. He wiped his hands and turned to face Logan with a grin.

"You don't think so?"

"I *know* so," Josh said. "For starters, are you trying to do a bun or a French twist?"

Logan stared at him. Then he looked at the phone. Caleb looked a little confused too. "I have no fucking idea," Logan told him. "She said it had to be up and be twisted."

Josh sighed. "Well, there are lots of variations of both of those things."

Logan leaned in. "If you're messing with me, I'll kick your ass."

Josh laughed at that. "I'm not messing with you. But you do have to find out what exactly you're supposed to be doing."

"And then you can show me?"

"Sure."

"Bullshit."

"I'll prove it." Josh turned and called out, "Hey, Alli, can I borrow you for a second?"

A pretty blonde at the second table from the bar, looked over. "Sure." She pushed her chair back and came over. "What's up?"

Josh gave Logan a sly grin, then said, "Come here," to her, crooking his finger.

Alli rounded the bar and came to stand right in front of Josh, looking up at him with a flirtatious grin. "Like this?"

"Yeah, just like this." Josh brushed her hair back from her face. "Can I use you to show Logan something?"

"Sure. What do you want me to do?"

Josh gave Logan a wink. Yeah, yeah, the girl was willing to do whatever Josh wanted. Got it. Great. Logan twirled his finger in a get-on-with-it gesture.

Josh smiled down at Alli and put a hand on her head, stroking down along the length of her hair. "Can I show Logan how to put your hair up?"

"My hair?" Her eyes got a little wide. And interested.

"Yeah. He needs to help his baby mama's little girls with their hair. Okay?"

Alli looked from Josh to Logan and back to Josh. She seemed a little...amazed. She nodded. "You know how to do that?"

"I've got a lot of secrets." Josh gave her a wink.

She laughed lightly and then turned around, presenting her back to them. Her long blond hair hung to her shoulder blades in loose waves.

Josh waggled his eyes at Logan. Logan frowned at him. He'd better fucking know how to do this and not just be using it as a way to come on to this woman.

Josh ran his fingers through Alli's hair, combing it out.

Alli's eyes slid shut as she slightly tipped her head back. And she gave a sexy little sigh.

Logan felt his eyebrows rise. Josh shot him a little told-you-so nod as he kept combing Alli's hair out. Logan rolled his eyes.

But he was, admittedly, interested now.

"Your hair smells amazing," Josh told Alli. "And it's so soft."

And damned if she didn't lean back against him a little. "Thanks." She sounded a little breathless.

Okay, okay, that was all fine and good, but Logan wasn't trying to seduce anyone here. He gave Josh a bored look. Josh just grinned.

But he kept working with her hair. He started gathering it back into a ponytail, holding it with one hand while his other fingers acted like a comb. When he held it all at the back of her head, he twisted the ponytail around one of his hands and then wrapped the ends of the ponytail around the knot in his hand. Then, like magic, he slid the hair around his hand over the wrapped ends. He grabbed the pencil that he always kept behind his ear and slid it into the knot of hair. He lifted his hands in a *ta-da* gesture and, sure enough, the bun stayed.

Logan stared at it. Then at Josh. No bobby pins? No ties?

Alli's hands went to the back of her head, feeling the bun. She turned with a wide smile. "Wow."

Logan had to agree.

"How did you learn to do that?" she asked Josh.

"I have a little sister." He lifted his shoulder. "We were required to do her hair before school."

"Oh, that's so sweet!" Alli said, her eyes wide. And clearly impressed.

Josh laughed. "It didn't seem sweet when I had to hold her down while Sawyer did French braids, or the time we used a jump rope to tie her to a chair when we had to do something fancier for Christmas Eve service at church."

Alli laughed. Logan gave a low whistle. He knew Kennedy Landry. He couldn't imagine making her do anything she didn't want to do. Even when she'd been a little girl. And he definitely couldn't imagine how spitting mad she must have been to be held down and braided. But he grinned. That would have been something to see.

"Who taught you to do it?" Alli asked.

"My mom would do it on Kennedy once and then Sawyer and I were on our own," Josh said. He leaned in. "But I'll tell you one of my secrets...it was a great way to get girls my age to spend time with me. Like two or three at a time. They loved showing me how to do hair."

Holy crap, Josh *had* been using hair to get close to girls for years.

Logan couldn't help but think about Dana's hair. It was long and silky and a fascinating combination of browns. And he loved running his fingers through it. So maybe he needed to practice some hairstyles...

"And I'll tell you another secret," Josh said to Alli. "I find watching girls do their hair extremely hot."

"Well," Alli said, definitely leaning into Josh's personal space now. "It just so happens that I have a wedding to go to this weekend. If you want to go with me, I'll let you watch me put my hair up into a very elaborate twist style."

He put his hand on her hair again and looked down at her with a half smile. "If you let me help you with it, I'm in." He leaned in. "And I'm *very* good at taking hair *down* at the end of the night."

"Definitely," Alli said, her voice breathless and her cheeks pink.

Jesus. Logan rolled his eyes. That was almost embarrassing. If it hadn't been damned impressive.

Not only did Josh know hair, but he'd just turned a girl on *and* gotten her to ask *him* out, all by doing a bun. And he'd done it with a *pencil*. Logan would never admit it, but that that was super-power level in his book.

"Damn."

Logan realized he'd forgotten that Caleb was on video chat on Logan's phone. He looked down as Josh walked Alli back to the table where her two friends were sitting, also looking captivated by him.

"Right?" Logan asked Caleb. "Our boy has some moves."

"Tell me I'm not the only one thinking about inviting him over for beer and brats...and hair tutorials," Caleb said.

Logan laughed. "You're the only one, man."

"Seriously? He knows things."

"He does. But he also gave us some very important intel."

"What's that?" Caleb asked.

"Girls love to *show* guys how to do hair. I've got Dana and you've got Lexi. Why not let gorgeous women show us instead of a cocky guy who spends his time in the swamp?" Logan asked, carrying the phone down the length of the bar. He needed to get going on work tonight.

Caleb was frowning. "That would work for you and Dana, but it's not like that with me and Lex."

Logan wasn't so sure Lexi thought that was true. "Lexi is sweet and gorgeous and saves your ass repeatedly," Logan said. She cooked and did laundry and errands for Caleb, not to mention picking Shay up from daycare at least twice a week. Of course, Caleb paid for all the groceries and insisted Lexi drive his truck on the errands so she didn't have to fill her car with gas as often. "You'd be a dumbass to pass up a chance to run your fingers through her hair. Period."

Caleb scowled. "Stop it. She's like a little sister. She's my babysitter, for fuck's sake."

Logan had no idea why the babysitter thing made any difference. But he knew from experience that Caleb didn't like it when his friends pointed out that there was a *ton* of babysitter porn out there that proved it was anything but a turn-off.

"Whatever, man. Run your fingers through Josh's hair then. I know how *I'm* going to handle this."

Caleb shook his head. "I gotta admit—if you show up with those ladybug barrettes at Dana's house, that's gotta get you big points."

Logan grinned and grabbed said barrettes, along with a few others, off the bar top and slid them into his front pocket. "I've got to make up for tying her daughter's hair up with a shoestring."

Caleb laughed. "I think you're going to be okay. And think about it—if you can master that pencil move of Josh's, you won't need to worry about shoestrings or barrettes."

He had a point. But Logan was determined to never *not* have ponytail holders and barrettes again.

"And hey, if you don't want those kitty barrettes, Shay would love those," Caleb added.

Logan nodded. "They're all yours. If," he added, "you never use the word 'kitty' in front of me ever again."

Caleb laughed and gave him the finger.

———

I
t was after ten and she was in her pajamas, but when she heard the light tap on her front door and looked out the window to see Logan's truck in her driveway, Dana's heart flipped a little and she happily pulled her front door open.

"Hi," she greeted.

He'd clearly come from the bar. He wore blue jeans and a Trahan's Tavern T-shirt with a couple of spots of blue—some kind of liquor, she assumed—and something that could only be mustard on it. He looked great.

But when he held out his hand and said, "Help me," she had to blink a few times.

There were four ladybug barrettes in his palm.

She looked up. "With what?"

"Girl hair."

She laughed and reached to grasp his wrist, pulling him inside. "You need help with girl hair?" she asked.

"Well, I can't keep getting by with shoestrings, you know?" he asked.

"Shoestrings?" She led him to the couch and wondered how long they needed to talk before they could make out.

She didn't know if it was pregnancy hormones, or the fact that now she was pregnant she really didn't have to worry about anything and could just let go, or if it was just Logan's effect on her libido—which had, admittedly, been like this since she first met him—but she definitely wanted to climb into his lap like the other night.

"Chloe didn't tell you?" he asked as he sunk onto the couch.

Dana took the cushion beside him, tucking her feet under her and facing him. "Tell me what?"

"That I had to tie her ponytail with Grace's shoestring last night."

Dana just looked at him. "What?"

He nodded and told her the story. She was grinning by the end. "That was very...resourceful, of you."

"But she didn't tell you?" he asked again.

She shook her head. "Nope. Didn't say a word."

"Huh." He seemed puzzled by that.

"You thought she'd tell me?"

"She was upset."

Dana nodded. "Probably. But why would she tell me about it after it was over?"

He frowned. "I don't know. To let you know that I'd messed up."

Dana thought about that. "Well, either she didn't think you did. Or she didn't want me to know."

Logan's frown cleared. "Huh."

She laughed again. "Which of those surprises you?"

"Both." He turned to face her and ran a hand up her thigh.

She had thin cotton pajama pants on but she felt the sparkles of sensation from his touch anyway.

"I guess I had this idea in my head that she might not want me taking her to dance class. And that if I messed up, she'd tell you and you wouldn't have me do it anymore."

It was going to take a lot more than a bad hairstyle to get Dana to not have him take Chloe to dance class anymore. He'd brought the girls home after class, had given them a snack, and had reviewed Chloe's homework folder all before Dana got home. They'd been in their pajamas and reading books in their bedrooms by the time Dana had washed her makeup off and changed into lounging clothes. Logan had kissed her sweetly— hotly, but sweetly—at the door, but he'd headed to Trahan's after she was settled in.

She'd never stayed at the office that late, ever. But it had been nice not leaving things on her to-do list because she was rushing out the door. The next day at work had been so great without having to catch up. She was feeling organized and more relaxed now than she had in, maybe ever, and it had only been one week.

There really was something about having someone there helping out a little, and it felt amazingly...light. Much better than having to rely on Lindsey, who had her own kids and boss to manage.

Dana put her hand on Logan's, running her fingertips back and forth across his knuckles. He had strong hands. His skin was rougher than hers and she loved the way he touched her with confidence and how his palms felt running over hers. She really hoped maybe he wouldn't leave with just a good night kiss tonight.

"Well, even if she had wanted to tell me about it—and I don't think she did—she couldn't have gotten a word in edgewise," Dana told him. "Grace didn't stop talking about the cemetery all during the bedtime routine and breakfast this morning."

He grinned and Dana felt a hitch in her breath. God, he was so good-looking. And now he was grinning about taking her baby girl to a cemetery. This was so weird. And great.

"I showed her my dad's and great-grandmother's graves," he said.

Her heart thumped. She wanted to hug him so badly.

"I heard." Her heart had ached when Grace had told her that. "She also told me that you both decided your great-grandma's not there because she's hanging out at the tavern."

He continued to rub her thigh but it seemed absentminded now. Like he just wanted to touch her, but wasn't really tuned in. He was clearly thinking about his time with Grace.

"That's the story," he said. "That she's haunting the tavern because she was sure that no one else would run it right. My grandmother, her daughter, claims that you're doing a good job if the ceiling fans all work. If they don't, she's annoyed. Kind of annoyed is one or two not working. Very annoyed if three or four won't work."

Dana laughed. "And do they sometimes not work?"

Logan looked more thoughtful than amused. "Yeah, actually. And I've been up there fixing them several times. There's no reason they wouldn't work. We've always chalked it up to old wiring, but now Grace has me thinking."

"Oh my God, my six-year-old has you believing in ghosts now?"

Logan shrugged. "She just...makes some good points."

"Such as?" Dana had honestly not talked about the ghosts that much with Grace. She'd just rolled with the subject, just like she would with any other topic. It was something that came up once in a while—like every night at bedtime when the globe needed moved—but otherwise Dana didn't dwell on it or make a big deal of it.

"Well, why would someone leave a place they were happy if they didn't have to?" Logan said. "If someone is a spirit and they *can* hang around someplace, maybe sometimes they choose to do that."

Dana wasn't sure what to say to that. Or to the idea that Logan was buying into, and encouraging, Grace's fascination. "I don't know if we should make a habit of hanging out in cemeteries," she finally said.

"Why?" He turned more fully. "Cemeteries are where you go to remember people, right? To honor them? Well, the stuff I told Grace about my dad and great-grandma were things I hadn't thought of in a long time. They're stories my grandma told me. Which made me think of my grandma too. Which prompted Grace to tell me about her grandmas. It was all very nice. Not morbid at all."

"Except the part about your grandmother haunting your bar," Dana pointed out.

"Nah, that's not morbid. It's kind of nice." He gave her a little smile and squeezed her leg. "Except when she's annoyed with us and the fans don't work."

She honestly didn't know what to do with this guy. He was…
something. He was a grown man who related best to her six-year-
old, Dana reminded herself. But she couldn't help but note that
Grace had been completely happy after her time with Logan and
that it wasn't like Grace was scared or having trouble sleeping or
anything. It had been generally harmless.

And Logan fully accepted Grace and her little idiosyncrasy.
That was really nice.

Dana leaned in, pulling his hand further up her leg and
around to her butt. "You know, you're a really nice guy." She
shifted forward, putting her lips against his. "And you have no
idea how sexy it is that you're so sweet to my girls."

But instead of kissing her, or pulling her into his lap, he said,
"Let me play with your hair."

That sounded sexy. Then she remembered the ladybug
barrettes. She sat back. "You want to play with *my* hair?"

"I need hair to practice with."

Her eyes went round. "You would rather practice braiding
than make out? Or more?" she added, running her hand up
his chest.

He grabbed her hand and, much to her surprise, stopped it.
He lifted it to his mouth and gave her palm a kiss. That shot right
to her core. Then he said, "Yeah. Except *not* braiding. I'm not
ready for that."

She laughed and groaned at the same time. "*I* am coming on
to *you* and you're resisting me in favor of ladybug barrettes?"

He shifted and dug in his front pocket and pulled out
barrettes with frogs and pigs as well. "I've got more in the truck."

She took them from him. "You have *more* barrettes? How
many do you think two little girls need?"

"I've got bows and headbands and ponytail holders and
combs and—"

Dana covered his mouth with her hand. "If you're trying to
dial *back* my sex drive, that's not helping." She felt him grin under

her hand and she moved it. "What?" she asked about the big smile.

"Guys know that women go all gaga when we're sweet with kids, you know."

"Well, that would be kind of hard to miss." It was hardly a secret. "Is that why you were so great with the kids at all the support group family gatherings?"

"Of course."

It had worked, she couldn't deny.

"I mean, that and the squirt guns. And because dodgeball is the greatest game ever. And because I'm awesome at hide-and-seek, thank you very much. And that I can justify eating extra snow cones when I'm hanging with them. And extra marshmallows in my cocoa. And—"

Dana slapped her hand back over his mouth, laughing. "Okay, I get it. There are lots of perks."

He wrapped his fingers around her wrist, but before he pulled her hand back, he gave the center of her palm a little lick. She sucked in a quick breath as her core clenched. He gave her a look that was hot and sweet at the same time. "But yeah, making this baby with you was the biggest one."

And the quick breath that lodged in her chest grew into a giant ball of emotion.

She sniffed.

"Oh, no," he said. "There's no crying in accidentally getting knocked up by the hottest bartender you've ever met."

She laughed again. And sniffed again. "That's ridiculous. That's the perfect thing to cry about."

"Okay, maybe," he conceded.

"But," she felt compelled to add, for some reason, "there's no crying when that hot bartender is actually a really great guy who doesn't think my little girl is a weirdo and doesn't throw his hands up at the idea of ladybug barrettes."

Emotion that looked a lot like affection and maybe a touch of surprise flickered in Logan's eyes. But he said, "Yet."

"Yet?"

"I haven't thrown my hands up about the barrettes *yet*."

She smiled, feeling the ball of emotion behind her breastbone warm into a gooey, sweet blob.

"And I definitely think Grace is a weirdo," he said. "But I get it. And I like it."

Dana felt the tears threatening, but he was right. She had no reason to cry over any of this. It was amazing. "Logan," she said seriously. "There is something really important you need to know."

His brows drew together. "Uh-oh."

She nodded. "Yeah."

"Okay."

"Those barrettes are nowhere near big enough to work in Chloe's hair."

Logan stared at her for a long moment.

Then all at once Dana found herself tossed onto her back on the cushion behind her, the hottest bartender she'd ever met looming over her.

She giggled. "We have plenty of barrette—"

And he started tickling her. She shrieked and rolled. "No! Logan, no!"

He laughed wickedly and put his mouth against her neck, even as she continued to try to escape his fingers. "I love it when you wiggle against me."

"I *offered* lots of wiggling," she reminded him between gasps. "You're the one who wants to play beauty salon."

His fingers stopped, his hand splaying over her ribs as he pressed a hot kiss to her neck, then her lips. "You're right." He leaned back, pulling her up with him. "Stop distracting me."

She was still trying to catch her breath, but she smacked his arm. "Your fault."

"Your fault," he told her. He gave her a look that made her pause. "It's so fucking hot that you're pregnant with my baby."

Wow. That was out of the blue. And sexy. And yeah, that was *not* helping her horniness. "It is?"

"It is," he told her, with all seriousness. "And it could be another girl."

She nodded. "It could."

"So I *really* need to understand barrettes."

Dana laughed. "Okay, already."

"Because no matter how hard I try to get her into fishing and alligator hunting and catching crawfish, she might still want barrettes sometimes."

Dana pushed herself up from the couch, but stopped to plant a hand on her hip. "There will be no alligator hunting."

"That's really sexist," he said. "I'm surprised you wouldn't want our daughter to do all the things our son would do."

Holy crap, it had to be the hormones because when he said "our daughter" and "our son," everything in Dana got warmer and her stomach felt like she was going over the top of a roller coaster.

She cleared her throat. "No alligator hunting for *anyone*."

"Oh, there has to be alligator hunting," he said. "It's a tradition with me and the guys."

She already knew "the guys" meant Gabe, Caleb, and Josh and Owen. She also knew that they all spent a lot of time in the little town of Autre where Josh and Owen lived and worked. "Then you and the guys can keep doing it. But," she added as she started for the stairs. "I will have less use for you if you ever lose any of your fingers to an alligator. Or God forbid, any other parts."

Logan just laughed. "I've been doing it all my life."

Dana paused at the bottom step. "And does Stella know that you're *killing* alligators?"

Logan pivoted on the couch cushion quickly. "No. And you

can't tell her or Cooper," he said, seriously.

Dana shook her head. "They won't hear it from me. But you wouldn't be able to keep...our daughter or son from talking about it to their cousins."

Yes, she'd stumbled a little over the "our daughter or son" thing, but mostly because she'd known that once she said it out loud she'd like it. A lot. Maybe too much.

Logan blew out a breath. "Noted."

She grinned. "I'll get the supplies. Be right back."

She headed upstairs, thinking that teaching Logan Trahan about hair bows was just about the last thing she'd ever expected to do. But because of that, it was maybe even better. She liked that Logan was surprising her. And he was definitely entertaining. Looking forward to seeing him, and even hearing about him from the girls, had quickly become a fun part of her day.

The girls were fast asleep when she tiptoed into their room and grabbed the plastic bin of hair accessories from the top of Chloe's dresser. Dana paused by each bed, gazing down upon the two best things she'd done in her life. Her hand went to her still flat stomach and she felt the flutter of butterflies. There were going to be three things she'd done well. And it was going to be a little easier, and a lot more fun, this time around, thanks to Logan.

Smiling, she brushed Chloe's hair back. Her oldest hadn't told her about Logan's improvising with the shoestring. She was sure that Chloe had hated not having her hair up like the other girls, but she hadn't tattled on Logan. That was something. Chloe liked him. Or was, at least, tolerating him being involved. That was good. That was very good. Logan would be taking her to class at least twice a week. She needed to like him. Or at least trust him. Chloe didn't really know what it was like to depend on someone other than Dana. Well, and Lindsey. Her girls knew that Lindsey was their first phone call after Dana. But now...

Dana suddenly had to swallow hard.

Her girls knew that they could depend on Dana and Lindsey. Their grandparents too, of course, but not for the day-to-day things they needed. No one else had been there consistently. Chad being home had been like...a vacation. He'd been fun. He'd been a novelty. For her too. At the back of her mind she'd always had the thought that things were temporary. So staying up late talking and having sex and being tired the next day was fine because it wasn't going to last. Letting the girls go out for ice cream after dinner two days a week was okay because it wasn't going to last. Lindsey was the one Dana had come to depend on to be her backup because her friend was, well, *there* and could handle the schedule and the routine and the rules the way Dana did.

But with Logan...he was going to be here. He wasn't leaving for the Middle East in a few weeks or months. So she had to be careful with what ways he disrupted their routines and rules.

Could she let her girls get dependent on Logan? Could *she* get dependent on him? Yes, he could give the girls rides and solve small problems like ponytails, but Dana had to make it clear that, while Logan was a lot of fun and was a grown-up who could pick them up once in a while, he wasn't a go-to all the time. He was already doing far more than she'd expected. Sure, he'd asked her to marry him, but she knew that had been just an impulsive offer in the wake of being dealt the biggest surprise of his life. He wanted to be involved with the baby and that was noble, amazing even, but Chloe and Grace weren't his. He was just trying to prove to Dana that he should have time and could handle responsibility with the baby. And he was doing a good job of it.

But she couldn't get too comfortable.

As long as she remembered that and continued to take the lead, Logan could be her right-hand man and no one would be disappointed.

Pressing a quick kiss to each girl's forehead, Dana headed back downstairs with the bows and ties and clips.

5

"Awesome." Logan clapped his hands together and rubbed them in anticipation. Then he looked at her face. "You okay?"

Dana forced her mouth into a smile. He *was* a great guy. And as long as she kept her expectations to him playing chauffeur, party-planner, and...yeah, okay...sex therapist, he was going to do great and they would all be happy.

"Definitely," she told him. She presented him with the little tub of hair accessories. "Here you go. Everything you could want and more."

He took it with clear trepidation. "I'm not ready for this."

"Come on, big guy," she said, grabbing one of the throw pillows and tossing it on the floor at his feet. "You braved the cemetery. You hunt alligators. I know you can handle some pink bows."

He took the lid off the box and looked at the contents. "Cemeteries make sense."

"They do?"

He looked up. "You know what Grace pointed out?"

"What?" Dana took a seat on the pillow by his feet, crisscrossing her legs, her back to him. She pulled the ponytail holder from her hair and shook it out.

"She said that people in New Orleans are happier in their graves than in other places where they're buried underground."

Dana frowned. "Why is that?"

"They're with their families and the graves are easier to get out of."

Dana sighed. These were the things that Grace said that had her teacher a little concerned. "They're easier to *get out of*?" She felt Logan's fingers in her hair, combing through the strands. He ran his hands from her scalp to the ends slowly and Dana felt her eyes slide shut. That felt amazing.

"Well, the graves here are above ground," he said. "And when I told her that they put families together inside the graves, she thought that made a lot of sense."

"You told her how they bury people here?" Dana asked, not quite able to pry her eyes open as Logan's fingers massaged against her scalp.

"Yeah. I mean, it's interesting. Something we do that no one else does. I thought she'd get a kick out of it."

He'd thought her six-year-old would "get a kick" out of knowing how people were buried in Louisiana.

And he was probably right.

It occurred to Dana that she should possibly be a little concerned about him giving Grace even more information about death and dead people to share at school, but with his hands in her hair, she couldn't do anything other than try to keep from purring like a cat.

He applied a brush to her hair and she almost lost the no-purring fight.

She tipped her head back with a sigh.

A moment later, she felt his lips against her neck. "That's the sound you make when I lick your nipples."

Her inner muscles clenched and she grabbed his ankle and

squeezed. "If you're not going to actually *do* that, you have to stop talking about it."

"I didn't say I wasn't going to do that," he told her huskily, dragging the brush through her hair. "But I have to do this first."

Thank God. "Then let's get on with it."

He chuckled. "I kind of love that *you* are the one needing *me* so badly."

She squeezed his ankle again. "Pregnancy hormones."

"Uh-huh." He licked just behind her ear and then bit her earlobe gently. "You tell yourself whatever you need to. As long as it keeps happening."

She gave a breathless little laugh. "You might not think that after I start getting huge and round."

He ran his hand down over one breast to her stomach and stroked over the thin cotton of her top. "I don't think so, babe."

She bit her bottom lip. He was so damned sweet sometimes. And sexy. All the time. "We could do hair later," she said, arching her back to get a little closer to his hand and hoping he might slip it up under her shirt. Or lower into her pants. Or one of each. He had two hands, after all.

Instead, his hands went back to her hair. "Once I get you naked, I tend to forget about everything else," he said, pulling the brush through her hair again.

She sighed. And not in the "wow, that's so hot" way from before. "Okay, fine," she mumbled.

He just laughed again and she couldn't help but smile. Yeah, he was feeling cocky about her being horny after all those months that he'd been flirting with her and asking her out. Fine. He could be arrogant about that. Because she really did want him. Badly.

Logan gathered her hair at the base of her head. "Okay, this is as far as I can get on my own."

She chuckled. "All right, so this might need some work after all. Hand me the box." She talked him through the steps for the

French twist that Chloe would need for her recital. Dana would be there to do her hair that night, of course, but she knew that the girls all liked to do their hair for rehearsals too.

Logan patiently went through the steps and was amazingly gentle with the bobby pins. Too gentle.

"You have to dig them in," she told him, holding the shank of hair that had fallen.

"Fuck. It doesn't hurt?"

"Well, sure if you get into the scalp it will, but you have to really get into the hair."

"Fuck," he muttered again, but he redid three of the pins.

She smiled. She assumed he'd watch his mouth when he was doing this with Chloe. She patted the spot. "Yeah, that feels good."

Dana heard him take a deep breath. "Thank you, Jesus."

She reached up and started taking the pins out. "Okay, now do it again."

He groaned. She looked back at him with a grin. "You have to practice. That took way too long, for one thing. And for another, you're not going to have someone sitting this still, coaching you. She'll be wiggly and you'll be distracted by Grace doing God-knows-what and dinner and the fact that you only have about ten minutes to do it all. So—" She put the pins in his hand. "Do it again."

And he did. A little faster and easier than last time. The third time was even better. By the fourth, she could tell he was getting bored. Internally shaking her head, because she knew all about people getting bored sitting still too long, she went up on her knees in front of him, still facing forward. "Okay, now you have to do it with distraction."

"Distraction? You gonna wiggle for me, Dana?" he asked, that low husky drawl distracting *her* for a moment. He ran his hands from her hips to her waist and pulled her back, nuzzling her neck. "I like your hair up. Gives me more access to skin." He dragged his prickly jaw up the side of her neck and she shivered as goose bumps broke out over her arms and back.

So *now* he was interested in seduction? Well, no. He needed to finish this hair thing first. His rules.

She pulled away and put his hands on her shoulders. "Twist. Again. Go."

But as he pulled the pins out and brushed through her hair again, she did wiggle. And she ran her hand up and down his calf under his pant leg. And thought of all the ways she could distract him so that they would both know for certain he could handle the hair thing when it came time. And just because it was fun.

"You want to be an expert at this, right?" she asked him, as he gathered her hair at her nape.

"Yep. No more shoelaces and disappointed dancers."

"Okay." Dana pulled away and stripped her shirt off.

"Uh," was his only response.

"Now go," she said, gathering her hair back for him again.

"What are we doing here?"

"Making sure you can do this while distracted."

There was a pause. Then he grasped the ponytail where she held it and tipped her head back with a little tug. He put his mouth right to her ear. "Take your pants off too."

Oh boy, what had she started? But she did as he said, sliding her pajama pants down and then kicking them off.

He held her hair tightly, something that always, surprisingly, made her hot. She'd never had someone do that before. Then again, she'd only been with one guy in college before she'd met Chad. Chad had been a dominant lover too. Sex against the wall and on the kitchen table hadn't been unusual. But for some reason, she felt like Logan was...dirtier. Not afraid to say what he was thinking, and he made the most everyday things hot. It was the drawl. Probably.

"Now touch yourself," he told her, twisting her hair in the first step. "Play with those pretty nipples for me."

Dana took a shaky breath and lifted her hands. She'd been turned on since he'd showed up, and while she would have loved to have *his* hands on her breasts, at this point she was fine with whatever. She cupped her breasts, running her thumbs over the tips, and giving a happy sigh.

"Don't stop," he said firmly as he twisted her hair again and lifted it.

She wasn't about to stop. Unless he wanted to replace her hands with his mouth. "No problem," she told him, her eyes sliding shut as she plucked at her nipples and relished the feel of Logan's hands in her hair.

He started with the bobby pins at the bottom. When he had four or five in place, he said, "Now stroke your clit."

Her body clenched at the words. She pulled one knee up and slid her hand down to her mound.

"Finger on your clit, Dana," he ordered gruffly in her ear.

He was watching, she knew. He was just holding her hair now, her head tipped back, his lips against her ear, watching her fingers.

She slid lower, circling her clit and giving a little sigh. She pressed and circled faster. This wasn't quite as good as him doing it, but this was fine. She was just *fine*.

"Now inside," he told her. "I want you to slide two fingers inside that sweet pussy."

Gladly. She needed the pressure, the fullness. She did it, unable to keep from moaning softly.

"That's in. In and out. Stroke deep," he coached her, his fingers tightening in her hair.

She let her knee fall out to the side and pressed deeper.

"Keep going. Make yourself come," he told her, starting to apply more bobby pins to her hair. "I want you slick and hot when I'm done here so I can slide deep."

She moaned louder this time and slid her fingers in and out, loving the sensation and the thought of Logan taking her after this. She kept moving as she felt Logan finishing the twist in record time.

"That's it, Dana," he told her, securing the last bobby pin, then dropping his hands to her nipples, plucking and pinching. "Come for me. Come all over your fingers. I'm going to suck them clean, then you're going to get up here in my lap and come on my cock."

Her breathing hitched and her muscles clenched, and as he squeezed one nipple and kissed her neck, she felt herself climbing to the peak.

"I can already taste you," he said huskily. "I want you on my tongue."

And she shot over the edge. She gave a little cry as the orgasm hit. Logan grabbed her wrist and pulled her hand from between her legs to his mouth. The ripples of pleasure kept going as she felt the hot suction on her fingers. He licked and sucked, then lifted her, bringing her onto his lap. She was still facing away from him and there was something strangely hot about not looking at him as he lifted her and then lowered her onto his cock.

It was him taking over. She knew that. There were no decisions to be made here, no responsibility, no keeping track of someone else. She didn't have to worry about birth control, he was telling her what to do, and she wasn't even looking at him. She was fully absorbed in *her* pleasure, her body. And it felt amazing.

Logan lifted and lowered her, talking dirty, his hand wandering from nipple to clit, filling her and moving her closer and closer to that delicious pinnacle. Yes, she'd just had an orgasm, but it just wasn't the same with her fingers. They would do—they *had* done for a long time—but having a huge cock on a sexy guy who knew how to use it...there was no replacement for that.

Dana let her head fall forward, bracing her hands on his

thighs and just moved with his thrusts. She closed her eyes and let the sensations take over, relishing the few minutes where she didn't have to do anything but *feel amazing*. But it didn't take Logan long to get her spiraling into another orgasm and Dana completely let herself go, not worrying about him or how wanton she sounded or...anything. And it was glorious.

Logan was right behind her, his hands gripping her hips hard and her name coming from between clenched teeth only moments later. She felt him rest his forehead on her back and take a huge, deep breath, and she gave a long, contented sigh.

"How's my hair look?" she asked.

She felt him chuckle. "Those bobby pins really hold when you put them in right."

Dana laughed and sat back. He wrapped his arms around her and sat back into the couch cushion, bringing her up against his chest. "And you passed the distraction test."

"Awesome." He stroked a hand over her stomach and Dana wondered if he was aware of the action.

"Stay."

The word was out before she could think twice about it.

She felt his surprise in the way his body tensed under her. "Stay the night?" he asked.

She nodded, wetting her lips. Okay, this was big. Having a guy stay the night with her girls just down the hall was huge, actually. It had never happened except for their dad. And this, with Logan, was fast. They'd had a one-night stand and now, a week after finding out they were pregnant, she was asking him to stay over. But...Logan was a part of this now. He was going to be around. A lot. For a very long time. And she'd seen him at the family gatherings. She knew how close he was to his brother and his mom and the kids. Logan was a good guy. He wasn't going anywhere.

"Yeah," she said, softly. "Stay the night."

"I'm asking this one time," he said. "And only one time. No matter your answer, I'm not asking again, so be sure."

"Okay."

"Are you *positive* that's what you want?"

She did. She really did. For very selfish reasons. Because she would *love* more of what he'd just done to her. And it would be pretty awesome to have someone hold her all night.

Remember he's the chauffeur, party-planner and sex therapist, she reminded herself. Sure, the cuddling would be a nice bonus, but she'd gotten by without that for a long time.

Chauffeur, party-planner, sex therapist, she repeated silently.

Okay, so he could give her another orgasm and then maybe he could run Chloe to school in the morning. Dana could take Grace, whose school was on her way to work, and Logan could take Chloe and it would save them all nearly thirty minutes. Heck, she could make a breakfast of more than cereal and peanut butter toast with that extra time.

"Dana?"

She focused on Logan and realized that yes, she wanted him to stay and that it wasn't just about the orgasms and school drop-offs. She wanted to wake up with him and make him an omelet and...start her day by talking to him.

But she forced herself to concentrate on the other stuff. Getting too used to having someone's scent on her sheets, some-one's hand in hers, someone's smile across the breakfast table made it really hard to go back to not having those things when they were gone. Lindsey would help with the chauffeur duties, Dana could muddle her way through the parties, and she had a pretty great vibrator. But that other stuff was really hard to replace.

She gave him a smile. "I want you to stay," she told him honestly. "And you can practice doing hair on the girls for school in the morning."

That would save her another ten minutes right there. That would be very *helpful*. Which was what Logan was going to be in her life. Not something that she would crave and want all the time and miss with an aching in her chest when it was gone.

She'd been there, done that. She'd fallen in love with a guy who couldn't be there all the time, who couldn't be a true partner in every sense, who had been a hell of a good time when he was around, but who wasn't there for...a lot of things. And she'd handled it. She was doing just fine. She didn't *need* Logan to be there. She'd enjoy the times he was, but she wouldn't let herself expect, or want, more.

Logan gave her a big grin, oblivious to her thoughts and the churning emotions she was trying to ignore. "Then let's go. I have some plans for your headboard."

Just like that, the melancholy thoughts dimmed and in their place was the happy sense of fun that Logan brought with him so naturally.

And that was good enough.

"You break my headboard and you're buying me a new one. A very expensive new one," she teased as she got up and pulled her pants and shirt back on.

"If we break your headboard, I'm hanging the pieces on the wall in the bar so I can tell everyone about it," he told her. Then he scooped her up in his arms and carried her up to bed.

And she only thought about how fun it was and *not* about how easy it would be to get used to this.

———

"We brought this last month. Everyone is going to hate me!"

Logan felt his eyes widen but he kept his mouth shut. Hating someone over homemade trail mix for snack time seemed harsh, but what did he know about fourth grade?

Dana sighed. "We don't have time to make anything else."

She was filling snack bags with a mix of pretzels, yogurt-covered raisins, almonds—except the two bags for the kids with nut allergies—and peanut butter flavored cereal balls. A few bags had chocolate chips in them, a few had fruit snacks in them, and a few had cheese crackers in them, but she hadn't had enough of any of those to go around. She'd basically just ransacked her cupboards after Chloe had reminded her that it was her turn to bring snacks to class.

"I *told* you about it last time," Chloe said.

Dana nodded. "You did. I forgot. I'm very sorry, but there's nothing I can do right now," she said. "Next month we'll do something else."

"You'll forget," Chloe muttered.

Dana didn't argue.

Logan grinned. Mornings with the Doucet ladies was chaotic. And he kind of loved it. He slipped the elastic band around Grace's ponytail. "Okay, pick a bow."

There were several bows and headbands that had black in them but only one that was all black. Grace was wearing black tights with a black-and-white striped dress, though, so Logan was assuming that her obsession with wearing black everyday didn't mean it had to be *solid* black.

She studied the choices in front of her intently. "What's your favorite color?" she asked him.

Surprised, he looked at the bows. "Purple," he decided. "Definitely."

Grace nodded. "Yeah. That one." She pointed at a purple one.

Logan leaned over to look at her face. "Really? You sure?"

She nodded. "Black is my daddy's favorite color, but you'll be my baby brother's daddy, so I'll wear purple for you."

The entire kitchen went quiet. Shock and an emotion he couldn't name rocked through him. Logan looked over at Dana. She was staring at Grace.

"Grace?" she asked, after clearing her throat. "Why do you think your daddy's favorite color was black?"

"Everyone wore it to his party," Grace said. She looked up at Logan. "So at your funeral, we'll all wear purple, okay?"

Logan fought the urge to grin. Because it was slightly crazy how comfortable this little girl was with talking about death. And because he would actually love to attend a funeral where everyone wore purple. And because wearing the deceased's favorite color was actually a brilliant idea. And because Grace was already planning his funeral.

He gave her a solemn nod. "Thanks, honey."

She looked at her mom. "And we'll all wear blue at yours."

Dana blinked at her. "Well...um...okay."

Grace looked at Logan. "My mom's favorite color is blue."

"I didn't know that," he told her honestly. "Thank you."

Grace lifted her shoe, with the bright blue shoelaces, one of which Logan had borrowed the other night for Chloe's hair. "This kind of blue."

Logan nodded. "That's the best kind of blue."

Grace picked up the purple bow and handed it to him, then turned again so he could put it in her hair. He looked over at Dana again and found her eyes shiny with tears. She met his gaze, and he could see that she was stunned by the fact that Grace was wearing blue shoelaces because it was Dana's favorite color. He gave her a wink. Her daughter was an adorable, sweet, and loving little weirdo. Or maybe she was the most normal of all of them. After all, everyone was going to have a funeral. Why not make it flamboyant and use their favorite colors?

"I wanted to take Rice Krispies bars," Chloe said, clearly unimpressed, and unconcerned, with funerals at the moment. As a ten-year-old probably should be.

"I have four," Dana told her wearily. "I have *four* Rice Krispies bars. Snack time is at ten. I can't get more before that."

"But everyone wants Rice Krispies bars!" Chloe insisted. "I told them that's what I was bringing."

"Then this is a good lesson in not making promises you're not sure you're going to be able to keep," Dana said, zipping the last little baggie shut and putting it in the box with the others.

"So they'll think I lied too," Chloe said. "Great."

"I've got *four*," Dana repeated. "Unless we cut those up into twenty little pieces, I don't know what you want from me."

"Make it a contest," Logan said. He picked Grace up and swung her down from the stool she was sitting on.

"Huh?" Chloe asked.

He looked up to find Dana and Chloe both looking at him. He shrugged. "Take the bars you do have," he said to Chloe. "But then give everyone a bag of snack mix and make it into a contest to see who gets the Rice Krispies bars. It's fun, no one will care about the snack mix because they'll be so focused on the contest, and no one's a liar."

"What kind of contest?" Chloe asked.

"You can't have an eating contest," Dana protested right away. "Someone could choke eating too fast."

"Okay, then it's a taste test," Logan said. "They get blindfolded, they eat the things in their bag, and have to identify each thing."

"But everyone else will hear their answers," Chloe said.

"They have to write them down. No talking out loud," Logan said.

"How can they write them down if they're blindfolded?" Dana wanted to know. She'd folded her arms, but she looked amused.

"Okay, it's a *memory* game, a *spelling test*, and a *taste test* all in one," Logan declared. "They eat their snacks blindfolded. When they're totally done, they take the blindfold off and have to write down as many things from the mix as they can remember. And they have to spell them right. First four to get it all right win Rice Krispies treats."

"They'll still be eating too fast and could choke," Dana said.

Logan rolled his eyes and Chloe actually giggled. He smiled at her. "Okay, no one wins for speed. When *everyone* finishes their list, the teacher takes all the right ones and picks four out of a hat."

Chloe nodded. "Okay. That sounds fun." She grabbed a headband and climbed up onto the stool next to him. "Will you put this in for me?"

Would he? Headbands were a piece of cake. He brushed her hair out, put the headband in, and lifted her off the stool. "Grab your backpack. I'll take you to school and carry that big heavy box of treats in with my big strong muscles."

Chloe giggled again and ran off to find her backpack.

"Man," Dana said, after Chloe had rounded the corner. "That's gonna get you another sleepover."

"I'm telling you. Snacks and games are my jam."

Dana was still smiling, but she had a soft look in her eyes. "I know."

He crossed to where she was standing and pulled her close. "What are you thinking?"

"You really want to know?" She looped her arms around his neck.

"I do." He was pretty sure.

"I was just thinking that, apparently, I have a type."

"Oh?" Logan asked, less sure now.

"You don't want to hear about my husband, though, do you?"

The thing was, he probably should. Logan shrugged. "Sounds to me like if he and I are both your type, he must have been a hot, funny, charming, sweet guy."

She smiled and nodded. "He was."

Wonderful. It was great that Chad Doucet had been amazing. Dana and the girls deserved that. It was also great that he'd been a soldier and had had all that military, tough-guy stuff going for him. Because that wasn't intimidating at all. Logan had, honestly, gotten the scoop about Dana's husband from Gabe, who'd gotten it from the support group, and then Logan had pretty stoically ignored the fact that Dana's husband had been a pretty awesome guy.

At first, it had been because he'd just been flirting. Then he'd been wrapped up in their one hot night. Then he'd been a little distracted by the whole we're-having-a-baby bit.

Oh, and he didn't really want to know how he measured up to the brave military hero who'd died protecting Logan's ass... amongst many others, of course.

"So that's your type, huh?" Logan asked. Might as well get the gushing over with.

"The cool, easygoing, make-everything-fun guy?" she asked. "Yeah. I guess so."

"Well, thank you," Logan said. He liked all of those adjectives.

"I didn't think I would do that again."

"Do what?"

"Go for a guy like that," she said.

"Oh?" Logan pulled back to look at her more fully. "Why not?"

"Honestly, I hadn't really thought about being involved with anyone again," she said. "But I guess if I *had* thought about it, I would have thought I'd go for someone more serious. But," she went on, before he could respond. "I think this is really good. It's a good balance. The girls need fun."

Logan wasn't sure why, but something pricked at the back of his mind. He wasn't sure that all of this was as complimentary as it sounded. But he couldn't figure out why it wasn't. "Everyone needs to have fun," he agreed. "Sometimes."

She nodded. "When Chad would come home, it seemed like the girls laughed more, played more, did new things. He was determined that they have fun and remember him when he was gone as the one they went on adventures with and got to just be silly with." She pulled away from Logan's embrace and started putting the plastic bags away. "It was always kind of annoying. He'd disrupt the schedule and he always got to be the good guy.

He wasn't fun-loving and silly when he was gone, of course. In fact, at first, I didn't understand what was going on with him. But then I realized, he needed a chance to laugh and play too."

Logan watched her, realizing that she was trying to keep busy because things had suddenly taken a serious turn. "I get that," he said. He couldn't imagine what Chad and the other guys went through over there. Wanting to just kick back and have fun with his girls when he was home made complete sense.

She turned away from the cupboard. "Yeah." She took a breath and met his eyes. "So, I let it go because I knew they all needed it."

He nodded.

"But now...now that it's been two years since the girls had that..." She swallowed hard.

Logan didn't know if he should grab her and hug her or if he should just let her be. He started to reach out, spurred on by *his* need to hug her, but she pulled herself up straight then and gave him a smile. "I just realized how much they've missed it and I'm glad they can have it again."

He watched her for a moment. Slowly he nodded. "I can totally do that."

She smiled and it was much more sincere this time. "I know. And it's good. It really is."

He finally gave in to the urge, took her hand and tugged her close. He enfolded her in a hug. "I'm going to make a lot of things good, okay?"

"I know you are."

But there was one thought that wouldn't leave him alone... he was getting off easy here. This woman and her girls needed someone they could be silly with, someone who would be fun and easygoing and make things a little lighter. He could definitely do that.

But he wanted to do more.

6

"Right there in the midst of the hair bows and pretzels, I wanted to drop my panties and push him up against the fridge."

Caleb made a choking noise, and Austin *actually* choked on the drink of coffee he'd just taken. Bea laughed and said, "Of course you did," while Gabe muttered, "Well, this is awkward."

Dana could only grin. She'd just told the support group about how Logan had insisted on learning to do hair and the other morning when he'd come to the snack-time rescue. She was... happy. This group had been the first people she'd wanted to tell about how great things were with Logan.

He hadn't spent the last two nights in her bed because he'd been closing the bar and didn't want to come over at two a.m. when she had to get up for work. But he'd been there four nights over the past week, had done the after-school pickup and the dance class run those nights, allowing Dana to stay at work a little later again. Her bosses had already noticed that she'd been around more, and Kevin had commented that having her along on their trip to San Francisco in July would be a lot of help. Could she travel that far for three nights, away from the girls? Maybe.

97

She'd need to talk to Logan about it, of course, and it was too soon to ask him to take on that responsibility. But...it was now a possibility where it never had been before.

And he just might go for it.

One of the nights, while Chloe had class, he and Grace had gone down to the most haunted hotel in the French Quarter, just two blocks from the tavern, and had talked to Bill, the concierge who'd worked there for twenty years and had some great ghost stories. He'd softened them up a little for the six-year-old—jealous wives killing mistresses and the kids who'd died in a fire there might be a bit much for a little girl—but he'd enjoyed talking to Grace about the ghosts. Logan had seemed just as giddy about the visit as her daughter, Dana had noted with some amusement and something that felt very much like affection.

The other two nights of dance class, Logan and Grace had sat in on the class, and Chloe had seemed as thrilled by that as Grace had about the ghosts.

"So, he's doing okay then," Corey, the unofficial leader of the support group—really the one that kept them all on track and made sure everyone had a chance to share each time if they wanted to—commented with a grin.

Dana nodded. "He really is. He um..." She wet her lips and looked over at Lindsey. Her friend was the one person who might not fully appreciate how much Logan had reminded her of Chad the other morning. It was what had kept Dana from telling the group about it at last week's meeting. Dana's experience losing Chad had, of course, hit close to home for Lindsey, and Dana knew her friend was watching Dana's progress through the grief process and life after Chad, carefully. "He's been with the girls and I hear the stories about what they do together so I know he's doing great, but actually *seeing* him with them, and their responses, reminded me of Chad and how great being with him always was for them. I guess I was just thinking about how helpful Logan could be, but not really about how good the fun and break from routine could be for the girls. For all of us, in some ways."

"But Logan will be there all the time," Gabe commented. "That's different from how things were with Chad, right?"

"Well, he'll be there a lot," Dana said. "And there won't be the times when we're saying goodbye." She thought about that. That was nice. The goodbyes had always been hard. "But not *all* the time," she finished. "It will still be something a little different when he's over and around."

"What about when the baby comes?" Gabe asked with a little frown.

"He'll get to do all the stuff he loves. Whatever he wants," Dana assured Gabe.

"Diapers?" Gabe pressed.

"Sure, sometimes." Obviously, the baby would need changed at times when he or she was with Logan. "But I'm not worried about that stuff," Dana said. "He's accepted Grace and all her quirks, he doesn't get fazed by Chloe's drama. The girls are happy when they're with him. I'm going to accept him just like that. Just go along with who he is and what he's good at and not worry about the rest." She gave Logan's brother a big smile. "It's all good. It really is."

"I thought you were going to have him really *help* you," Bea commented.

"Oh, yes, the parties and the pickups are so helpful," Dana assured her. "And you know how I've worried about Grace's obsession and Chloe's idea that everything has to be perfect all the time—and I know she gets that from me. Well, Logan listens to Grace and he's helping Chloe relax. He's actually taking Grace down to the Quarter on Sunday to see a jazz funeral. The path goes right by the tavern and they can watch from the balcony. And because all the girl stuff and dance stuff is new to him too, he's helping Chloe problem solve the things that don't go according to plan. The shoestring to tie her ponytail...things like that. Grace doesn't go on and on about ghosts at home and Chloe is a lot more relaxed."

"So..." Gabe started, "the diaper thing..."

Dana laughed. "Honestly, if he keeps making my girls happy, I don't care if he never touches a diaper."

Gabe shook his head. "He always gets out of the crappy stuff. Literally."

Dana just grinned.

"I'm sure that he'll be great at whatever Dana needs from him," Addison said, giving Gabe a look. "They'll figure out what works for them."

Gabe sighed.

Dana smiled at Addison. "Thanks. I know we're just getting started, but I'm very happy."

"We're all very glad," Roxanne told her.

"We are," Gabe agreed.

They moved on to the latest prison visitation Bea's grandkids had with their mom and Roxanne's issues with her fifteen-year-old's new boyfriend.

Dana listened and discussed, but in the back of her mind she couldn't help but think how good she had it. No jail visits. No worries about boyfriends. Yet. She'd always known that Chad would be an intimidating figure to any guys wanting to date his girls. The Special-Ops-military thing would surely make a boyfriend think hard about how he was treating that father's daughter. As happened at times, a wave of emotion hit her suddenly and she had to suck in a quick breath and give herself a second to get past it. Chad wouldn't be there for the first dates, the proms, the crushes and heartbreaks.

But Logan would. Kind of. He'd be around because of the girls' younger sibling. And maybe he could sit on the sofa and give the boys menacing looks.

She almost laughed at that, though. She wasn't sure Logan could do menacing if someone paid him a million dollars for it.

He'd welcome the guys into the house, chat them up, and have them laughing by the time they left for the evening. Hell, he'd be the kind of dad that boys wanted to watch football games and go fishing with.

Dana sighed. That wasn't all bad either. Being friendly to the boyfriends could be a good approach too. But obviously Logan and Chad weren't exactly alike.

"So he slept over?" Lindsey asked during their break in the middle of the meeting.

Dana glanced around to be sure no one could hear—especially Gabe. "Yeah. I know it's fast. I just...he was practicing doing my hair and...I didn't want him to go." She shrugged. She couldn't explain it other than that.

"Wow."

"I know." Dana sipped her coffee. Wow was a really good word for, well, everything right now.

"I mean, Chad never did hair, did he?"

"Oh, no. I kept all the dance drama away from him." She smiled. "But I don't think Logan finds it dramatic." She thought about that. Yeah, that was definitely part of it. The drama didn't get to him. "He's not that good at hair," she said. "I saw Chloe's when I got home the other night. It was up but it was...crazy. To get it to stay, I swear he used every single barrette he bought." She'd been right that the little barrettes he'd bought weren't big enough to hold Chloe's hair. Until he used six ladybugs, four frogs, and four pigs. Then it stayed up. "But Chloe doesn't care." Dana had been amazed. Still was. "She laughed about it. Said that he decided they needed to choose a theme, though. Either bugs or amphibians or barnyard animals. He told her he'd try to find cow and chicken barrettes if she wanted him to."

There was a long beat of silence and Dana realized she'd gotten lost in her thoughts for a moment. She looked up at Lindsey. Her friend was giving her a slightly puzzled look, while also smiling. "You would have done her hair right the first time."

Dana nodded. "And that would have been that. It wouldn't have gotten ridiculous."

"You're not really the ridiculous type," Lindsey commented.

"No," Dana agreed. She stirred the plastic stick around in her coffee. "But maybe my girls are. Or should be. Sometimes."

"Maybe. Sometimes," Lindsey said.

They were quiet for a moment. Then Lindsey asked, "Are you worried about him sticking with it? Do you think he's just trying to get on your good side for the baby?"

Dana felt her heart trip at that thought. But she shook her head. "Honestly? I think he was just trying to get Chloe's hair up and that was his solution." She blew out a breath. "Okay, maybe I think that the big picture—getting Chloe to dance class—might be about proving to me that he wants to help out. I think he's sincere about that. And he's getting it done. But the silliness and fun...that's just him. I don't think he intends any of that. I think the ghost stories at the hotel were as much for him as they were for Grace. I think he can't *help* but think of things like how to make snack time into game time too. That's just him. So—" She shrugged. "I keep him in his wheelhouse and he's happy, the girls are happy, and I'm happy. No worry about him sticking with it if it's all stuff he really likes and that comes naturally to him, right?"

That would be easy enough. It was how she'd always handled Chad's time at home. She made sure everything was good for him too so he'd always be happy to come home. She hated the idea that he might feel like being with her and the girls was more work. His time at home was happy and fun for everyone.

"And I do want him to stick with it," she said, blowing out a breath. "Kevin and Dave are hinting at upping my responsibilities. Which would mean more pay. And some travel."

Lindsey's eyes widened. "Well, good for you. You deserve it. Hell, you deserve more pay now."

Dana shrugged. "They're very flexible with me. If the girls are sick or I need to come in late or leave early, they're good about it. That's the trade-off."

"But now with Logan you think you can do more at work? Be away sometimes?"

"For a couple of days," Dana said. "I mean, it might be peanut butter and jelly and horrible hairstyles and cemetery tours for two or three days—and they might have to call you." She grinned. "But I think they'd survive. If Logan is willing."

Lindsey laughed. "Of course they would. They always survived Chad's time at home."

Dana nodded. Things had definitely been more relaxed when Chad had been home. It just...could be. Having an extra pair of hands and someone to keep an eye on things while she was doing something else, meant things could be less rigid and didn't take as much pre-planning.

"Is it weird?" Lindsey asked after a moment, her voice quieter, more thoughtful.

Dana focused on her friend. "Is what weird?"

"Having someone there...in Chad's place?"

Dana pulled in a breath. She had to be honest with Lindsey. "No. Not weird. Because...I didn't really think about it until the other morning. He isn't really in Chad's place."

"Isn't he?" Lindsey asked. "He's sleeping with you, getting the girls ready for school, picking them up."

Dana gave a little laugh that wasn't really amused. "But Chad wasn't really there doing those things," she said. "When he was home, he did. But it wasn't ever permanent. None of us got used to it." She sighed. "This, with Logan, just feels like having someone extra helping. Like when you help me out. Or my mom comes over. Or when Chad was home. It's an extra, temporary person." She shrugged. "There isn't really...anything to replace."

There. She'd said it. Logan being there and doing hair and going on ghost tours was new, so that wasn't a replacement for anything. And him being there to pick the girls up was a little thing that other people could, and had, done for her.

She gave Lindsey a small smile. "Does that sound extra bitchy?"

Lindsey looked a little sad, but she shook her head. "No. Because you're right. It's like...having a nanny."

"Well," Dana said, needing to lighten the mood. "Having a really hot nanny who I can have amazing sex with."

Lindsey, thankfully, laughed.

"Of course, I'm also really hormonal, so maybe that's not really Logan either," Dana added.

"You weren't the first time with him," Lindsey reminded her with a knowing look.

Dana couldn't deny that. "Okay, the sex is amazing. But that's not a replacement for Chad either."

Lindsey smiled, though there was a touch of sadness in her eyes. "But you can have it on an ongoing, booty-call-him-when-ever-you're-in-the-mood way with Logan."

Yeah, there was that. And that was no small thing.

"I'm glad about all of this," Lindsey said. "I really am. I do want him *helping* you, though. With real stuff."

"Trust me—making my girls happy, making them giggle, making them okay with just being them even when it isn't 'normal' or like everyone else—that is a *ton* of help. I don't want them sad or focused on doing everything right. I want them to remember Chad and everything, but I don't want them to have a hole in their lives where he should be."

Lindsey looked surprised. "You think Logan could be a real step-dad to them?"

"Oh, I won't dump all of that on him," Dana said quickly.

"Dump?" Lindsey said, clearly offended on Dana's behalf. "He'd be lucky to have you and your girls full-time."

Dana shook her head. "I don't mean that. But the finances

and legal stuff. The everyday boring, blah stuff. He'll be a very positive adult male for them to look up to and have fun with."

"They have fun with you," Lindsey said loyally.

"Eh." Dana waved that away. They did. The girls laughed with her too, of course. They had days at the park, going to the aquarium, reading under the covers with flashlights, movie marathons with chocolate chip cookies. Of course they did. "But I also discipline and harp and make a point of making Chloe's hair perfect and forget treat day."

"You mean, you're a mom."

"Exactly. And Logan is...a fun uncle." He really was. The girls were lucky to have him around. When he was around. She'd told him initially that he couldn't just be that. That being a dad would require more from him. But truthfully...she hadn't realized how great and important that fun uncle could be. And he was just so damned good at it.

"He won't discipline or ever do any of the hard stuff?" Lindsey asked with a frown.

"I've got that covered," Dana insisted. "I mean, Matt doesn't do that stuff."

"He's not *here*," Lindsey said. She seemed a little frustrated.

"And Logan's not their dad. He's good at green slime and ghost stories. The girls need someone doing that stuff. And he's happy doing it. It all works."

"You think the serious stuff would scare him off?" Lindsey asked.

"Well, tantrums and projectile vomiting and explaining racism and dealing with self-esteem issues in a ten-year-old all scare *me* sometimes. I wish *I* could just go home after the barrettes and green slime is done."

Lindsey finally sighed. "Yeah, I hear you. But *I've* got you. We've got each other."

"The best BFF-mom-dad combo ever, right?" Dana asked, putting her arm around Lindsey and squeezing.

"Yes. You definitely have me," Lindsey said, squeezing her back.

And Dana knew she did. The mom gig wasn't easy.

But having a fun uncle in the wings was definitely making it better.

———

"Hey, babe."

Dana pivoted in her seat quickly to see Logan standing in the row of seats behind her in the school auditorium the following Tuesday.

"Hey!" She hadn't expected to see him tonight. It was her night with the girls—school pickup and all—and he was supposed to be at the bar. "What are you doing here?"

"It's dress rehearsal."

She took in his grin and tipped her head. "Yeah, it's *dress rehearsal.*"

Chloe and her team had regional competitions starting soon, and they were rehearsing in a couple of the costume options to see which looked and moved best.

"That's why I'm here."

"You work on Monday nights."

"Not when it's dress rehearsal."

Dana pivoted fully in her chair. "Do you know what a dress rehearsal is?"

"Of course." He frowned. "Why are you so surprised to see me here?"

"Because..." She gestured toward the stage where twenty little girls were milling around in pink leggings. "It's dress rehearsal."

"And why do you keep saying that?" he asked.

"Because—"

"Logan!" They were interrupted by Amy Morris, one of the other moms. She approached with a huge smile. "Oh, hi, Dana," she said as she came up the middle aisle. "I didn't think you'd be here tonight."

"Hey, Amy. Why not?"

"Well, it's dress rehearsal."

Dana felt her eyes widen. Did *anyone* understand that term? "Right. That's why I'm here."

"Oh." Amy glanced at Logan. "I just thought when Logan was here, you weren't."

That was true. That was how this thing was supposed to be working. Logan was here when she couldn't be. When she could...well, then *she* was here. And at home. And wherever else she needed to be. "Yes. Because Logan's been helping me out," Dana said. She glanced at Logan but he just shrugged. "But, obviously, *I'd* be here for dress rehearsal." For fuck's sake. This was Chloe's first year with this group and she was the youngest of all the girls. They were going to Baton Rouge for a weekend competition in two weeks. Dana had to know any changes or tweaks to the costumes and the hair and even the travel plans.

"Well, great," Amy said. "I'm glad you're here. And I'm *really* glad to see you," she said, turning a bright smile on Logan.

Dana watched the slow, easy grin spread across Logan's face. The grin he couldn't seem to help but give females of all shapes, sizes, and ages, in all situations.

"I'm ready." He held up a hairbrush.

"Awesome," Amy practically gushed.

"I already did Chloe's hair," Dana told him.

"That's okay," he said. "I can redo it."

Dana frowned. "Redo it? But—"

"Come on, everyone's waiting," Amy said, starting back down the aisle.

Logan glanced at Dana. "I'll be back in a little bit."

"But— What's going on?" she asked.

"It's dress rehearsal," he told her with a wink.

And over the next fifteen minutes, Dana watched with a mix of amazement and, if she was honest, lust.

The guy was doing hair. *All* of the hair. All twenty little girls' hair. In some crazy twist...with lots of barrettes.

Dana had no idea what was going on.

Logan was here for dress rehearsal and was, evidently, the hair guru.

She looked to her right as Amy came into her row and took a seat three chairs down. "Thank goodness I finally figured that out," she said with a little laugh.

"Figured what out?" Dana asked.

"How to do that hairstyle." Amy pointed at the stage. "Logan was practicing on my hair last week so I never really *saw* him do it, you know?" She lifted her hand and touched the back of her head as if remembering Logan's hands in her hair.

"Logan practiced that on you?" Dana asked, feeling a stab of jealousy. And *that* was stupid. No way his playing with Amy's hair had gone the way playing with *her* hair had.

Still...she didn't love the idea of his hands on another woman. She also didn't love that it bothered her. A lot.

"Yeah, while we watched rehearsal." Amy laughed. "He wasn't very good at it, but he kept doing it over and over. It started the night with all the barrettes in Chloe's hair. He wanted to get better at it, but then at the end of the rehearsal, Chloe told him that everyone wanted to do a style with lots of sparkly barrettes."

Dana shook her head. Of course it had turned out that way. Was there anything Logan Trahan could do to a woman, of any age, that she wouldn't think was absolutely amazing and magical?

"So you and Logan are together?" Amy asked, looking away from the side of the stage where Logan was finishing up the last couple of hairdos.

Dana gave her a big smile. And remembered that Amy was single. "We are," she said firmly. In fact, she and Logan were going to have a talk about whose hair he did from here on out. "Very together." He was at her house every single night that she wasn't. And he stopped by on some of the nights she was. And stayed over.

"Lauren told me that Chloe said you're having a baby," Amy said of her daughter.

Dana nodded. "Yep. Me and Logan."

Amy gave a little shrug. "Well, I had to ask." Her eyes went back to Logan.

Dana's gaze followed. She almost hoped their baby *would* be another girl. Logan had a magic touch with females. Maybe they'd get through the teenage years with no drama. Maybe with all three girls.

Dana swallowed. She shouldn't think about Logan and her girls long-term. Sure, he'd be around, in and out, because of their baby. But she couldn't put a bunch of expectations on him with Chloe and Grace. She shouldn't make plans. Not making long-term plans was something she was pretty good at.

Of course, the more fun he had with all of it, the more likely he was to be around more often, she thought as she watched him laughing with the girl he was styling. Dana found Chloe off to the side, watching. With a smile. She looked...affectionate, and maybe a little proud. Dana felt her chest tighten. She'd love if her girls loved Logan. He was a really good guy and, well, there weren't going to be any *other* men in their lives. She was having a baby with Logan. She had no interest in juggling a relationship—whatever that ended up looking like—with him *and* someone else.

But if her girls fell for him, she'd really need him to stick around. At least, he'd need to be consistent. If Chloe and Grace came to expect him to be around for birthday parties and a weekend a month at the zoo or the occasional ghost tour, then he needed to keep up with that. So Dana would keep the boring or not-as-fun stuff—like dance dress rehearsals, parent-teacher conferences, and homework projects—and would let him have the fun.

When everyone's hair was appropriately twisted and pinned up, Logan came back up the aisle.

She watched him, acutely aware that he was incredibly good-looking and that her body responded to that damned grin of his, just like every other female on the planet. She was not immune. Nor did she really want to be.

"No playing with other women's hair," she said, as he slid into the seat next to her.

He looked over at her. "They're little girls."

"I mean Amy." She gave him a look.

He chuckled and reached for her hand, bringing it to his mouth for a kiss. Then he said, as if they were talking about the weather, "You're the only woman I want riding my cock after I brush her hair."

Dana was hit by a sudden streak of heat and had to clear her throat.

He laughed and put her hand on his thigh, covering it with his. She knew she should expect him to talk like that, whether they were in the middle of a school auditorium or not, but he had a gift for catching her off guard.

They watched the girls line up for the first number, and Dana noted that Chloe looked a little nervous.

"You didn't have to come tonight, you know," she said, leaning in closer to Logan, but with her eyes still on the stage.

"Of course I did," he said. "I'm the Hair Honcho."

She glanced at him. He gave her a grin. "Get it? Hair Honcho? Instead of Head Honcho?"

She snorted. He was such a goof. And she really wanted him to stick around. That thought jabbed her in the chest and she fought to keep the smile on her face. "You know Head Honcho would still kind of apply," she told him. "Hair is on heads, after all."

He gave her a little smile. Like her teasing pleased him. "Or I could just go for it all and be Head Hair Honcho."

She laughed and tightened her hand on his. "I still can't believe you came and did this tonight. You could have told me. I would have done the hair."

He nodded. "Yeah. But I wanted to come."

"You've seen this routine probably eighty times by now."

"That's okay." He settled into the seat, still holding her hand, his eyes on the stage.

"But really, Logan. You shouldn't have to be here. I've got tonight."

"I know you do. But I wanted to be here."

She sighed. Geez, she was trying to let the guy off the hook here. "I thought our deal was to take turns. You help out when I can't be there, but when I'm around, you're free."

He looked over. "I'm free?"

"Yeah." Dana shrugged. "You're off for the night."

The music started and the girls started going through their routine, but Logan was still watching Dana. He ran his thumb back and forth over her knuckles. "I thought it would be fun to do this together. When we're taking turns with the girls we don't see each other much."

She laughed. "You saw me two nights ago, as I recall."

He lifted a brow. "You mean the booty call? Where you called me while I was at work and said some really delicious dirty things and *made* me come over and pleasure you?"

Dana felt her cheeks heat, but...yeah, that was pretty much how it had happened. "You saw quite a bit of me that night."

He gave her one of those slow, naughty grins that made her panties practically melt off. "Yeah. But not what I'm talking about. We haven't really talked, or just hung out, or anything." He leaned in. "And saying 'I love your cock' and 'harder' is *great,* but not what I mean by talking."

She felt her blush deepen even as she laughed at the "great" description of the naughty things he got her to say when they were together. "You *made me* say those things," she reminded him.

He sat back in his seat with a cocky smile. "Yeah. And you were a good girl about it."

Her pelvic muscles clenched.

"But, still not what I mean by *talking*," he said.

She shook her head. He really wanted to just talk? Logan Trahan? After *months* of pursuing her for a fling, he was now telling her that he wanted to spend time doing other things?

"Well, that's kind of how this goes. How it will go with the baby," she said. "We take turns. One of us does kid duty while the other gets other stuff done."

"Do you want to go?" he asked, turning his gaze back to the stage. "I'm staying, so if you have other stuff to do, go."

Did he sound a little irritated? Did she have other things to do? Always. At the top of the list was getting reports together for the conference call her bosses were doing with Beijing on Thursday. At the bottom was cleaning her oven. And there were at least forty things in between those. Which meant that her oven wasn't going to be getting cleaned. Again.

"I'm just saying that I thought this was what we'd worked out," she said. "We take turns. I do the sitting around, waiting, organizing, routine stuff, and you do the fun stuff." She'd dropped Grace at a friend's house to play for a couple of hours while she came to Chloe's rehearsal because Dana wasn't the type to traipse around a cemetery. "And I don't mind," she said quickly. "But I don't want you to think you have to do *all* of this. It's boring to watch this over and over, but I can work on paperwork or answer emails while I wait." In fact, she'd sent the reports for Thursday over to the printers from her phone just thirty minutes ago and she'd pick them up on her way home.

She could have sworn she saw Logan clench his jaw before he said, "I knew you'd be here tonight. I didn't feel like I *had* to come,

Dana. I wanted to. I wanted to help with the hair and I wanted to see you."

Dana swallowed. That was nice. It really was. But how long would it last? "I just don't want you to get burned out before—"

He looked over. "Before what?"

"Before the baby even comes."

He didn't say anything to that. But she was certain his jaw clenched this time.

"Babies are more work than the girls," she said. "I just want...I want you to be around for a lot of the baby stuff and if you get tired of all of this...not as fun stuff...then..." She trailed off as his fingers tightened around hers.

"Tired of it?" he asked. "Is that what you think will happen?"

"It's just...a lot," she said.

"Do parents actually get tired of their kids?" he asked, his eyes flashing with emotion.

She frowned and shook her head. "That's not what I mean. But yes, the activities and worry and schedules and...the *stuff*... can definitely get tiring."

"All the more reason for you to like having me around."

"Of course. And it's very nice. I just..."

He squeezed her hand again and she realized she'd broken eye contact. She met his intense stare again. "You just what?" he asked.

"I don't want to scare you off," she told him honestly. "I do love having you around and I want it to last. So I don't want to wear you out on all of this now."

He leaned in. "The only way you need to worry about wearing me out is in the bedroom. And you're going to even have to up your game there, Ms. Doucet. Though I look forward to you trying. Now, if you'll excuse me, I have something I need to do."

He started to get up and for a stupid moment, Dana panicked that maybe he really was leaving. Suddenly she really didn't want him to. "What are you doing?" she asked, not letting go of his hand.

Logan glanced toward the stage. "Chloe's forgetting the steps in that part again."

Dana looked in that direction. She could see that the girls had all stopped and their director was talking to them. Chloe looked like she wanted to cry. Dana frowned. "What's going on?"

"There's one spot where she and two other girls have a little solo," Logan said. "Though is it really a solo if three people are doing it?" But he shook his head. "Anyway, she's nervous because the other girls are older and do it right every time and she ends up stumbling because she's thinking about them instead of the steps. She thinks they all think she's an idiot who can't get it right." He slipped his hand from hers. "I'll be right back."

"What are you going to do?" Dana asked, watching him move down the row of seats to the aisle.

"Well, no one can look like a bigger idiot doing that dance than I will."

Dana felt her eyebrows climb her forehead as Logan made his way to the front row and took a seat right on the end.

The director started the music again and the girls moved into their routine. About two minutes in, Logan got up and started doing the dance in front of the stage. He got every step right—further testament to just how many times he'd actually seen this rehearsed—and he got the girls smiling and laughing as they went through the steps. When they got to the part that had tripped Chloe up earlier, Logan moved through it perfectly...and Chloe followed him. She didn't miss a step and when the routine ended, the director clapped. And Chloe beamed. At Logan.

Dana felt her eyes stinging and started blinking as she watched Logan pivot away from the stage with a grin on his face. She knew that he'd given Chloe a little wink at the end. She just knew. That was Logan. He'd make the moment right, covering it with a sweet layer of fun-frosting, and then he'd just wink about it. Like it was no big deal. When those few minutes might have been the biggest in Chloe's whole week.

He said he wanted to be around for everything and wouldn't get tired of the not-as-fun stuff, but he didn't even realize how important what he did do was. She couldn't lose that. Her girls couldn't lose *him*.

He reclaimed his seat next to her and took her hand again.

"Come home with me after this," she said.

"What for?" he said, a teasing glint in his eye.

"Yes. For that," she said honestly. How could she not want this man?

"I'm starting to think you only want me for my body."

And she was starting to fear—no, she was way past *starting*—that she wanted him for way more than that. "Well, we can watch TV or something boring like that," she said with a little shrug. "But if I *don't* give you a blow job for *that*"—she gestured toward the stage—"I could lose my woman card."

"Yeah?" he asked. "That's in the rule book?"

"*Dancing* with a woman's daughter to help her get the routine right, in front of her classmates? Oh, yeah. Definite blow job stuff."

He settled back in his chair with a smug look. "Okay, I'll *let* you give me a blow job. But," he said before she could respond to that, "we have to spend at least twenty minutes talking about a current news event first."

Dana had no idea what to do with this guy. So she just nodded. She could do that. Probably.

"And I want something serious. And nothing that has anything to do with the girls," he added.

"Wow, something serious in the news. We might have to really search, but we can probably find *something*," she said dryly.

He smiled. "That's my girl." Then he added, "But we can stop for ice cream on the way home, right?"

And there was *her* guy.

7

_____

"He wasn't just in the army. He was Special fucking Ops." Logan looked around the corner from the kitchen into the dining room where Chloe was doing her homework at the table and Grace was coloring and realized he needed to keep his voice down.

It was three nights after the dance dress rehearsal and he was knee-deep in stories about Dana's dead husband—her Special Ops soldier dead husband—for a report Chloe had to do about a family member who was a hero.

It had been Logan's idea to call Chloe's grandma, Chad's mother, for information since Dana wasn't around.

Now, two hours later, they had *plenty* of information about how amazing and heroic and badass and *amazing* Chad Doucet had been.

Gabe chuckled on the other end of the phone. "Probably a good thing he's dead. You wouldn't want to be messing with that guy's wife if he was alive."

"You're hilarious," Logan said. "Seriously. So glad I called you."

"What do you want me to say? That you're special in your

own way and not to worry about the gorgeous, intelligent, independent woman who is too good for you, comparing you to her strong and brave soldier husband who died a hero?"

He had definitely called the wrong guy. Logan scrubbed a hand over his face. "Yeah, something like that."

Gabe laughed. "You're fine. Unless you told her you're like a secret agent or that you moonlight as a brain surgeon or something."

"Uh, no. I've actually been pretty up front about what I do." Which wasn't fucking much, really.

"Then you're fine. Because she got into bed with you, more than once, brought you to meet her kids, and asked you to help out with them, knowing exactly who you are."

Logan thought about that. Gabe had a point. "So um...*why* do you think she did all of that stuff?"

Gabe laughed again. "Because maybe you're not so bad."

"But really."

"I mean it," Gabe said. He sounded mildly amused but not like he was actually laughing now. "Look, Chad was a hero. Thank God for guys like him. But also...maybe there's something to being here. Like you are. You know?"

"Being here. I'm making green slime, practicing doing hair— and by the way, French braids are way harder than they look— and helping Chloe write a report about her amazing dad. So, yeah, I'm here."

"Yep. And Chad didn't do any of those things."

"Because he was protecting *our* asses in the middle of a fucking desert surrounded by people who wanted to kill him. While I was pouring beer and screwing a new woman every night, he was carrying seventy-pound packs of equipment around in one hundred degree weather so that...I could pour beer and screw women as a free man!"

There was a long pause on the other end and Logan peeked around the corner at the girls again.

"Are you okay?" Chloe asked.

"Yep. You?"

"Yep," she said with a grin.

He gave her a wink. Then he lowered his voice and turned back into the kitchen. "Chad Doucet was *amazing*. What the hell is Dana doing with me?"

"Wow," was Gabe's reaction to that.

"Well, seriously. The guy led his unit. He *wanted* to be a soldier. He enlisted right out of high school, knew he wanted this to be his career. He saved *two lives* when he died." Logan worked to lower his voice again. Of course, it wasn't like Chloe didn't know all of this. She was the one writing the report, after all, and she'd been on that speakerphone with her grandmother just like Logan had.

"*How* are you getting this information?" Gabe asked. "Dana's never told us any of that."

"From his mom," Logan said. "Chloe needed info about her dad and I didn't want to go digging through Dana's stuff, so we called her grandma. I'm telling you, man, Chad was a badass. I can't believe Dana hasn't told you this stuff."

Gabe was quiet for a long moment. Then he said, "So this is what you're like when you're in love."

Logan pulled up straight. Love? "You think I'm in love with Dana?"

"I think you're in love with *Chad*."

"Fuck off."

Gabe chuckled. "Seriously, you need to relax. Dana was just talking about you the other night at group. She thinks you're awesome. She was all smiles and compliments."

Logan frowned. "Really?"

"Yep, said that she likes you just the way you are."

Logan frowned deepened. "What the hell does that mean?"

Gabe sighed. "She *likes* you. Jesus, are we in junior high? She likes you. You don't have to be like Chad. She said things are going well."

"So, I'm definitely *not* like Chad."

"For fuck's sake," Gabe muttered. Then said, "She said that you're great at the fun stuff and she's realized that's really important and so she's totally fine with you being yourself and just having fun with the girls, making them laugh, that stuff. She's not even going to make you do diapers."

Logan ran a hand through his hair. "She doesn't think I can do diapers? Fuck."

It all made sense. The way she was surprised he'd been at the dress rehearsal. The way she'd been *shocked* he was doing everyone's hair. The way she'd insisted that if she was there doing the routine, boring stuff, he didn't need to be. The way she'd said she didn't want him to burn out on all of this.

She didn't think he could handle the serious stuff long-term.

And the hell of it? He wasn't sure either. He'd never done a long-term committed thing. And he made everything into a game. Why would Dana think he could handle serious?

"I think she actually doesn't *want* you to do diapers," Gabe said. "And by the way, Addison does not share that feeling about *me* and diapers."

But Gabe was going to be fine with diapers. And every other thing having to do with babies. He'd done it once before. And because Gabe was...Gabe. He just took things a little more seriously than Logan did. Fun came naturally to him. It seemed to him that if a six-year-old was curious about death and funerals and ghosts, then they should look into it and help her understand it as best she could. It seemed to him that if a girl was having trouble remembering the steps to a dance routine because all eyes were on her, or so she thought, then it made sense to take the eyes off of her and put them on someone else. It seemed to him that if you had a classroom full of kids expecting Rice

Krispies treats but you only had four, then you had to figure something out.

But Dana's reactions told him that these were a bigger deal than they seemed to him. And he'd been feeling pretty good about them all. And the blow jobs, he wouldn't lie.

Now, though... He peeked back into the dining room. Now he got it. No one could be a bigger serious guy than a guy who not only took care of his own family, but took care of the entire country—hell, in some ways the fucking *world*—in his job, every damned day. Chad Doucet took care of business. Serious, big, global business.

Logan Trahan poured beer.

Yeah, he could kind of see why Dana wanted to be in charge of the serious stuff and let him handle the fun and games.

"I'm going to fucking do diapers," Logan told Gabe.

Gabe laughed. "Okay, but you may want to rethink just how adamant you are about that."

"I can do the serious stuff," Logan said. "Dammit."

"But she wants you to do the fun stuff. She's got the other stuff handled. She doesn't want you to—"

"Burn out," Logan interrupted. "Yeah, I know. And the fact that she thinks I could burn out on taking care of my kid says a lot, don't you think?"

"But you're not taking care of your kid," Gabe said after a moment.

Logan's eyebrows slammed together. "What the hell does that mean?"

"Grace and Chloe aren't your kids," Gabe said. "That's all."

"But they're Dana's. And I'm here now. So...they are. Kind of." Logan wasn't their legal guardian or their step-dad or their adopted dad. But he was absolutely good with all of those ideas.

"That's what I was hoping you'd say," Gabe told him, his tone sincere. "If you're going to do this right, then it means doing it right for those girls too. For good. Even after the baby comes."

"Of course it does," Logan said with a scowl.

"That's the right answer."

"Well, Jesus, the baby won't even be able to talk for what, a year? It will take a couple for him or her to be *interesting*," Logan said. "Grace and Chloe are already there. I'll probably like them more than the baby for a long time."

Gabe chuckled. "Don't know about *more*, but there is room for all of them. Trust me."

"I'm not worried."

"Good."

"Dana is." Logan's scowl was back.

Gabe sighed. "It's okay for her to be worried, Logan. You don't know each other very well yet and she's been doing this a long time on her own. Single moms are...amazing. And special. Not like other women. They don't *need* us. You know? So if they want us around, it's just because they want us around. That's pretty awesome."

Logan took a deep breath and blew it out. "That's a good point."

"So, just look at what you can do for Dana. Just be there with her. Remember you're lucky. And just roll with it."

Logan felt his shoulders relax a little. He could do that. Rolling with it was one of his specialties. "Okay. Thanks."

"No! Stop it!" Grace suddenly yelled from the other room.

"I can say that!" Chloe yelled back.

Wide-eyed, Logan started for the dining room. "Uh, gotta go."

"Yeah." Gabe chuckled, having clearly heard the yelling. "You got this, Logan," Gabe assured him. "All of it."

Yeah, well, if he didn't now, he would.

They disconnected and Logan shoved his phone into his pocket as he stepped into the dining room to find Grace standing on her chair, her face red, glaring at her sister. Chloe was frowning right back from her seat across the table.

"You can't say that! You don't know!" Grace told her sister.

"You don't know either!" Chloe said. "You don't know everything!"

"Whoa! It's not MMA time, girlies," Logan said.

That distracted Grace for a moment. "What's MMA time?"

"MMA is fighting," Logan said. "And there's no MMA in this dining room."

"Tell Chloe to not say stuff about Daddy!" Grace said, remembering the cause of her ire and glaring at her sister again.

"I can say stuff about him!" Chloe shouted. "He's my dad too! This is *my* report!"

Logan raised *his* voice slightly. "Girls! Someone tell me what you're talking about."

"Chloe says Daddy's favorite color was red!" Grace said.

Logan could see the tears in her eyes. He looked at Chloe. "True?" he asked.

"I said that because *Grandma* said so!" Chloe said.

Logan frowned. He'd gone into the kitchen to get snacks partway through the conversation with Chad's mom, so it was possible that she'd said that when he hadn't been there to hear. He looked at Grace. "Honey—"

"His favorite color is *black*," Grace said. She stomped her foot on the seat of the chair.

"Grandma said red," Chloe told her.

Logan scrubbed a hand over his face. "Maybe he liked both."

Chloe shook her head. "People don't wear black at funerals because the person liked it. Everyone wears black at all funerals." She looked at her sister. "My teacher said so."

Grace's face scrunched up and—shit—the tears started to roll. "No!"

"Grace—" Logan started.

"*What* is going on?"

They all turned as one to face the doorway that led to the front of the house. The doorway where Dana was now standing.

Damn, he really liked her in those dresses she wore to work. And the heels... He shook his head. "Little disagreement."

Dana took in the details, including Grace's tears and the papers spread all over the table in front of Chloe. She crossed to her youngest and plucked her off the chair. "No standing on the chairs," she said. She sat in the chair, putting Grace on her lap. "Okay, what's going on?"

"Chloe said Daddy's favorite color is red, not black," Grace said.

Dana looked at Chloe. "Why did you say that?"

"Because Grandma told me." Chloe pointed at the papers in front of her. "I'm doing my report on Daddy and Logan said we should call Grandma for some stories and so we did and she told me lots of stuff and one thing was that his favorite color is red."

"Is not!" Grace shouted at her sister.

Dana smoothed her hand over Grace's hair. "Okay, we don't have to yell." She looked up at Logan. "Sorry."

He gave her a quick shake of his head. "Nothing to be sorry for."

"Chloe said that people always wear black to funeral parties," Grace said. "And that's not true."

"It is too!" Chloe exclaimed. "My teacher told me! It was in a story we read in school! Right, Logan?"

Oh boy. He looked from Chloe to Dana. What the hell did he say? His instinct was to go with the truth, of course, but Grace was clinging pretty hard to that favorite color thing and who was he to mess with that? He took a deep breath. He knew who he wanted to be—the guy who knew what the fuck to do and say in these situations.

But before he had to come up with anything, Dana said, "Girls, I'm going to say good night to Logan and then we'll talk about this."

She was rescuing him. Or rescuing the girls from his answer.

Whatever that would have been. Logan felt surprise, and annoyance, ripple through him. "I'm good," he said.

Dana shook her head. "It's okay. We can do this later."

Logan started to reply, but thought better of it. Okay, then. He'd let her lead this. Until they got to the foyer. You didn't argue in front of the kids. Everyone knew that.

Until you got to the foyer.

Dana put Grace on the chair and kissed her head. "No more yelling. I'll be right back." Then she looked at Chloe. "You too."

Both girls nodded.

"'Night, girls," Logan said to them both. "I'll see you tomorrow."

"Bye, Logan," Grace said, giving him a little smile.

"Thanks for helping me with this," Chloe said. "I liked talking to Grandma."

"Anytime, sweetheart," he said. For just a second he was tempted to drop a kiss on top of their heads the way Dana did, but he resisted. It was too soon for that. Probably. Fuck if he knew, really. Instead, he just put a hand on both heads. "Sleep tight."

He followed Dana down the short hall to the foyer.

She stopped by the door, turning to face him. She took a deep breath. "I'm—"

"I swear to God," he interrupted. "If you apologize, I'm going to...not kiss you good night."

They both knew that was an empty threat. He'd never leave without kissing her. But his point was made.

Her eyes widened and she said, "Oh really?"

"Really. An apology is bullshit and you know it."

She put her hands on her hips. "I'm not sure I do know it. They don't fight a lot, but they do squabble. And this is obviously a bigger topic than just who gets the last cookie, or if we get strawberry or bubblegum-scented shampoo. You shouldn't have to deal with that."

"Why not? I was here. I was a part of the conversation since I suggested we call Chad's mom. Grace and I have talked a lot about funerals and stuff. I don't see why I couldn't be a part of this too."

"Yeah, we'll get back to calling Chad's mom," Dana said. "But you shouldn't have to deal with questions from my girls about their dad. Chloe shouldn't have argued with Grace about that, she knows how important that is to her. But at the same time, now that it's come up, I need to figure out how to talk to Grace about mourning and wearing black and that funerals are, usually, for most people, sad."

"I can help with all of that," Logan said. "We saw the jazz funeral. We could talk about why it's sad, but why it can also be happy and be a party like she wants it to be. We can talk about how different cultures do it differently." He moved in closer and put his hands on her hips. "And by the way, I really liked learning more about Chad tonight."

She looked up at him, a tiny wrinkle between her brows. "You did?"

"He was a hell of a guy."

She nodded. "He was."

"I mean he was *badass*," Logan said. "Did you know that he once rushed into a building that was about to explode to save a dog?"

Dana let out a little laugh. "I did. But you see, talking to Chad's mom gives you a little bit of a biased view. Yes, he did that. *But* the building wasn't going to explode until *they* detonated it. He saw the dog go running in and he went after it. But it wasn't like he was risking his life."

Logan nodded slowly. "I'll admit, I kind of like that story better." He pulled her closer. "I was all set to tell you about the turtle I saved from an alligator once. Scooped him right up out of the water just before the gator got there."

She lifted a brow. "Really?"

"True story. I swear." He paused. Then gave her a grin. "You can ask my mom."

Dana smiled. "Not your brother? Who was probably *there*."

How did she know that? "Admittedly, their versions of the story are a little different from each other's. But only in how far away the gator was from the turtle, and my hand, at the time," Logan said.

"And maybe if there was a gator there at all?" Dana asked with a knowing smile.

"There was," Logan assured her. "I mean...there had to have been, right? They're all over down there."

She outright laughed at that and ran her hands up his chest to link her fingers behind his neck. "You don't have to tell me stories. I like you just the way you are."

Yeah, Gabe had said that she'd said something like that at support group. "And how am I?" he asked.

"You're fun. You're charming. You're sexy. You make things lighter," she said, smiling up at him.

And dammit, he *knew* she meant all of that as a compliment. They were the things she *liked* about him. As Gabe had said, she'd let him close, let him get even this involved, knowing who and what he was. And she didn't *need* him. For him to be here, it meant she *wanted* him here.

Except that she was trying to throw him out before any big, serious conversations happened.

"So why would you not want me to stay for this conversation? I can maybe make it better." For some reason, he *really* wanted to make things better for her. And the girls.

Dana's smile faded. "This isn't a light conversation."

No, he supposed it wasn't. "I'm sorry I stirred things up. I really thought talking to Chad's mom would be a good way for her to the get info she needed."

"It was. That's fine. These conversations come up from time to time." Her smile was a little sad now. "And they always will, I guess."

"Yeah," he said, his voice a little rougher. "They will. I still wonder about my dad. Things still come up sometimes that lead to a story I've never heard."

Dana's smile was a little more genuine now. "Does your mom like telling the stories?"

"She really does." He paused. "You know, you could talk to her about it all sometime. Anytime. I'm sure she'd have some great advice and she'd love to share it."

Dana seemed surprised for a second, but then she nodded. "I'll keep that in mind. That might be nice. Corey, from the support group, lost his wife. He's great to talk to too. But his kids were older and remember their mom better than the girls remember Chad."

Okay, well, that was kind of something he could give her and help with. "Yeah, we were young."

She nodded. Then rose on tiptoe and kissed his cheek. "Thanks."

When she started to settle back on her heels, he palmed her ass and pulled her up against him. "Come on now, you know that's not enough."

Then he kissed her. Deep, and long, and sweet.

When he finally let her go, she looked a little dazed and turned on.

"Man, I needed that," she said with a little sigh.

And something Gabe had said echoed in Logan's mind. *Just look at what you can do for Dana* and *maybe there's something to being here.* Okay, so one thing Chad hadn't been was *here.* Logan was doing that. At least. "So, you think I'm a pretty good time, huh?"

"Best time I've ever had." There was a sweet sincerity in her tone and her expression when she said it.

He had to admit, that word "best" kind of made him feel

better. And there was definitely something in the way she was looking at him. "Okay, then. I'll see you tomorrow."

"Sounds good." She unlinked her fingers from behind his neck and stepped back. She sighed. "I wish you could stay."

"I could."

She shook her head. "You did the St. Patrick's Day party today, right?"

He couldn't help but grin. "I did. The leprechaun poop was a *huge* hit."

"Of course it was." She laughed. "No, I'll handle the daddy's favorite color and funeral conversation since you did the party and homework."

He sighed. They didn't have to argue about this now. They didn't really need to argue at all. She was going to go in and settle an argument with her girls, have a tough conversation, and then get them to bed. She didn't need the add-on of arguing with him too.

He pulled her in and kissed the top of her head the way he'd wanted to with the girls. "I'll give you a massage next time I see you," he told her.

"I will *not* forget you said that," she told him.

Yeah, he could lighten things up for her. If she thought he was the best time she'd ever had, then that's exactly what he'd be.

As Gabe said, Logan was lucky Dana was letting him be anything, really. He'd be the best at whatever she'd let him be.

———

Dana shut her computer down and rolled her head. It was finally Friday. Her bosses had headed out about two hours ago, and she now had everything done from this week and a huge start on her to-do list for Monday. That felt good.

It also felt good to think about ordering pizza tonight. And not having to set her alarm in the morning. And seeing Logan. He was at her house with the girls right now and, if there was a God in Heaven, everything would be calm and cool there, and he could spend the night. Because she had *not* forgotten about the offer of the massage from last week. This week had been crazy and they hadn't really had time for a massage. At least not the kind she really wanted. Especially considering that both nights he'd stayed over, she'd fallen asleep on him before they'd been able to...massage anything. But tonight would hopefully be different. He wasn't working, they didn't have to get up in the morning for anything, and maybe she could get the girls to bed early tonight.

Her phone pinged with a new text just as she grabbed her purse and shut her desk lamp off. She looked down, praying that it was Logan saying that he'd already ordered the pizza and that it would be there when she got home. And that he'd ordered one of those mega chocolate chip cookies too.

The message was from Logan. But it didn't say anything about pizza. It said, *Ever have sex in an elevator?*

She laughed. *No.*

Wanna try it?

Um...no.

Come on. No one's here. The security guy said that everyone has left except you. He said for twenty bucks, he wouldn't even watch the camera in the elevator while we're in there. Though I don't believe him.

Yeah, she didn't either. Then she frowned. Wait, what? *What elevator?*

Your elevator.

At the office? Which was a dumb question because she didn't have any other elevators.

She stepped into the foyer as said elevator stopped on her floor and whooshed open.

And sure enough, Logan was inside.

And damn, he looked good. He was in blue jeans and a button-down short-sleeved shirt. He had about a day's worth of scruff on his jaw, and he'd obviously just run his fingers through his hair because it was tousled on top.

"What are you doing here?" she asked.

"Picking you up." He put a hand on the elevator door to keep it open and tipped his head. "Let's go."

"Where are the girls?" But she stepped into the elevator. What was her option, really?

"I got a sitter."

She shook her head. "Oh, no, Logan, Lindsey had a long week. She can't—"

He let go of the door and pushed the button for the first floor. "Not Lindsey. They're with my mom."

"Oh, she doesn't have to—"

He turned to her quickly and backed her up against the wall. He braced a hand next to her ear and leaned in. He smelled damn good too.

"Dana. Breathe. It's all good. They're there with Stella and Cooper, and *everyone*, including my mother, is thrilled."

"But...what are we doing?" She could pretend that she wasn't a little breathless with him leaning in like that and that she wasn't focusing on his mouth. But why? This man affected her libido in crazy ways. And she loved it. As much as she hated feeling out of control, she didn't mind the way Logan made her heart race and her breathing quicken and her body heat.

"We're going to have some fun. Just us. Not with the girls. Not at the house or the school."

"A cemetery?" she asked, with a smile.

He grinned too, but shook his head. "Nope."

She reached out and took the front of his shirt in her fist. "I'll admit, the idea of having you all to myself for a few hours is tempting."

"More than a few hours," he said. "They're having a sleepover at Mom's. I was told we're not welcome back before breakfast."

She should maybe protest this a little more. She should

maybe say one more time that his mom didn't need to do that. But Chloe and Grace loved Stella and Cooper, and Dana trusted Caroline completely and...well, that meant the entire night with Logan. Starting right now. "Okay, I love this idea. I have some whipped cream in the fridge that I got for hot chocolate, but I suddenly have a different craving."

He caught her hand as she tried to run it inside his shirt at the top where the two buttons were open. He laughed. "We're not going to your house."

"But we *could*."

"Listen, you little horn dog," he said, his tone part affectionate and part exasperated. "We're doing something that doesn't involve the girls or sex."

No sex? Now hang on. "But—"

"Okay," he conceded. "There will probably be sex."

She let out a relieved little breath at which he laughed and shook his head.

"*But*," he went on. "There's more."

"I'm *really* okay with...less."

The elevator dinged as they arrived on the first floor and Logan ushered her out. "Yeah, well, you get to have the deep, meaningful conversations and do all the boring stuff, and I get to be the fun one, right?"

She narrowed her eyes, but nodded. "I guess that's what we decided."

"So, I'm being the fun one." He led her to the security guard's desk. "Sorry, Ed, no twenty bucks tonight." He held out his hand.

Ed chuckled and leaned over to grab a red gift bag. He handed it to Logan and said, "Well, I'm here every night. There's always next time. Ms. Doucet's been working late more often recently." He gave Dana a little wink.

She laughed. "I see you two already became friends." Of course they had.

"Hey, if you're going to get frisky in an elevator at a posh office building, it's good to have friends running the cameras, you know?" Logan said.

"You really think Ed won't look?" Dana asked, teasing the older man who'd been sitting at this desk for as long as she'd worked here.

"Oh, I mean so that I'm sure to get a copy of the video," Logan said.

He and Ed laughed and Dana just shook her head. But she had to admit one of the most attractive things about Logan Trahan was how easygoing and friendly he was with *everyone* he met.

Except the moms of the other dance girls. He didn't need to be friendly with them at all.

"Here." Logan handed her the bag. "This is for you."

"A gift?" They hadn't done the gift-giving thing yet.

"For tonight."

She was definitely intrigued.

"Addison helped me," he added.

That was good. And she was *very* intrigued.

"And the fact that there are no panties is not a mistake or oversight."

She paused, Ed snorted, and Logan grinned. So, of course, she did too. "Got it."

She headed into the ladies' room off the lobby. Ten minutes later, she emerged in a brand-new sunshine yellow sundress that hit her mid-thigh and yellow sandals. The straps of the dress were thin, leaving most of her shoulders bare, and crisscrossed in back in a way that needed a different type of bra. Or no bra. And, as Logan had warned her, there were no panties included with the outfit. Which made her think that the no bra thing was part of the plan too. Logan might not understand dress straps and bras, but Addison did. It all also made her glad she'd shaved that morning and that her pedicure was only about a week old.

Logan was leaning on the front desk, talking to Ed, but he

looked in her direction as the bathroom door bumped shut behind her. He froze. Then slowly straightened, turning to face her as she approached, her work clothes—including bra and panties—in the gift bag in her hand.

"Holy." He paused. "Shit."

What woman wouldn't smile at that reaction? She stopped a few feet away from him and turned, giving him the full view. "How did you know my size?"

"Addison," he said. "She guessed."

"She's good."

"She really is. I almost bought the red."

Dana laughed. "I like red too."

Logan nodded slowly. "I know you're talking but I can't concentrate on anything you're saying." He gave a low whistle. "If I hadn't already knocked you up, I'd really be working at it tonight."

She blushed hot and looked at Ed. She hadn't told her bosses about her pregnancy yet. Not that Kevin and Dave spent a ton of time chatting with Ed. But Logan had. And since the security guard didn't seem the least bit surprised, she could only assume that the topic had already come up. Logan seemed to have no trouble telling people about their situation.

And that was kind of...nice. Weird, maybe. But nice. She liked that he wasn't trying to hide it and wasn't embarrassed by it.

Which made her decide that she would tell her bosses on Monday.

"That's a very caveman thing to say," she told Logan.

Logan didn't look a bit apologetic when she looked back at him. "Yeah. You bring out the best in me."

"Being a possessive, mark-your-territory, keep-me-barefoot-and-pregnant caveman is your best?" she asked, crossing the rest of the distance between them.

He reached for her, a hand on her hip, the other on her bare shoulder. "I think so. Never been possessive before," he told her, his voice a little husky. "And hell yeah, I want everyone to know you're mine."

Heat unfurled in her stomach at that. She was fully independent. Could handle anything. Had a pretty great life, even having lost her husband. But dang, there was a little bit of her that liked that Logan had never felt like this before. And that liked the idea of being Logan's. Because that would make him hers too. And she liked that a lot.

"But don't you dare go barefoot all the time," he said, tucking her hair behind her ear. "Because these fucking sandals are hotter than hell. In fact, they're staying *on* tonight. All night. No matter what we're doing."

She laughed, her entire body warm—including her heart. His words weren't flowery or romantic, but they were sincere. Logan Trahan, French Quarter playboy, was totally into *her*.

And vice versa.

"So where are we going?"

His thumb was stroking over her bare shoulder and she was kind of hoping that he'd change his mind about not going to her house.

"Autre."

Okay, that wasn't what she'd been expecting. "What's there?" Well, other than his buddies and their tour and fishing company.

"Crawfish boil."

Her eyebrows went up. "Really?"

"Really. Crawfish, beer—sweet tea for you—music, and a bunch of crazy Cajuns."

That sounded...awesome.

"You up for it?" he asked.

"Absolutely."

He gave her a grin that curled her toes. "That's my girl."

Damn, she really liked when he called her that.

8

The bar was owned and operated by Ellie Landry—Josh, Sawyer and Owen's grandmother. It didn't have a name. Because when *her* grandfather opened it, it was a shack that sold beer and whiskey to fishermen and it was the only place in town, so it hadn't needed a name. It had never needed a name. There were other bars in town now, but if someone said they were going to "the bar", they meant Ellie's place, and pretty much everyone in the area just called it that—Ellie's.

And honestly, the place was pretty much like visiting Ellie at her house. She spent more time there than she did at home, she personally poured eighty percent of the drinks, and all the food was prepared according to her recipes and was cooked by her or her best friend Cora. Ellie knew every person who walked into her bar within five minutes of them being there and once you'd visited, you couldn't wait to go back.

Logan would never admit it, even under threat of death, but Ellie's pecan pie was better than any woman in his family could make, and if you hadn't been at a crawfish boil at Ellie's, you hadn't really been to a crawfish boil at all.

Her ex-husband, Leo, and her new boyfriend, Trevor, did the

actual boiling, but Ellie kept a careful watch over them and she was in charge of all the fixins' and extras. Including the best sweet tea in the South. Logan would fight anyone who said differently. As would everyone else who'd ever tasted it.

Logan watched Dana take the first sip. Her eyes widened and she swallowed quickly. "Wow."

"I know. I'm tellin' you, you have never had food like you're gonna have tonight."

She smiled up at him. "This is nice."

It was. It was peak crawfish season and the time of year with some of the nicest weather to be had in Louisiana. It wasn't cold, but the heat and humidity hadn't climbed yet. It was the perfect time to be outside, with twinkle lights strung from poles stuck in the ground, live music playing, great food, and friends gathered around. These were the nights that made Logan feel the most content, and he was surprised for only about two minutes that it felt even better with Dana there. He'd never expected that it could feel better. But this woman just made him happy.

Well, not when she was insisting on doing all the heavy, hard work herself with the girls, but that was...a conversation for another time.

Which was what he'd been telling himself for a week.

Dana had come home late Tuesday and Thursday this week, his nights off from the bar so he could go to dance class, and she'd fallen asleep on him before they could really talk. Or do anything else. He couldn't fight with her when she was snoring softly against his shoulder. Especially when she felt so bad about it when she woke up, blinking and brushing her hair back from her face, confused about where she was and what time it was.

But Logan loved that she could lean on him—literally—and relax enough to fall asleep. He guessed that she hadn't done that much before. Because more often than not, there was no one there to prop her up.

And now, tonight, having her away from the house, away from

her responsibilities, and surrounded by good people, good food, and good music, he wasn't going to bring anything difficult up. Tonight was all about his specialty. Having fun.

"Let's dance." He took her cup from her hand and set it on the table where they'd sit for dinner. It was still a little bit until the food would be ready, the band was playing, the moon was rising, and he wanted to get his hands on her.

"No one else is dancing," she said with a laugh, letting him lead her to an open area on the side of the bar's building where the band was set up.

"Why's that matter?" He spun her once, then started two-stepping her around the space.

Her hand flew to the skirt of her dress and she laughed. "Whoa, okay, if we're going to do this, we gotta take it easy on anything that's going to make this skirt fly up too high."

Right. No panties. He gave her a wicked grin. "Yeah, I'm not sharing that."

So, he dialed the spinning back a little. But much to his surprise, and delight, she knew what she was doing. They were soon swinging all over the dirt patch and four other couples were right there with them.

When the music stopped, he dipped her back—carefully. Bringing her upright again, he said, "You dance."

She smiled and nodded. "I dance."

"I love that."

She seemed to think about that for a second. Then she said, "Yeah, me too. I haven't done it in a long time."

The dinner bell rang just then—yes, Ellie had a big old cowbell that she rang when it was time to eat—and Logan took Dana's hand, linking their fingers.

"How about crawfish?" he asked. "You know how to do that?"

She looked up at him, clearly offended. "Where do you think I'm from, Mr. Trahan?"

He thought about that. She did have the soft Louisianan

accent. And she danced like a southern girl. But he obviously didn't know that much about her.

"I have a crazy idea for the night," he told her as they took their places at the long wooden picnic tables covered with paper and big metal buckets spaced at intervals down the middle for the crawfish shells. "How about we talk? Tell each other about ourselves? Share some stories."

She looked at him. "Huh. That is kind of a crazy idea. For us."

He leaned in. He suddenly wanted to know everything about this woman. "I'll tell you what—for every story you tell me, I'll give you a kiss. And you can choose *where* that kiss goes."

With a smile that was sweet, and cute, and sexy all at the same time, she said, "You're on, Mr. Trahan. But then you better find us a quiet, *private* place to talk."

He knew just the spot.

But before they headed that way, they ate, drank, talked and laughed with his friends. And yeah, Dana was clearly a Louisiana girl. Or at least, she'd lived here long enough to know how to eat crawfish and knew that you couldn't do it without corn and potatoes and that you had to do it with your hands. She dug in with the rest of them, twisting the heads off of the crawfish, eating the corn right off the cob, and she put back at least three glasses of sweet tea.

Logan was also grateful for the nosiness of his friends. Of course, none of them could leave a pretty girl alone if their lives depended on it, but in this case, they got her talking about her job and bosses, about her girls, and he found out that she was actually from Layfette. She shot him a little smile when she said it. Well, that made sense. She *was* a Louisiana girl. He also discovered that, while she loved pralines, her favorite dessert was bread pudding.

"Ellie makes amazing bread pudding," Owen said. The guys referred to their grandmother by her first name, because they had three grandmothers living in Autre who had lived there all their lives, and if they simply said "grandma," the instant question was "which one?"

"Ellie makes amazing everything," Leo, Ellie's ex-husband but best friend, said.

It was a strange relationship, but it worked so everyone just rolled with it. Knowing both Ellie and Leo, Logan could imagine that they were both a lot easier to like if you weren't living with them.

"Ellie's gator sausage is the best, hands down," Gabe agreed from down the table.

"I don't love alligator," Dana said, twisting the head off of a crawfish. "I don't hate it, but it's not my favorite."

"Well, then you *have* to try mine," Ellie said. "I only use wild and the ones I get myself are always the best."

Owen laughed. "You always say that, but you don't know which is which."

"The hell I don't." Ellie lifted her bottle of beer.

Owen just shook his head.

"You actually hunt alligators?" Dana asked Ellie.

"Of course."

"She's the one that took us out when we were kids," Owen said. "Our dads and Leo went along too, but Ellie's the one who taught us to shoot."

Dana's eyes went round. "Wow."

"You wanna go sometime?" Ellie asked. "You could bring your girls."

Dana's eyes widened further. "Um...I don't..."

Logan laughed. "Stella would never speak to any of you again." He shot Ellie a wink. "Though you could teach Dana to make bread pudding."

"Can't," Ellie said. "That recipe goes with me to my grave."

"I told you I'm selling that recipe at your funeral to the highest bidder," Cora said, returning to the table with a pitcher of sweet tea and heading straight to Dana's cup.

"You're just gonna get up there next to the preacher?" Ellie asked her.

"Yep, right after the eulogies when everyone's feeling mellow and fond of you. Before they think about how much quieter it'll be around here."

Ellie flipped her friend off and Cora laughed.

Logan glanced at Dana. The two older women were in their late seventies but hunted alligators and swore and flipped each other off. But Dana was just grinning as she held her cup up for Cora to refill.

"You sure you don't want some of the rum punch? *I* made that. I'm no Ellie, but I'm not all bad," Cora said.

Dana shook her head. "Oh, I'd love it actually, but I can't." She looked around the table. "I figured...you all...knew." She looked at Logan.

He grinned. The guys knew she was pregnant, of course. But he hadn't told Ellie and Cora yet. He hadn't seen them since *he'd* found out about the baby. And for all the things his friends were, they didn't run their mouths about stuff that wasn't theirs to blab about.

"Knew what, honey?" Ellie asked.

"Uh..."

"Dana's not a big drinker," Logan started. If Dana wasn't ready to share their news with a big group of virtual strangers, he was okay with that.

"Logan and I are having a baby," Dana said right on the heels of his statement. She took a deep breath and looked up and down the table again. "I'm due in mid-September."

"Hoo-eee!" Ellie exclaimed, clapping her hands together. "Logan Trahan, that's the way to do it, boy!"

Logan felt something happen that hadn't happened in *years*. He blushed. He gave Ellie a grin. "Thanks. I'm pretty...proud of myself, too."

Ellie cackled at that. "Sometimes it's better to be lucky than to be good."

And Logan nodded. He couldn't deny that getting Dana pregnant really did seem lucky.

"This really is good," Cora agreed, taking her seat now that all the tea glasses were topped off. "Little Cooper looks so much like Logan. It's only right to spread those genes out a little more."

"Um, excuse me," Gabe said from three seats down.

Cora grinned at him. "Oh, you're a good-looking guy, Gabe," she assured him. "And we're all hoping your new baby looks like you. Because Cooper could be Logan's." She turned back to Dana. "It's the brown eyes and the smile. That little Trahan boy is going to be just as much trouble as his daddy and uncle."

Addison laughed. "I don't know. Cooper isn't quite as...carefree as Gabe and Logan."

Cora gave her a knowing smile. "You just wait, Mama. Once that little one learns what a sucker girls are for big brown eyes, you're gonna be in trouble."

Addison grinned, but she didn't argue.

"Well, I'm kinda hoping for a girl," Logan said, draping his arm around Dana's shoulders. Damn, this felt good. Having her here with these people that he loved so much. Having her so comfortable. Seeing her laugh and smile and eat and just relax.

"Are you now?" Ellie asked.

"Oh, be careful about those kinds of wishes, boy," Leo said.

"No, really," Logan said. "I know how to do barrettes now. I'm set."

They all laughed. But there really were a lot of boys represented in this family as well as his own. A little more estrogen could only be a good thing. Speaking of girls, Logan realized that Kennedy, Josh and Sawyer's sister, was missing from the party. So was Sawyer, as a matter of fact.

"A little girl that's a combination of you and Dana?" Ellie

asked. "The mamas of Louisiana better be locking their boys up, because she'll have them all wrapped right around her finger."

Dana laughed and Logan looked down at her. "Shit," he said.

"What?"

"I just realized I'm in trouble."

"Yeah? Just now?" she said with a grin.

He nodded. "If this baby *is* a girl, she will definitely take after you and...well, being a guy who became a sucker for you far too easily, I just realized there's no chance *I* won't be wrapped around her little finger."

Dana's eyes softened and she put a hand on her stomach. "I've seen you with my girls. I already knew there was no chance of you not being putty in her little hands."

He laughed and hugged her close as the rest of the table chuckled with them.

Yeah, he was in trouble. But there was nowhere he'd rather be.

———

"Are alligators nocturnal?" Dana asked a half hour later, as Logan drove them about half a mile down a dirt road toward the edge of the bayou.

"Yep."

"So going *closer* to the swamp in the dark is maybe not a great idea?"

He shot her a smile. "We'll be in the bed of the truck."

"They can't jump?"

"Uh..."

She snorted. She knew gators could jump. The chances of one jumping into the truck bed were minimal, of course, but she was definitely not setting foot on the ground out here.

"I'll keep you safe," Logan said, pulling into a little nook in the midst of some trees and shutting off the engine. "I'd fight a gator for you."

"Well, how about we just avoid that whole situation? I would prefer if you kept all of your body parts intact," she said.

He turned on the seat, settling his hand along the back of the seat. "All of 'em? Not just your fifteen favorites?"

"I have *fifteen* favorites?" She also turned, tucking a foot under her butt.

"Well, there's the obvious one," he said.

She nodded. There certainly was.

"And then there's lips and tongue."

She swallowed. Uh, yep. Those were certainly on the list.

"And then there's all my fingers and both hands."

She laughed softly. "Each finger counts separately?"

He tipped his head. "I like to think they're each worthy of individual mention."

"Maybe you could use them each and demonstrate—"

"Nope." He pulled back and opened his door. "You're not tricking me into that. We're gonna have a *talk*."

"Tricking you?" she repeated. "Is that what I do?"

He looked back at her. "You and that magic pussy of yours."

Dana's eyebrows rose. "Magic? Really? Well, thank you very much."

He snorted. "Get out here. We're going to be romantic. And *not* naked. And no one's allowed to say the word pussy again. For...like an hour."

"You're the one who said it, not me," she reminded him.

"You're not above saying it, if you think it might get me naked."

Well, that was true. "But I'm not getting out."

"Why not?"

"Gators."

"Gators aren't going to get you."

"Not if I don't get out, no."

Logan shook his head, got out and slammed his door. A minute later he was by her door, pulling it open, scooping her into his arms, and carrying her to the back of the truck. He set her on the open tailgate and then climbed up beside her.

"We shouldn't let our legs dangle," she said, scooting back deeper into the truck bed.

He followed.

"And put the tailgate up," she told him.

He did. Though she could hear his sigh. But she knew a gator wouldn't jump up and climb over a closed tailgate. At least, she was ninety-five percent sure.

"Here." He reached for something and a moment later had a sleeping bag unrolled for them to sit on. He also had a lantern that cast a soft yellow glow over the back of the truck. That was nice. "Gator jerky?" he asked, holding out a packet.

She laughed. "No. Thank you."

He grinned and tossed it back with the pile of supplies.

"What is all of this?"

"Hunting, fishing, and camping stuff," he said, moving to sit beside her on the sleeping bag.

"You spend a lot of time down here?"

"I do. Love it down here. Love the city, but love getting away too."

"I can see why you like to hang out with these people," she said. The whole evening had been so nice. So comfortable. It was clear that the family had adopted Gabe and Logan into their fold. It seemed anything went—you could wear, do, say, and think whatever you wanted to. They would call you on your bullshit, but they would accept you. "How did you meet these guys?"

"The bar," Logan said, stretching his legs out and bracing his hands behind him. "Josh and Owen came in one night and we got to talking. They came back and watched the Saints game at the bar the next weekend. They told us about their business and we decided we had to check it out. And it's just evolved from there. They definitely know how to have a good time."

That was clear. And Logan fit right in. "And now Josh works for you."

Logan nodded. "He was working at a place over on Bourbon. He still fills in over there sometimes. And he's been around Ellie's place his whole life. And he doesn't sit still or do downtime very well. So when he saw that Gabe needed more time off with Addison and the kids, he offered to help us out."

"He was there the night I came in," Dana said, referencing the night she'd finally taken Logan up on his flirtatious offers of a night that would rock her world.

And he had certainly done that. Far beyond the bedroom. She had to swallow hard at that thought. Logan Trahan had blown into her life, turned it upside down, mixed things all up, and yet... walking into his bar that night in January was possibly one of the best decisions she'd ever made.

That realization seemed to suck the air from her lungs for a moment.

"I remember," he said.

"Yeah?"

"I remember Josh was over by the door when you walked in. He gave a whistle, I looked up, and I think my heart stopped for a second."

Dana felt *her* heart skip a little beat. "Really?"

"I knew you walking in there meant something."

He was looking up at the stars, but Dana knew he was totally tuned in to her.

"You comin' to me was something," he said, his voice a little rough.

It was. It had been a big decision. It hadn't been him hitting on her and her finally saying "okay." She'd dressed up, driven down to the Quarter, and walked into the bar all with the understanding that *she* was initiating everything that night. "I was nervous."

He looked over at her then. "No way. There was no way you thought I'd say no."

She wet her lips, keeping her eyes on the sky, wondering how much she should admit here. She hadn't been nervous about him turning her down. He'd kissed her under the mistletoe at the support group's Christmas party and well, he'd *kissed* her. It had been clear he'd wanted her.

She'd been nervous about something a lot bigger. Should she tell him? He was in her life now. They were *involved*. Very involved. What did it hurt to confess now? "Not that," she finally said. "I knew that once I was with you, you'd be very hard to get over." She glanced at him. "I guess I had a feeling everything was going to change."

Logan gave her a slow smile as he processed that. He clearly liked that admission a lot. "Guess your gut was right."

"Guess so." Though, if she had to say, she wasn't so sure it had been her gut so much as...her heart. She blew out a little breath.

"So, yeah, Josh said, 'if you don't take that girl upstairs right now, I'll never forgive you.'"

Dana laughed at that. "Is that right?"

"Not that there was a second of hesitation from me. But yeah, guess he knew it was a pretty big deal too."

They sat quietly for a few seconds. The stars were so bright out here away from the city lights. The water lapped at the edge of the shore. Crickets sang. A frog croaked here and there. And Dana took a huge deep breath. Maybe the deepest she'd taken in a long time.

"I like that sound," Logan told her.

"Me too."

"I guess I've been pushing to be involved with the harder stuff, but if I can make you make that contented, happy sound, then I'm good with whatever it takes."

God, how could this *not* involve her heart? "You're *really* good at contented and happy," she said. "I know I keep saying 'fun,' but it's not just that. It's just...happy. You just remind me—everyone—to take things easier."

"I'm glad."

And she believed him.

"So, you know how I met these guys," he said. "Tell me how you met Chad. Is he from Lafayette too?"

She shook her head. "New Orleans. His mom and dad relocated to Houston when his dad got a promotion, but that was after we were together. He grew up in New Orleans."

"How'd you meet him?"

"Blind date. My friend was dating his cousin. She wanted me to come to New Orleans to party with them for a weekend." Dana shrugged. "His cousin brought him along so I wouldn't be a third wheel. We hit it off and started dating seriously right from that weekend."

"How long ago?" Logan asked.

"Eleven years." She swallowed. It seemed like another lifetime. "It was the summer after we both graduated from high school."

Logan was quiet for a moment. Then he said, "His mom told me that he enlisted right away."

Dana nodded. "He enlisted before we met. He left that August. We had about two months together before he went to basic training." She took a breath. "I was pregnant when he left."

Logan shook his head. "Damn, girl, you really are the most fertile woman in Louisiana."

She swatted him on the arm. "You said New Orleans before."

"Changed my mind."

"Well, *anyway*, we got married after basic," she said. "Before he started his specialized training."

"But," Logan said, clearly working things through in his head. "That means you never really lived together full-time."

She shook her head. "Nope. We only knew each other two months, his plans were in motion, and of course we didn't expect to get pregnant. But"—she licked her lips and moved her hand to cover Logan's—"I think I'm learning that the stuff I don't plan can turn out just as good as any plans I put together."

He lifted his brows. "Whoa. That's pretty huge."

She loved that he knew that.

Logan turned his palm up and linked their fingers, pulling their joined hands onto his thigh. "So he wasn't around much. With the girls. Or really with you."

"He'd be home for several months at a time, but then gone for up to a year. Sometimes longer, depending on the mission. We never knew until the last minute when he would be home. And we never knew exactly how long he'd be home each time. He was Special Ops and basically on call all the time. If something came up, he had to go. So it seemed that even when he was home, the idea that he could get a call and have to go with little notice was always in the back of our minds." She took a breath. "But he loved it. He loved what he did. It was his passion. So I never minded." Much. It had always been hard to say goodbye. Being apart was hard. But then again, she'd never really known any different.

"And when he was home...you made it fun. Took care of the bigger, not-as-fun stuff so he wouldn't have to," Logan said, his voice gruffer.

Dana swallowed hard. So he'd figured that out. "I wanted him to be happy to be home," she said softly. "We hadn't planned any of what happened. We'd barely talked about *us*, not to mention a family and everything. He never, ever made me think that he regretted anything. He loved the girls and was great with them. And of course, we talked and Skyped and all of that stuff."

"But you can't really change diapers or do hair or help with nightmares over the phone," Logan said.

Dana nodded. "I just wanted him to really look forward to

coming home. Especially considering what he did all the time he was away. It was never just us when he came back. And I didn't want him to wish it was different." She'd known she couldn't compete with his passion. The military always came before family and she'd known that going in. But she'd wanted to be a solid, happy plan B for him.

Logan squeezed her fingers, and she knew that he understood she was comparing the situation with Chad to what she and Logan had going on. They sat quietly for nearly a minute.

"Okay, so you told me some stories," he said. "Where do you want a kiss?"

She smiled. Nothing made Logan Trahan serious for long.

And, honestly, she had all kinds of ideas about where she'd like his mouth. This was the perfect opportunity to make things sexy and get off of the serious conversation topics. But it only took a flicker of a moment for her to realize she wanted this to be...different.

"On my head." She lifted her other hand and tapped the top of her head where he often dropped kisses, almost without thinking about it.

He was clearly surprised. "Yeah?"

She nodded. He tipped toward her slightly, cupped the back of her head with his free hand and kissed her head. He lingered for a moment, taking a deep breath, but then sat back.

She snuggled closer to him. "I love when you do that."

"Really?"

"Yeah. It's...sweet. Makes me feel taken care of."

"Huh," was his only reaction to that.

They were quiet again for a stretch. Then he said, "For the record, even though we didn't plan any of this either, I'm very happy here. With you. Just the way things are. I don't wish they were any different."

Dana's throat tightened and she couldn't respond. She squeezed his hand. And that was enough.

She tuned into the night around them. The stars overhead twinkled brightly, and the air was cool but had the lingering feel of the warmer day. "It really is nice out here."

"Yeah," Logan agreed. "Lots of people don't think the swamp has much appeal, but..."

"It's easy," Dana filled in. "It's the epitome of laid-back."

Logan nodded. "Definitely. It's all about the slow pace and come as you are. It's just about the good things in life—good food, people, music."

"I like it." She paused, then added, "That all reminds me of you. Appreciating life. Loving the moment you're in."

Something flickered in his eyes. "I'm really glad."

She wet her lips. She knew she could run her hand up under his shirt, and it would be about two minutes until his hand was up under her skirt. But she didn't move. Instead she asked, "Is your favorite color really purple?"

He met her gaze. "I don't know. I honestly never thought about it until she asked."

"Kids make you think about a lot of things you never did before," she agreed.

"Is blue really your favorite color?" he asked.

She laughed softly. "Yeah. I've been asked that question before so I had to decide."

"I like purple," he said.

"Probably a good thing since Grace thinks that's your favorite. You should probably expect gifts and coloring pages in various shades of purple for the foreseeable future."

Logan grinned at that. "I would love a coloring page from Grace."

And she knew he meant that. Her heart squeezed. "I didn't know that red was Chad's favorite color."

"No?"

She shook her head. She wasn't sure how much she should confess to Logan about Chad and their relationship. It felt a little like a betrayal to say anything that wasn't good. And really it had been good. The big, handsome soldier had swept her off her feet. Chad had been a very loyal, dedicated, life-loving guy. In that way, Logan definitely reminded her of her husband. Chad had lived big. He'd believed in the way of life he'd known growing up and had felt strongly about protecting it. They'd had a whirlwind two months together, but it had felt right. She'd never had a moment's hesitation telling him she loved him and wanted to be with him, even if it meant half a world would separate them a lot of the time. Sure, she'd been young and in love and a little naïve about how that would all play out in actuality. But she'd been proud of him, and she'd often thought that maybe the way things had worked out had been perfect. They hadn't really gotten used to being together, so being apart was easier. She was naturally programmed to be independent and so she handled the separation pretty well most of the time.

"We didn't talk about stuff like that," she said. "I guess we didn't get to those basic things."

"How did that conversation with Grace go the other night?" he asked.

"Okay, I guess." She shrugged. "There are a lot of conversations like that where I'm never quite sure how they go. I don't know if I made sense or made a point or made anyone feel better."

"What did you tell her?"

"That it didn't really matter what his favorite color was because the fact that she was doing something with him in mind was all that mattered. And that if black wasn't his favorite color before, now that she's been wearing it for him, it is now."

Logan nodded. "Good answer."

"You think?"

He gave a soft laugh. "If that little girl asked me to make yellow my favorite color or kale my favorite food or snails my favorite animal, I'd do it without thinking twice."

And Dana felt a sudden stab of emotion that she was pretty sure meant she was falling for this man. Oh, boy.

That wasn't all bad, of course. They were having a baby together. He wanted to be around. He'd given her this night with these new people who already felt like close friends. And this was Logan. Charming, sexy, fun-loving, good-guy Logan. It was probably inevitable that she'd fall for him. She just had to figure out how that was going to work.

"I've been meaning to ask you," he said. "The other night, talking to Chad's mom on the phone, she didn't seem surprised that there was some strange man staying with the girls. Does she know about me and the baby?"

Dana nodded. "The girls told her right away."

He grinned. "I love how excited they are."

She did too, actually. It was going to make things, at least some of it, easier.

"Did she take it well?" he asked, of her mother-in-law.

Dana met his eyes. "She did. She wants me to be happy. She told me about a year ago that she hoped I'd find someone. She's pretty great."

"I want you to be happy too," he said. "I'm glad that she and I will get along on that point."

A prickle of surprise made her ask, "You think you'll need to get along with her?"

"I assume the girls see her at least once in a while?"

Dana nodded.

"Well, if we're both a part of your lives, then it's good if we get along."

She hadn't really thought about how Logan would get along with the other people in her life. But the idea of him interacting with them wasn't as strange as she would have expected. And both her mother-in-law and her own mother would love Logan. They were females, after all.

"I like you, Logan Trahan," she said.

He smiled, but it was a different smile than usual. It wasn't playful or sexy. It was...sweet. "I like you too, Dana Doucet."

Stupidly, she heard herself ask, "Why?"

An eyebrow rose and he asked, "Why do I like you?"

She nodded, feeling silly and vulnerable suddenly. But it was so obvious why Logan was likeable. Beyond his general outgoing, friendly, fun personality, he was sincere and accepting and, well, the grin. But she was...a working mom. She was more than a little bossy, because she had to be. She was never totally on top of things. She didn't kick back very often, and she tended to be thinking an hour...or a day...ahead to be prepared, rather than really being in the moment.

"The first time I ever saw you was at my first of the family potlucks for the support group," Logan said.

She remembered seeing him the first time too. *Damn*, had been her first thought.

"I showed up after Gabe and Cooper got there," he said. "And I walked up into that little shelter thing at the park, and the first thing I saw was Cooper talking to one of the most beautiful women I'd ever seen. I thought 'that's the way to do it, buddy,'" he said with a grin.

Dana laughed.

"You chatting with my nephew was the perfect reason to come over and introduce myself," he said. "And as I walked up, I heard him telling you a joke."

"I remember the joke," Dana said.

"You do?"

"Why did the teddy bear say no to dessert?" Dana asked. "Because she was stuffed."

Logan grinned. "I'd just told him the joke the night before. And you laughed like you'd never heard anything funnier. And the look on Cooper's face made me like you instantly."

That was sweet. She ran her hand up his arm. "Well, that's a pretty good joke."

"Yeah, and then *I* told you a joke," Logan said. "And you gave me a look that said *you're no way cute enough or charming enough to get me to fall for that.*"

She laughed. "Your joke was terrible."

"Other women had laughed at that one. And given me their numbers."

She had no trouble believing that. "You were using your *nephew* to try to get my number."

"And you weren't falling for it for a second," he said. "That's when I got really interested."

"I was a challenge?"

"You were too good for me."

She shook her head. "Come on."

"I watched you the rest of the afternoon. With your girls, with everyone else's kids, with your friends. It was all so...effortless."

Dana definitely laughed at that. "Effortless. Wow, *that* is not a word I would ever use about the things I do."

"But it is," he said. "You were standing by the food table having this conversation with Lindsey. I could tell from your expressions that it was a serious topic. You were totally focused on her. But one of Bea's grandkids ran by and you handed him a napkin, you refilled Corey's coffee cup, and you redid the barrette in Shay's hair, all without any of them asking you and without missing a beat. I doubt *any* of them, even Lindsey, realized that you'd taken care of all of that. But you did it. You took care of everyone and you didn't even blink."

Dana was staring at him. "You really saw all of that?" She didn't remember any of those things.

"I did."

"And you were drawn to the idea of having someone take care of *you*?" she asked, kind of teasing. And kind of not.

He laughed. "I was just *impressed*. And you were gorgeous. And you were unimpressed with me. And...yeah, I got a little crush. And it grew every time I was around you. You're so fucking *capable* and yet, when you look at your girls, you go all soft. And when someone in the group needs something, you're there. There was one party where you gave your sweater to Bea, your cookie to one of Austin's girls, and twenty bucks to Lexie."

She felt her mouth drop open. "You were *really* watching me."

"I couldn't help it." He lifted his shoulder. "You sacrifice for other people. That's sexy to me."

Dana tucked her hair behind her ear, feeling a little flummoxed. "Cookies and sweaters are hardly a sacrifice."

Logan reached to tip her chin up with his finger. "Bullshit," he said softly. "Those are just examples. You put other people first. Without even thinking about it." He paused. Then added, "I'll be honest—" He brushed his thumb over her chin. "I probably didn't put all of that into actual thought before all of this with the baby and everything. It was just a general impression of you. Something about you drew me in. But I do know what it is now. You think I'm fun and the life of the party and make people comfortable and happy. But so do you. Not with the same techniques, but being *with* you is easier on people than being without you."

She sucked in a little breath. That was, by far, no question, the best thing anyone had ever said to her.

She wet her lips. "You know how the no-panties thing was a little bit of a drawback for dancing?"

His eyes darkened and he moved his thumb to run it over her bottom lip. "Yeah?"

"Well, there are no drawbacks to it in the back of a truck in the dark down by the bayou."

"You decide where you want your next kiss?" he asked, his voice rougher.

"I have. But I also think that I've racked up way more than one."

He nodded slowly. "I do believe you are right." He laid her back onto the sleeping bag. "Just tell me where to start."

"My mouth," she said. "And then just...don't stop."

The man did exactly as she asked. The dress pulled down from the top and up from the bottom perfectly, allowing him to get at every inch they both needed him to get to. The touching, talking, kissing, and stroking was hot, but slow and sweet, and when her body tightened around him, taking him over the edge with her, Dana *felt* the way he said her name as he held on to her. And when it was all over, he rolled to his side, pulled her in against him, and kissed the top of her head.

9

Two weeks, three dress rehearsals, and another cemetery tour later, Dana answered the front door and came back into her kitchen carrying a huge plate of brownies.

"These are for you," she told Logan. "From your fellow dance moms."

"Oh?" he asked, pretending he had no idea what would have prompted such a gesture. "That's nice."

"You're considered one of the dance moms?" she asked, setting it down.

He was. By some of them, anyway. He shrugged. "I guess so."

She turned and gave him a smile. "What happened?"

"What do you mean?"

"I mean, why did Molly Anderson just bring you a bunch of brownies from her and all of the other moms?"

Well, they weren't from *all* of the other moms. "Because I'm awesome?" he guessed.

She laughed. "Maybe. But you've been awesome for a while now. What happened that suddenly deserved brownies?"

He looked at her. "Did she tell you and you're trying to corroborate the story, or she didn't tell you and you want the story from me?"

"So there is a story."

Crap. "And you really don't know it?"

"Do I need to ask Chloe?"

He sighed. "No." He leaned back against the counter. "There's just this one mom, who hasn't, by the way, been to *any* of the dress rehearsals and almost no classes at all, who suddenly has an opinion about the hairstyles."

It was clear that Dana was fighting a smile. "*I* haven't been to many of the rehearsals or classes."

"That's different."

"Why?"

"Because I like you. And you give me blow jobs."

She snorted. "Okay, maybe I get a little leeway there. But you get along with a lot of people who *don't* give you blow jobs."

He shrugged. And realized that he probably looked a little...pouty.

She grinned. "Is it maybe because she's not appreciating you and you're not even a little bit used to being criticized? Especially by women?"

"Maybe." That was exactly it, actually. "But Tiffany thinks she can just come in now, without being there at all, without contributing anything up to this point, just when everyone is really good at the style and likes it, and change everything?"

Logan realized that he was ranting about little girls' hairstyles for dance class. He knew that Josh and Gabe and Owen would get a huge kick out of this. He knew he should reel it in. It was *barrettes,* for fuck's sake. But dammit. He'd come up with that style and everyone loved it. Especially Chloe. That was really the bottom line. Chloe was proud to have him there and involved. And now Tiffany was trying to screw it all up.

"Okay, so what happened?" Dana asked, crossing her arms. "Tell me the story."

"Fine." He blew out a breath. "So last night, we're all there, everyone's ready and she and her kid—"

"Jada," Dana supplied.

"Right. Jada. The diva."

Dana's eyebrow rose and Logan nodded. Yes, he'd just used the word diva. Out loud.

"Anyway, Tiffany and Jada just blew in there last night, late, and started talking about how we needed to rethink the style. I've never even seen her there so I was just kind of hanging back, but I'll admit, I was getting annoyed. But then the other moms pointed out that I'd come up with it, and she looked me up and down and said, 'I guess that explains it.'" He paused. "She said it with this *tone*."

Dana bit her bottom lip.

Logan sighed. "I know. I hear myself. But—"

"Welcome to mom-hood."

"God, women can be such bitches."

"This is a surprise to you?"

"I guess..." He blew out a breath. "Kind of. I mean I *know* it, intellectually. Just like men can be assholes, women can be bitchy. But I've never really been the target."

"Even with girlfriends? Exes?" Dana asked.

He shook his head. "I tend to stay friendly with women. And I mean..." He trailed off and actually dropped his gaze.

"You mean what?" Dana asked. She sounded amused.

He felt completely sheepish, but he looked up and confessed. "I don't let things get too serious or let expectations build to the point where breakups are super dramatic." *Until now*. He didn't say it. He didn't need to. He knew Dana realized this was different for him. And yeah, a breakup would be dramatic. That was one word for it. Another word was devastating. And that scared the shit out of him.

Dana nodded, clearly not surprised that he hadn't had a serious relationship before. At all. "Okay, so Tiffany is one of the point three percent of women in the world who don't think you're amazing. I can understand how that might be hard to deal with," she said.

"You're hilarious," he said. Then he frowned. "I don't care if she likes *me*. But she made it all dramatic for everyone. Unnecessarily. And Chloe was upset. And *that* pissed me off."

Dana looked surprised. "She was?"

He lifted a shoulder. "I think she liked that the team was doing something that she and I came up with."

"Okay. I can see that." Dana paused. "And?" she said after a moment.

"And what?"

"Are you telling me that those brownies are just don't-feel-bad-we're-on-your-side brownies?" she asked.

He could lie. But she could ask Chloe what had been said. Or *any* of the other moms. "No. Those are you-said-something-we-all-wanted-to-say-but-couldn't brownies," he admitted.

Dana nodded, obviously not surprised by that either. "So what did you say?"

"Oh, trust me, I know all about what looks good and what doesn't."

Dana's eyes widened. "Did you say it in that drawl of yours?"

"The one that makes your panties melt off?" He gave her a grin.

"And with that grin?" Dana asked, pointing at his nose and not admitting—or denying—what his drawl did to her.

"The grin was probably more of a I-know-you-think-you're-all-that-but-I-disagree."

Dana nodded. "And you looked *her* up and down when you said it, and it was perfectly clear that you thought she was in the 'not' column, right?"

Logan nodded.

"And it didn't work. She didn't actually care what you

thought," Dana guessed. "And that annoyed you as much as her perfect hair and snotty attitude."

"Not quite as much," Logan said. "But yeah. A little."

Dana chuckled. "She's a piece of work. And I wish she hadn't stirred things up. But I gotta admit, it would be funny seeing you meet a woman who doesn't swoon for you."

"You didn't swoon for me. At first."

"I did. I just hid it."

He liked that. He narrowed his eyes. "Maybe that's what she's doing."

Dana laughed. "I don't think so. Tiffany Custer is not the swooning type."

Well, then, yeah, he didn't know how to deal with her. "Does she *always* dress like that for dance class?" The woman had been wearing a short skirt, heels, about five pounds of makeup and a bottle of hairspray. Yes, she had the body for the skirt and heels. But it was clear that she liked to be looked at and knew how to accentuate her assets.

"She's beautiful. Always very put together. Always dressed to the nines," Dana said. "She's a plastic surgeon. And a yoga instructor."

Jesus. Logan tipped his head. "She's high-maintenance."

"For sure. But you have to admit she looks good."

"But that's not how the girls should look. They're ten. And they're already wound up enough about getting the steps to the dances right. We hardly need to pile on with how they look and if their hair is perfect. That was what I was trying to do—show them that it wasn't all such a big deal and that it could just be fun and be...them. You know? They each picked the barrettes they liked the best, and it's something everyone can do because it works for all the hair types and doesn't have to be perfect."

Dana was watching him with an expression that was part wonder and part amused. "I can't believe how worked up you are about this."

"She offered to pay for a hair stylist to come with the team to do everyone's hair!" he exclaimed. "That's ridiculous."

Dana agreed.

"So then she was super pissed when I suggested we vote, and insisted that everyone *write their votes down* instead of just a show of hands because I could tell the girls were getting intimidated by her. And then she lost. There were only three votes for the hair stylist, which means one person besides her and Jada." He knew he should *not* be this into this. He glanced at the brownies on the counter, though, and felt a stab of triumph. "I hate that the other moms don't feel like they can stand up to her."

Dana sighed. "Well, in some cases, they're just tired and don't want a fight or for things to be awkward among the families or the team. Some of them just don't see it as a big deal and are more focused on things like getting off work to go to the competition and living out of a hotel room with a bunch of little kids for the weekend. And yeah, some probably just don't really care as long as the girls are happy."

He narrowed his eyes. "Which one are you?"

"Maybe a tiny bit of all of those?"

"So I'm making a big deal out of this?"

"I'm not saying that. I think it's great that you care about this. And Tiffany could use a little opposition." Dana glanced at the brownies. "Clearly everyone agrees."

"Almost everyone," Logan muttered.

Dana laughed and crossed to him, wrapping her arms around his waist. "Don't worry, Trahan, I like you enough to make up for all three of those females who voted against you."

He hugged her and grinned in spite of himself. But he made his voice solemn when he said, "Yeah, you know, that was really hard on my ego. I might need someone to reassure me that I'm amazing."

She pulled back and looked up at him. "Gosh, how can I help?"

"How about you meet me in your bedroom thirty minutes after the girls go to bed and by then I'll have a list."

"Okay," she agreed with a grin. "And how about tomorrow night, instead of hanging out at Chloe's rehearsal, you and Grace go find a haunted house or something."

"Stay away from the drama at dance?" he asked.

"You won the vote. They're staying with your idea. Just let that be."

"But—"

"Logan."

"But I like dance class," he mumbled.

She laughed. "You like being the only dance dad."

Emotion speared through him with that. A feeling of *yes*. But not because he liked the attention of being a one of a kind. But because of that last word. Dad. Yeah, he liked that. A lot. He nodded, without a touch of humor. "I do. I like feeling that I'm doing something important. Something that matters to Chloe. And you."

"And it does. You've helped me a ton by handling all of that, and Chloe loves having you involved. And Tiffany can't change that, okay? She's just a mean girl. In the end, the hairstyle doesn't matter as much to Chloe as just knowing that you care about it for her. I'm sure Chloe is fine. Okay?"

"So I should just back off and go with the flow."

She nodded. "You're good at that, remember?"

Yeah. He was. Supposedly. At least he used to be. Until someone messed with one of his girls' happiness.

And the phrase *his girls* caused that same flash of emotion that went through him when Dana used the word *dad*. A mix of possessiveness and pride and happiness and...love.

He was in love. With all three Doucet girls. And he was going to make sure they were happy. Dammit.

"Fine. I'll take Tuesday night off from dance," he said. He hadn't taken Grace over to Muriel's yet.

Muriel's was commonly known as the most haunted restaurant in New Orleans and was right across Jackson Square from Trahan's. One of the waiters, Ken, had worked there for twenty years and knew all the stories. And he was great at reading his audience and embellishing. He'd love Grace. And vice versa.

"Yes, do that," Dana said. "Hang with Grace. Have some fun. Let the drama go."

He nodded. "Fine. But you know, that whole thing with you getting your way with me because of the blow jobs?"

She ran her hand up his chest. "Yes. I remember that theory."

"Oh, it's not a theory," Logan said. "Tell me again about letting it all go after you use that sweet mouth on me. I'll be a much better listener then."

Dana rose on tiptoe and put her mouth on his. "Deal."

———

"I can't believe I heard it!" Grace said. Again.

Logan chuckled. Ken had done a great job regaling Grace of tales of the things he'd seen, and heard of, at Muriel's over the years and then he'd taken them up to the séance lounges on the second floor, and Grace had fallen head over heels. The rooms on the second floor were decorated in deep jewel tones with plush sofas and heavy curtains and elaborate wall hangings, lamps, tables, and even two crazy, huge, gold Egyptian sarcophagi.

The rumor was that the upper rooms were the ones where the primary ghost that haunted Muriel's spent his time. It wasn't uncommon for people to hear the sound of someone knocking on the brick wall up there. Grace swore she'd heard it tonight.

And instead of being freaked out like most six-year-olds would be, Grace was completely enthralled.

"I'm glad you liked it, honey," he told her sincerely. Yeah, okay, so this had been more fun than arguing with Tiffany Custer about hairstyles.

Grace had wanted to know what a séance was and instead of being creeped out by the idea of actually communicating with dead people, she'd been fascinated. Briefly, Logan wondered if he needed to reel all of this in. He didn't want her asking for a crystal ball or tarot cards for Christmas, and he didn't want her to be the weird kid at school. Then again, he knew the majority of people who lived in New Orleans, particularly the ones who had grown up here, had a pretty open-minded view of the fact that the place was haunted. A combination of the age of the city and numerous traumas, from fires to the yellow fever epidemics to the slave revolt of 1811, almost guaranteed there were some spirits hanging around. Most New Orleanians would claim to have had a paranormal experience or two in their lives.

Logan saw Chloe coming down the steps of the school a few minutes later as Grace was wondering if she could have her birthday party at Muriel's. Yeah, okay, that might be weird. He would put pretty good money on the fact that Muriel's had never hosted a little girl birthday party in the haunted séance rooms of the restaurant. And what would the party favors be? But as he thought about it, he decided that, as a matter of fact, he and Grace could throw a kick-ass séance-themed party. Everyone could have their own turban, and they could use dry ice to create a spooky atmosphere. Everyone could write their own epitaphs...

Every thought was derailed as Chloe opened the door to his truck, her cheeks streaked with tears.

Concern coursed through him—a cold, icy feeling that he had felt rarely in his life and never with the power he felt it now. He forced his voice to stay steady. "What happened?"

She sniffed and climbed up into the truck. "I hate dance."

Oh...shit. She definitely did not hate dance.

He shifted on his seat, resting his arm along the back of the seat, still working to keep his posture and expression calm. "Tell me what happened."

She took a deep breath. "I hate Jada."

Ah, okay, well at least that was more specific. Logan gripped the steering wheel with one hand. "What did Jada do?"

"She told everyone that your hairstyle doesn't matter because you're not a real dad," Chloe told him, staring at the dash of the truck instead of looking at him. "And when I told her that you were going to be my baby brother's dad, she said it didn't count, and *then* she said that my brother and I wouldn't be *real* brother and sister because we have different dads and wouldn't have the same last name."

Logan's heart was pounding and his body felt completely cold as Chloe looked over at him, her expression completely forlorn.

"I want my brother to be my real brother and I want to have the same last name," she said.

Logan swallowed hard. "The baby will absolutely be your real brother," he said evenly. "Or sister," he felt compelled to add.

"What about our last name?" Chloe almost whispered.

Fuck. Fuck, fuck, fuck. He made himself breathe deep. He couldn't tell her that they definitely would share a last name. That was something he and Dana needed to figure out, he supposed. But he was fighting the urge to declare that these girls were his in every possible way, and they *would* absolutely have his last name. Tomorrow. And that if Dana wouldn't marry him, then he'd adopt them anyway and... He was going a little crazy, obviously. But damn, the urge to make everything okay, to protect and claim these girls, was causing a physical knot in his gut.

"It doesn't matter what your last name is," he said, finally. His voice sounded like he was pushing it past sandpaper. And he wasn't sure he sounded convincing. Because *he* wasn't convinced. It *did* matter. He wanted them to be *his*. All of them.

"But kids have their dad's last names, right?" Grace asked from the back seat. "If we don't have the same name, how will people know you're our dad too?"

Logan felt like she'd just punched him in the heart. The organ gave a weak thump that hurt.

"Jada said you're not our dad," Chloe said. "And that you're only helping with dance because you're having a baby with our mom and that you don't really care about dance."

Logan squeezed the steering wheel and blew out a quick breath. "Chloe, look at me."

She was turned in his direction, but wasn't meeting his gaze. Instead, she was staring at the front of his T-shirt. Her eyes lifted slowly. When their eyes met, he said, "I *promise* that I care about dance. Because I care about *you*. And I do want to be your dad. I really do. I want you to have my last name. But whatever happens, I love you. And I will be here to help you with things. And the baby will be your *real* brother or sister. Jada is wrong about all of that." He looked up into the rearview mirror. "Grace?"

"Yeah?"

"I mean all of that for you too," he said, his voice steady and sure, his chest hurting with how much he wanted to make everything perfect for these two little people. "I love you and I'll be here for you and the baby is your real brother or sister too."

Her bottom lip trembled. "So I can have your last name?"

Jesus. *Yes.* That was all he could think of for a moment. Then he said, "Your mom and I would have to get married to make that happen."

"Why don't you want to get married to Mommy?" Grace asked.

And that was when it occurred to him that he might be in over his head here...and he was going to get in trouble. But that didn't stop him from saying, "I do want to marry your mom."

"Did you ask her?" Chloe wanted to know.

He looked at the older girl. Yeah, he'd already messed this up. This was exactly the kind of conversation that he should not be having with the girls without Dana there. Or on board. Or even aware of it.

But dammit, whatever happened, he wanted these girls to know that they were wanted. By him. Completely. He loved them and they could depend on him. There was nothing wrong with telling them that. "Yes," he finally said. "I did."

Grace's eyes got huge and she clasped her hands together under her chin, her expression the same she'd had on her face when she'd first seen the sarcophagi at Muriel's. "We get to have a wedding!"

So...yeah, Dana was going to have his hide.

"Soon?" Chloe asked.

He focused on her again. "I don't know." He was, of course, going to do whatever he could to get Dana to say yes. Soon. And he thought he was closer to a yes now than he had been when he'd first asked her. But...they hadn't talked about it again.

"Can you ask her when tonight?" Chloe asked. "I want to tell Jada she's wrong." She frowned at that.

Logan wanted to tell Jada she was wrong too. In front of all the girls. Just like she'd done to Chloe. But, of course, Jada had gotten all of this from Tiffany. No way had the ten-year-old come up with all of that on her own. Likely she'd overheard Tiffany talking to the other moms about why Logan shouldn't be so involved.

Well, that was going to stop right now. She thought he was involved because he'd been doing hair? She hadn't seen anything yet.

"You know what?" he asked, turning off the ignition and unbuckling his seat belt. "I think we should go talk to Jada right now."

"Right now?" Chloe asked, her eyes widening.

"I think maybe it would help if *I* told her she was wrong," he said, opening his door. "Unbuckle, Grace. We're going inside."

Grace scrambled to unhook the belt on her booster seat, while Chloe tucked her backpack down on the floor by her feet. They were both out of the truck by the time he rounded the bumper and hit the sidewalk. He took one little girl hand in each of his and headed for the front doors. The adrenaline was pumping as they climbed the steps. He was going to have to use his nice words, he knew, but damn he wanted to call Tiffany Custer out. He knew women like her. The ones that made others feel small so that she could feel big. He didn't know what her deal was with him, but he didn't fucking care. She just needed to stop bringing this into the girls' consciousness. He would not have Chloe hating dance. And he was done staying out in the truck while sending Chloe in by herself.

They stepped into the gymnasium a minute later. Rehearsal was over, but it seemed that everyone else was still there, girls and moms. The teacher was up on the stage with three girls, but the rest were in two clusters. The one that had Jada Custer at the center and the one that didn't.

Logan headed for Jada.

"Hey, girls," he said, easily, shutting the entire group up instantaneously. Nine pairs of eyes looked up at him and got round. "Sorry I missed practice tonight," he said, giving them a grin that worked on females from four to ninety and had his whole life. "How are things coming along?"

"Good," one of the girls, Sarah, said.

"Yeah, good," another, Lanie, said.

He nodded. "I'll bet. You guys are a good team. I can't wait to see you at the competition. And I've decided that I'm going to put together a set of pump-up songs for you. You know what that is?"

A couple of the girls nodded and a couple shook their heads. "Well, when I was playing football and basketball in high school, I always put together a list of songs that got me excited and focused on the game to listen to while I was riding to the game and in the locker room. It pumped me up for the competition. I'm going to make a disc for you girls. You can each have a copy to listen to on the way to the competition or while you're waiting to go on. So all I need is to know your favorite songs. The ones that make you happy, that make you want to dance. You can tell Chloe and she'll tell me. Or you can come up to me at rehearsal." He looked at each of them, focusing on Jada last. "I'll be here."

"Dads don't really do stuff with dance," Jada said. "But my *mom* could make us discs."

"Nah," he said. "I really want to do it. Chloe's just really lucky to have a mom *and dad* who care about dance, I guess."

Emphasis on him being a dad? Check. Dig at the other dads? Check.

Jada looked at Chloe, then back to him. "Are you really her dad?" she asked.

Without knowing what Jada had said to Chloe earlier, he might think that she was actually asking an innocent question. It seemed like something a ten-year-old might be legitimately curious about. But he *did* know what she'd said. "Yes," he said firmly. "I am now."

For a second, Jada had a *yeah, right* look on her face, but she covered it. "My mom said that you're not married to her mom."

"I'm not. Yet. But you don't have to worry. I'll still be around here and be able to do hair and make those song discs and just generally be a lot of fun to have around." He gave her a smile that he didn't think a little girl would be able to tell was completely forced. And then he went too far. "So even if your dad isn't at the competition, I'll be there cheering extra loud for *all* of you. Because you're a team and we don't worry about silly things like what people's last names are and who comes up with the great ideas."

Except that obviously *he* was worried about both of those things. And taking on a ten-year-old over it.

"What is going on over here?"

But *there* was the female he most wanted to talk to about all of this. He turned. "Hi, Tiffany."

"Logan, isn't it?"

She fucking knew his name. He didn't bother to force a smile with her. "Yep. I'm here with Chloe."

"You're her mom's boyfriend, right?"

"Fiancé," he said. Because he was already in deep here, so why not? "And the hair guy and the guy who's in charge of the pump-up songs and the guy who's been helping out around here quite a bit because you working moms need someone who can pitch in, right?"

Why the hell did this woman have a problem with him? He was *helping*. Not just Dana and Chloe. He'd done a juice run the other night. He'd brought cookies another night. Best chocolate chip cookies in the state made by his own mother, thank you very much. He'd assured the painfully shy Hannah she was doing a great job. He'd noticed something was off with Lauren and had gotten her off the stage just as she was having an asthma attack. He had called her mom and let her walk him through the inhaler thing and kept Lauren calm waiting for her dad to show up to get her. And, dammit, he'd come up with a hairstyle that would work for all the hair types, including Abby, who had a birthmark on the base of her head that she wanted to cover up.

"Right. You're a bartender. I guess that means you have a lot of free time?"

He laughed. "In New Orleans? I don't think many people work more or harder than restaurant and bar staff around here." Then he gave her a look. "And I own that bar with my brother. So, you know, there's a little more to it than pouring beer."

Tiffany—*Dr.* Tiffany to be exact—crossed her arms. "Yeah, I guess you probably pour wine and vodka too."

He nodded, refusing to let her get to him. He dealt with worse than her—and kept his sense of humor and charming disposition, thank you—on a weekly basis. Of course, none of the drunk frat guys or crazy tourists were making Chloe feel badly. It was a lot harder to laugh things off with Tiffany. "A bit of bourbon and even a margarita here and there too."

She didn't look impressed. He felt the same way. And fuck

her. He didn't care what she thought or said about his job or his bar. But he *did* fucking care what she said about, or to, Chloe.

"Well, you don't have to worry about being around and helping at the competition. We've got things covered."

"Oh, I'm not *worried*. Not even a little. I can't wait to see all the girls looking stunning and kicking butt." He shot the little group a smile and had several returned.

"What I meant was, that since you're not officially a dad of any of the girls, you won't be allowed back in the prep area anyway, so you don't need to worry about getting off work."

He narrowed his eyes, turning his back on the girls enough so that none of them would notice. "Oh, I'll be there. Chloe's my girl. No one will keep me away."

Tiffany gave him a bored look. "Well, the team will have a list of parents who are allowed in the prep and staging area."

"Great. I'll be sure Mrs. Morgan is spelling my name right." He started to move to walk toward the dance director. To his shock, Tiffany put a hand on his chest, stopping him. He looked down at it, then back up at her.

"I think we're covered," Tiffany told him.

"Really? By the moms who haven't been here for ninety percent of the rehearsals?" he asked.

"You don't *actually* think that we can't step in and take care of things without being here every night?" she asked. "I mean, we've all been doing this for *five years*. You just got here. And we need to know that people will show up for sure."

"Why wouldn't I show up?" he asked, knowing she thought she knew a reason.

Tiffany shrugged, dropping her hand. "Well, I mean, you're a *boyfriend*."

"Fiancé," he said, through gritted teeth.

"Okay," she said placatingly. "Still not really...committed to... things." She gave him a small smile. "And what if you have a bar emergency or something and can't make it? It's probably best for us to rely on the *real* parents to be there."

He stepped closer to her, leaned in, and said lowly, "Lady, just because *your* husband can't be counted on, doesn't mean that Dana and Chloe are in that same boat. And if your husband *is* going to do something for this team, I'd suggest he take you to bed and give you an orgasm or three. Clearly you need something to loosen you up."

Tiffany actually gasped at that and pulled back. Logan wouldn't have been surprised if she'd slapped him. And he probably would have deserved it. But *damn*, he could not let her talk to him that way. She could fuck right off. He was here for Chloe, period. No matter what this uptight, full-of-herself bitch thought.

"Jada, it's time to go," Tiffany said, stepping around him.

He nodded. Yeah, it was past time. Jada took her mom's hand and Tiffany led her out of the gymnasium, her back ramrod straight, her shoes clicking angrily on the hard floor.

"Whoa."

Logan looked over to see that Amy had joined them. She was watching Tiffany leave. "What was *that*?"

Logan blew out a breath and shoved a hand through his hair. "That was me *not* being easygoing."

"What's going on?" Amy looked up at him.

"She wants to keep me away from helping with the team at the competition. Well, probably with everything."

"She's just jealous, you know," Amy said. "Her husband never comes to any of their girls' stuff. He only goes if their son is playing sports."

"Is he a brain surgeon or something?" Logan asked. "Horrible hours saving lives or something?"

Amy snorted. "He's a self-employed financial guy. Works at home, sets his own hours. Spends *a lot* of those hours on the golf course."

"Bitch," Logan breathed. "Putting down my bar while her husband is out on the ninth green?"

"She's got to make herself feel better somehow. It makes her crazy to see a guy who's not even a dad stepping up the way you are—"

"Don't say that," Logan said crossly. He never said anything crossly. "I haven't signed adoption papers or whatever, but dammit, there are lots of ways to be a dad."

Amy's eyes got wide. "Are you going to be signing adoption papers?"

He glanced over at Chloe and Grace. They were holding hands, and Chloe was now talking to the other girls from class since Jada had left. His heart turned over in his chest. He'd made that better. Okay, he'd made a for-sure enemy of Tiffany. And he was going to have to tell Dana about everything, and he had a gut feeling *that* wasn't going to go well. But yeah, he'd done something good here. He'd stood up for Chloe and Grace. He'd claimed them. And he didn't regret a word. He nodded at Amy. "Yeah. I am. Definitely."

Amy's eyes got soft. "Wow. That's amazing. They've all been through so much. I'm so glad Dana found you."

He gave her a small smile. "Thanks. But I'm the lucky one." And he somehow kept from asking if she'd be willing to write him a recommendation for Dana.

Because yeah, he was going to be in trouble for this.

10

Dana heard the front door open and felt an equal rush of relief and exhaustion. Logan and the girls were here. She knew he'd run out for ginger ale and crackers, but that also meant that she now needed to deal with bedtime for the girls and she, quite frankly, had *no* energy.

She'd gotten cocky, thinking that maybe she was going to skip the morning sickness this time around. She'd made it through almost three months with nothing.

And now...Mother Nature was making up for lost time.

"Babe?" she heard Logan call up the stairs.

She took a deep breath and started for the staircase. Her stomach roiled and she paused. *Man, give me twenty minutes without wanting to hurl. Please.*

"Dana?"

"I'm up here," she called back.

The next thing she heard was the sound of four little feet pounding up the stairs.

"Mommy!" Grace said, skidding to a halt in front of Dana. "We're going to have a wedding!"

"We...are?" Dana wasn't sure how to respond. Were they

talking about a pretend wedding? Stuffed animals getting hitched? A friend from school? Someone Logan knew? Had he invited the girls along to a family wedding or something?

"Yes! And then our last name will be the same as the baby!"

And it all became clear. Quickly. Dana felt shock rock through her and she had to work to keep her face composed. Had it come up while they'd been wandering a cemetery or something? Chloe was standing behind Grace, and Dana focused on her. "You were talking about last names tonight?" she asked.

Chloe nodded. "Jada said that Logan can't help with dance because he's not a real dad and that he's only helping because you're having a baby and that he's the baby's dad, not ours, and that we won't have the same last name."

All of that came tumbling out, and Dana was surprised to see Chloe's eyes fill with tears. "Oh, honey," she said, reaching for Chloe. She came forward and let Dana wrap her arms around her. "It doesn't matter what our last names are," she said against Chloe's head. "You know that we love you and of course Logan will still help with dance. Jada is just confused."

Chloe shook her head. "No. Her mom said that only real parents can help." She pulled back and looked up at Dana. "But it's okay. Logan told her that he's going to help anyway and that you're going to get married so he *will* be our dad and it won't matter."

Dana wondered why she wasn't more shocked to hear that Logan had made such a declaration. But it was exactly the kind of spontaneous thing he would do without thinking through all the consequences. Like how her girls would take that information. She sighed. Of course, she also wasn't surprised that Tiffany had run her mouth and that it had gotten to Logan. That woman rubbed her the wrong way too, but it had been funny to see how much she'd bothered Logan.

Though, maybe not so funny now...

"Logan wants to help out because he cares about you," Dana

said. "And he would hate it if someone was making you mad or sad. But that doesn't mean we're going to get married."

Grace frowned. "But what will the baby's last name be then?"

Okay, well...that wasn't a bad question. They hadn't talked about that. They hadn't talked about first names either, for that matter. "We have some time to figure it out," she said.

Grace's frown deepened. "You have to give the baby a last name," she said. "Our baby can't not have a name!"

Dana smiled at Grace's sudden protectiveness of the baby. "The baby will have a name," she assured her. "Logan and I just have to talk about it."

"But I want the same name as the baby," Grace said.

"I understand, but—"

"I want the same name as Logan," Chloe said quietly.

Dana looked down at her oldest. She gathered her thoughts and worked on sounding calm. "You don't have the same last name as your grandparents from Lafayette," she said. "But they are still your family and love you. You know that. Last names don't matter that much, sweetie."

"But when you have the same last name, people know you belong together," Chloe said.

Dana blew out a little breath.

"I want to belong with Logan," Chloe added.

Dana's heart squeezed in her chest. She hadn't been expecting any of this and she had no idea how to respond.

"I do too," Grace said, flinging herself forward.

Dana wrapped her other arm around her youngest.

"I want to belong with Logan," Grace said against her shirt. "He said we can have the same last name. He likes that idea."

Dana held her girls, her mind spinning. Dammit, Logan. Why did all of this have to come up like this? They needed to talk about some things, and maybe she should have warned him about being careful about how he worded things about the baby. He was great with the girls, but he didn't have vast experience in talking with them and explaining things in a way they could understand, that they wouldn't blow up into a...wedding.

Then again, she had *no* trouble believing that he'd jumped right into that conversation with both feet. Logan didn't hold back. Which made her really wonder about the rest of that conversation with Tiffany Custer, come to think of it.

Her stomach twisted a little and she sucked in a quick breath. Lord, she'd already thrown up three times. Why couldn't that be enough for one night?

"Hey, ladies, can you head in and start getting ready for bed? I need to talk to Logan."

"He's making us pump-up songs," Chloe told her. "And he told Tiffany he's doing hair at the competition no matter what she says."

Oh, Dana bet he did. "Pump-up songs?"

"Discs of songs that will get us excited about the competition."

"Ah," Dana said with a nod.

"He said that he's okay being the only dance dad. And he said something to Tiffany that made her *really* mad," Chloe added.

"What did he say?"

"I couldn't hear it," Chloe told her. "He said it quiet. But Tiffany's face got really red." Chloe giggled. "And then Tiffany took Jada home."

Great. Tiffany was mad. It wasn't like Dana's path crossed Tiffany's much, but the dance team had to be, well, a team. The weekend competition in Baton Rouge could be a long three days if people weren't getting along.

Chloe was new to this team. She'd just moved up. It wasn't good to cause waves just before competition season.

"Okay, I'm going to go say goodnight to Logan. You two get jammies on and stuff. I'll be back up in a little bit."

She headed downstairs. Logan was pacing the foyer. He looked up as she hit the middle of the staircase.

"Tiffany Custer is a bitch."

Dana sighed and came the rest of the way down. "What happened?"

His eyes flickered to the steps behind her. "What did the girls say?"

Dana wanted to smile. Oh, he wasn't going to volunteer any information she didn't already have, huh? But she lifted a brow instead. "Why don't you tell me your side?"

"She made Chloe cry."

"Who did?"

"Tiffany. Well, Jada. Because she was repeating things Tiffany had said."

Dana frowned. "She was crying?"

"Yes. And she said she hated dance." He blew out a breath. "Jada told her I couldn't be involved and that I wasn't her real dad and she wouldn't have the same last name as the baby and that I was there helping only because we were having a baby together."

Dana sighed and turned, heading down the short hallway to the kitchen. She needed to get out of earshot of little girls who might hang out at the top of the steps. Logan followed her. She crossed to the fridge and got a bottle of water. Her stomach was queasy, but she wasn't at risk of throwing up all over him at this point. She took a drink, then met his eyes across the middle island. "I thought you and Grace were going to go do something instead of sit in on rehearsal."

"We did. I took her to Muriel's. I thought she was going to faint when she saw the sarcophagi."

Dana lifted a brow. "Wow. She didn't even mention Muriel's. She was so caught up in the wedding we're going to be having."

He winced slightly. "Well, some girls are really into weddings."

Dana nodded. "Right. So how did you end up talking to Tiffany if you were ghost hunting?"

"I went into the school after Chloe came out to the truck crying."

Dana frowned, feeling her heart squeeze. "And you confronted Tiffany?"

"I actually talked to Jada first."

"You confronted a ten-year-old?"

"I told her, and the other girls, that I would absolutely be at the competition, with pump-up music, because that's what a good dance dad does."

Dana felt a prick of trepidation at that. Her phone dinged and she reached into the pocket of her bathrobe. She swiped the screen and saw a message from Amy and another she must have missed from another mom, Leslie.

Heads-up. Some moms are riled up, Amy's said.

Leslie's read, *I don't think your boyfriend should be telling the girls that the other dads don't care about their daughters just because they don't show up for rehearsals.*

Well, shit.

She looked up at Logan. "You told the girls that their dads don't care about them because they don't come to rehearsals?"

He frowned. "What? No. Of course I didn't say that." He paused and added, "Though..."

Dana's eyebrows went up. "Though? What's that mean?"

"Just saying that you can't tell me a couple of those guys couldn't show up once in a while if they wanted to."

"Maybe it's just easier for the moms to be there. Or maybe the moms don't want the dads there because the moms are the ones who need to be in charge of the costumes and stuff. Or maybe the girls want their moms there. You don't know the situations."

Logan shook his head. "The dads could do it sometimes. It's not brain surgery. Which of those ladies wouldn't like a night off? If they're not working, they could go to dinner with friends or... just do nothing. They could sit at home and read a book. I mean, seriously."

Dana took a second to marvel that playboy bartender Logan Trahan was currently lecturing her on equal co-parenting.

"Okay, that's all fair. But you can't make those decisions and judgments about other people." Dana blew out a breath. "Tell me how this conversation went."

Her phone dinged again. *Logan won't start anything with the other dads, will he?*

That was from Amy, but Dana suspected the question had been asked of Amy by another mom. Or three. Or more. Oh, geez. She looked up at him. He looked pissed. And stubborn. She didn't *think* he'd start something, but...four months ago, she wouldn't have thought that he would be standing here telling her *any* of this either.

She finally typed back. *I'm handling it.*

Okay, Amy responded. But then she added, *Congratulations, btw. I think he's going to be an amazing step-dad.*

Dana pulled in a deep breath. Then looked up at Logan. "So the girls are not just assuming there's going to be a wedding? You told other people that too?"

Logan's jaw tightened and he drew himself straighter. "I don't think I've ever made it a secret that I want to marry you."

She sighed. "Logan—"

"If you would just marry me all of this would be taken care of. The girls would be mine, we'd have the same last name, the baby would have the same last name, I could go behind-the-scenes and everything."

"Is that what this is *really* about? You can't go behind-the-scenes and do hair?"

"No. This is about people denying me the chance to be involved with things that are important to my—" He broke off and swore under his breath.

Dana crossed her arms. "Your what?"

Again, he clenched his jaw and narrowed his eyes, but met her gaze directly. "I was going to say daughter."

Dana felt a sharp stab in her chest. It wasn't unpleasant, exactly. It was just...surprising. She'd expected him to be good with the girls. He was good with all females. But when she'd actually seen him with them, and the way they responded to him, she'd realized that she'd completely underestimated him. Or the girls. She supposed that she'd thought the girls would be a little slower to warm up to a new man.

And maybe they would have been, with any *other* new man.

She swallowed hard. "You think of Chloe and Grace as your daughters?" she asked.

"I'll tell you this, I would take a bullet for either of them. And if someone makes one of them cry, they are going to hear from me."

Dana felt her throat tighten. "That's...so...nice, Logan."

"Nice?" he repeated. "This isn't *nice*, Dana. I'm not doing this to get on your good side. This isn't a show or me playing around or trying to get laid or just doing something silly for fun."

She pressed her lips together.

"That's why I do ninety-percent of the things I do," he admitted. "But now, with them, I'm all-in. And the way to keep them is to marry you."

Dana blinked at him. Then frowned. She opened her mouth. Then closed it. Then opened her mouth again. "So now you're with *me* so that you can stay with the *girls*?"

He frowned. "Not exactly. But yeah. Maybe." He shoved a hand through his hair. "I don't know. But I don't like Tiffany and Jada telling Chloe how they think things are with us. I want Chloe to feel secure and if she and Grace want my last name, then, dammit, they can have it."

Dana shook her head. Part of her was completely turned on by this possessive, protective side of Logan. The other part of her was concerned. This was happening fast. He was getting in deep. The girls were getting in deep. She loved the idea that he really wanted to be around and involved, but...this was the tip of the iceberg. And this issue, the first one that wasn't fun and games that he'd handled, well, it was a little sticky.

"I appreciate what you're saying," she told him. "I really do. I know that this was the first time you've seen Chloe upset and that tears are probably not your thing—"

"Goddammit, Dana!"

She sucked in a breath. "Logan."

"I'm not overreacting here."

"You're sure? It's a little girl's dance competition." She tried to keep her voice calm and even like she did when the girls were upset.

It didn't work.

"It's so fucking much more than that!" He was looking at her like he couldn't believe what she was saying. "That bitch told her daughter who told the rest of the girls a bunch of shit about us because she was trying to put me down because she's jealous of us."

"So let her be jealous," Dana said. "That's on her, not us."

"It's on us when it affects Chloe."

"But she's right!" Dana exclaimed. He wasn't listening.

"What the fuck do you mean by that?" Logan asked, his eyes narrowed.

"You are not my husband. You're not Chloe's father. You are, at best, my boyfriend. We are having a baby together. And we haven't talked about first names, not to mention last names."

Logan gave a low growling noise.

She ignored it. "And the baby *is* why we're together, right? Tiffany is a bitch and I'm pissed she said that stuff to her daughter and that Jada repeated it to Chloe. I'm upset that Chloe is upset. But...it's all true. The last name stuff, the reason we're together...all of it."

"So, I should have just ignored it? Just gone along with it all? Just told Chloe 'yep, Jada's right?'"

"Of course not."

"What would you have liked me to do?" He leaned back against the counter behind him, gripping the edge until his knuckles were white.

"Come home. Tell Chloe that you care about her and that we will all sit down here together and talk it out."

"Let Tiffany, or anyone else, just say whatever the fuck they want about us?"

"It's just...hard." Dana sighed and pressed her hand against her stomach as it twisted a little. "There are a lot of battles we *have* to fight. There are a lot of hard discussions we *have* to have. I don't worry about arguing with people who don't really know us and don't get us and who, frankly, don't really matter."

"You don't care what Tiffany is saying?"

She shrugged. "No. I don't care what she's saying or what she's thinking. I just care about what *we* think. What we *know*. *We* know the truth about us and who you are to us."

"Do we?"

The way he said it, low and sharp, made her wince. "Of course we do." They did. Kind of.

"So never stand up to people? Never explain it? Never *say* to other people what we are?" Logan asked.

"Not *never*. But I just don't want to get into...who's doing barrettes."

"That's bullshit, Dana. She shouldn't—"

"Is it really that important that you're the fun dad?" she exclaimed, "that you're better at this than the rest of us? That they like you best?"

He stared at her. "Whoa."

Dana pressed her lips together. She hadn't meant to say that. But really? He *had* to be the popular one no matter what?

"Honestly?" he finally said. "Yeah. Kind of. I like being great at something that matters. And making Chloe and Grace feel accepted and laugh matters."

Dana sucked in a little breath. Damn. This guy...what

was she going to do with him? It had started out as him being someone who could just help her out. But he'd gone all-in. He'd fallen in love. With her daughters. And in his insistence to love them fully, he was making things complicated.

"It's hair," she said quietly. "You can and will be fun for something else. Fighting this is...exhausting. You can do Chloe's hair and—"

"It's not about the hair!" He pushed away from the counter.

"Then what's it about?" She suddenly felt like she could just lie down right here on the floor and go to sleep.

"People knowing that I'm...legit."

Surprise shot through her. She hadn't been expecting *that*. She studied his face. He looked completely earnest. "People knowing...or *you* knowing?"

"Yeah. Okay, maybe that."

She swallowed hard. "You only have to be legit to us."

"And am I?"

Dana's chest tightened. "You are—"

"Just fucking marry me," he interrupted. "That's the way to fix this all. None of it will matter if we're married."

"That is *not* a solution."

"Of course it is." He spread his arms wide. "I don't like being on the outside of this, Dana. I won't have it. That baby *will* be mine and I want the girls too."

"You won't have it?" she repeated, her eyes wide.

"I'm going to help raise those girls. It only makes sense—"

"Whoa." She put a hand up. "We haven't talked about any of this. We got pregnant, Logan. Accidentally. And there is *a lot* we need to figure out. But we can't just rush in because your feelings got hurt tonight."

"That's not what this is." His voice was low and firm, and he looked completely pissed.

She took a deep breath. "I understand that you're out of your element when things aren't fun and easy, but you can't go off on emotion here. We have to think—"

"Stop it. Stop saying that. I'm trying to be what you want here, but there are possibly things that you don't even know that you need."

"What I don't even know that I need?" She couldn't believe this. "You're supposed to be *helping*."

"I have been!"

"Until now. You were doing ghosts and dance class. That's it. And now there's angst and drama and texts that I wasn't getting before. My daughters are all confused and asking questions I'm not ready for."

He pulled in a long breath through his nose and let it out, his eyes glittering with emotion. "I should have just let it go? No. fuck that," he said without waiting for a response. "This is important. Okay, so I'm not great at this hard stuff. Yes, I'd rather it was fun and everyone was happy. But you know what? Maybe you're not great at it either."

Dana felt a *thunk* in her chest. "Excuse me?"

"You want everyone *else* to be happy. You make it all easy for *everyone else*. No rocking the boat, no putting responsibility on them, no calling them on their bullshit. But that's crap, Dana. You can be upset and you can ask people for things. They won't reject you if things aren't always perfect every second. Chad didn't leave you, or stay away, because it was hard here. Jada wasn't being mean to Chloe because Chloe is hard to get along with. People aren't going to leave when things get bumpy. Life gets bumpy sometimes. People understand that."

Dana felt tears stinging her eyes and her stomach flip, and she folded her arms tightly against her body.

Her phone rang, making them both start. Logan glanced at where it was lying on the countertop.

"You've got to be fucking kidding me."

It was Tiffany Custer's name that popped up on the screen.

Dana felt his intention before he even moved, and she reached for the phone as he did. She grabbed it a millisecond before he did, silencing the ringer and then tucking it into her pocket.

"You're not going to talk to her?"

"I'll call her tomorrow."

"Don't you dare apologize for me," he said, pointing a finger at her nose.

"Then stop making things messy!" she snapped.

"Life is messy, Dana. I'm not afraid of a little mess."

Dana opened her mouth to reply and…threw up on his shoes.

———

For the next hour, Logan cleaned up vomit, made cool wet cloths, poured sports drinks, and checked temperatures.

Chloe had met them at the top of the steps as Logan carried Dana to bed with the news that there was "puke everywhere!" in the bathroom where Grace had gotten sick.

Chloe seemed fine, so far, but he kept checking her as well.

At the moment, everything was quiet, all the bedding was in the dryer, and everyone was asleep. Logan slumped onto the couch, resting his head back. Dana had talked him out of rushing them to the ER or even calling the doctor, saying this was just a bout of the flu. Just? He didn't think his heart rate had been normal since Dana had gotten sick in the kitchen. Cooper had been sick in the past, of course, but Gabe and their mom had handled the majority of that so Logan hadn't realized how fucking exhausting it was to have people you loved not feeling well. Not the cleanup, but the worry. And the feeling of helplessness.

Logan scrubbed a hand over his face and sighed. He was staying over. Right here on this couch. He wasn't even going to leave to get more clothes or anything. He had to be here. Dana was annoyed with him, and they hadn't solved the issue of his involvement in the girls' lives beyond school pickup and homework help, but they would. Probably.

He pivoted his body, lying back on the cushions. Just for a few minutes. He'd go check on them soon. And knowing that they were sick, there was nowhere else he *would* be. Was this fun? Fuck no. But if anyone was going to take care of these girls, it was him. Maybe he didn't have the most experience, but no one loved them more. And as soon as she wasn't puking every fifteen minutes, he was going to tell Dana that.

At least it wasn't morning sickness. She couldn't blame him for this.

Of course, in a few months they'd be adding someone *else* to love and worry about. Someone else who would get sick from time to time. Someone else who would have to deal with hurt feelings and who would have questions about step-parents and half-siblings and ghosts and funerals. His heart thumped hard against his ribs at that, though. Someone *else* he would be responsible for, who would need him, who would make him act on pure emotion and do and say things that he never would otherwise.

He shouldn't have started shit with Tiffany. Okay, he knew that. But he also wasn't really sorry.

Was he better at green slime and ghost stories? Sure. But three months ago, he had no idea about the sheer number of barrette options that existed in the world. He'd learn the rest of this too. Or at least his kids would grow up knowing that he was doing his best and it was all out of love.

His kids. His heart flipped again at that. He hadn't labeled everything or thought about how others would define their relationships until Jada and Tiffany. But now...well, everything he'd said to Dana was true. Chloe and Grace were his in his heart, and he wanted it to be official and for the world to know. Not because he needed the attention or needed to officially be the fun dad or because he needed to be better at something than the other dads

—and moms—but because he wanted *everyone* to know that they all belonged together.

And yeah, okay, he'd been looking for something to be really *good* at besides bartending, and being the number one dance dad had felt like a pretty good option.

He ran his hand over his face again. This was all crazy.

Rolling to his side, he debated turning on the TV, going upstairs to check on everyone again, or just closing his eyes. He was just reaching for the remote when he heard a faint thump behind the couch. He paused. There was a rustle and he stifled a groan. Okay, he needed more bleach water and his rubber gloves.

But it was Chloe who came crawling on all fours around corner of the end table.

She was clearly trying to be quiet and go undetected. He wondered if she hadn't realized he was down here. He closed his eyes, watching her through just a slit in his eyelids. She glanced at him and then very carefully got to her feet. She reached for something on the end table, and Logan was startled to see her picking up the globe that Chad had given the girls. The one that Grace insisted moved each night. Chloe took the globe to the other end table and set it down where Grace would find it in the morning, supposedly moved by their father's ghost to let them know he was there with them.

Logan felt his throat tighten. It wasn't Grace moving the globe each night as Dana suspected. It was Chloe.

God, he loved these girls.

He lay still, watching her. She was staring at the globe. She reached out and gave it a little push, making it spin. She watched the countries and oceans slowly rotate.

Logan took a deep breath and stretched a little on the couch, pretending that he was waking up so as not to scare Chloe. But he wanted to talk to her. He cleared his throat and slowly opened his eyes. Chloe was watching him.

"Hey, honey," he said, giving her a smile. "Whatcha doing?"

She hesitated, clearly weighing what she should tell him.

"You feeling okay?" he asked, pushing himself up onto one elbow. "Your stomach okay?"

She nodded. "Yeah, I'm okay."

"Did you need something?" he asked. She didn't have to tell him about the globe. He'd keep her secret. But he kind of hoped she would.

Chloe looked at the globe and then back to him. "I came down to move the globe."

He looked at it too. The rotations had just stopped. "Oh."

She took a deep breath. "I'm the one that moves it every night," she said. "For Grace. I know she likes thinking Dad does it."

Logan nodded, his chest feeling tight. "That's nice."

She nodded, looking back to the globe. "Do you think maybe now she won't need the globe?"

Logan pushed himself up to sitting, his heart thundering. "What do you mean?"

"Now that you're here," she said. "Now that you're here, maybe she won't need to think Daddy's here."

Damn. See? This wasn't fun and silly stuff. This was not unicorn poop or ladybug barrettes. "I don't know," he said honestly. Because that's all he could do, really. He wanted to be honest with the girls. "For one thing," he went on. "I don't know that it's true that your dad's not here."

Chloe gave him a *yeah, right* look, but he shrugged. "I've been reading and hearing a lot about ghosts lately," he said with a little grin. "And I don't think it's crazy to think that he might be hanging around and checking on you."

And Logan hoped like hell that didn't freak Chloe out. Not all little girls thought this stuff was cool the way Grace did.

"But he'd be hanging around to be sure we're okay," Chloe said.

"Right."

"And if you're here, then we are okay and he doesn't have to do that. He can go to heaven."

Logan felt like she'd just punched him in the chest. Wow. He cleared his throat. "You don't think he's in heaven?"

"Not if he's still *here*, right?"

He took a breath. "Well, I don't know everything about it, but some people think that spirits can move back and forth."

She wrinkled her forehead, but then nodded. "Okay."

"Come here." He reached a hand out and she took it, letting him tug her up onto the cushion beside him. He put an arm around her. "Here's what I *do* know—when someone loves you, that doesn't stop just because they're not around all the time. And even if he thinks I'm here to take care of you, which is really nice and I absolutely promise that I'm going to do that, he might still want to visit so he can just see you."

She nodded again. "Okay." Then she looked up at him. "But he's not moving the globe."

"I know."

"Maybe I should stop moving it." She seemed deep in thought about that. "Maybe Grace will be okay."

Grace would absolutely be okay. Logan would make sure of it. Though he did need to convince Dana that she needed to let him stick around, even for the hard stuff. "You know what I think?" he told Chloe. "I think that you know the best way to handle this."

Her eyes were round when she looked up at him again. "I do?"

"I do. You love her. You know her. And anything you do will be because you want her to be happy and feel safe. So however you decide to handle it will be right." That was exactly what he wanted from Dana. The trust to maybe not do things exactly the way she would or even get it exactly right, but to do it with the right intentions and because he loved them.

"Okay," Chloe finally said. "I'll think about it."

He gave her a little squeeze. "Great. And if you want to talk about it, or anything, I'm right here."

She gave him a big smile. "I know."

And she couldn't have said anything that would have mattered more.

———

After Chloe went back to bed, Logan checked on Grace and Dana, but they were both passed out. Everything seemed quiet for the moment, so he returned to the couch and lay back, closing his eyes just until they needed him again.

A few minutes later, he awoke to the sound of soft knocking on the front door.

He sat up, blinking at the sunlight streaming in the front windows. Sun? He glanced at the clock and found that it was just before seven a.m. He'd been asleep for over six hours.

He pushed up quickly, heading for the steps to check on everyone, but the soft knocking stopped him. Right. Front door. Someone was here.

Frowning, he strode to the door, unlocked it, and pulled it open.

Lindsey was standing on the other side.

"Hi." She gave him a smile.

"Um, hi." He scratched his chest. He was not fully awake. "What's up?"

"I brought some supplies." She lifted her hands. In one was a grocery bag and in the other was a casserole dish.

Logan rubbed a hand over his face. He had more than a day's growth of beard, he was in the same clothes from yesterday, and he was sure his hair looked like he'd just spent the night on a couch. "Supplies?" he finally repeated.

"More Gatorade, some ginger ale, crackers, Jell-O, and soup. And this is chicken and dumplings. More for you, but once their stomachs settle, they might be able to handle it. Very starchy and not too spicy."

Everything sunk in and Logan sighed, bracing a hand on the doorjamb. "She called you."

"Yeah."

"Even though I was here."

Lindsey looked slightly apologetic about that. "Yeah."

"Dammit," he muttered.

"In her defense, she knew you'd need all of these supplies and knew that I could easily run them over."

"That's ridiculous and you know it," he said. "I'm right *here*."

Lindsey nodded. "But we talk every morning before work. It's just our routine. So—" She handed him the stuff in her hands. "Here you go. Take the help."

He took the bag and the casserole. "You know I can't let you in. I have to be the one here for her for this."

Lindsey smiled. "Good."

"Yeah?"

"Of course."

Of course. Okay, that had been easier than he'd expected. "Can I ask you something?" This was Dana's best friend. A fellow single mom. She knew things.

"Sure."

"She said something last night about me being the fun one and the girls liking me best. Do you think she really feels that way?" That had never been his intention. Not really. Yes, he liked being the life of the party, the fun uncle, the one that could make any girl laugh and blush, the owner of one of the most fun bars in the Quarter... Logan's thoughts trailed off. Okay, maybe he had been going for being the most fun person in Grace and Chloe's life. Because he'd wanted to be important to them and fun was what he did best. But now he was starting to think maybe he had more to offer. He could handle ghosts and hair emergencies and puke.

Lindsey seemed to be considering his question, and he appreciated that she was taking him seriously. "Well, let me ask you this," she finally said. "When you think of your childhood, what stands out?"

"What do you mean?"

"Without really thinking hard about it, when I say, 'what do you remember from when you were a kid?' what comes to mind?"

"Okay." Logan just let the word *childhood* go through his head. "Blanket forts with my brother. Playing baseball. Fishing and swimming in the summer. Parades. Going for waffles at the Camellia Grill on Saturday morning."

Lindsey nodded. "Exactly. You don't think about the times that your laundry was done or the lunches that were packed for you to take fishing or the homemade creams she concocted to put on the sunburn you got playing baseball."

Logan swallowed. "I only remember the fun."

"All kids do. And that's how it should be. Dana knows that. So she makes sure that everything else happens."

"She never has fun with the girls? I don't believe that."

"Sure. But while she's having fun she also has to think about when it's time to wrap up for dinner or bedtime. She has to think about the cleanup of the fun. Or the consequences of the fun— how much is it going to cost, how tired will the girls be tomorrow, what is not getting done while they're having fun. And she has to organize and plan the fun. It's never *just* fun."

"When Chad was home, did he help with all of that?"

Lindsey shook her head. "Chad was always here temporarily. Dana made sure that it was fun for him too. She made the plans and dealt with cleanup. And after he died, it reinforced the importance of making all of that happen even more. She's so glad the girls only have good memories of their dad."

Logan sighed. "I knew that she worried that Chad wouldn't want to be here if things here were a lot of work or not fun, but she also made it fun while he was here so the girls would really love having him here."

Lindsey smiled. "Yeah. The girls were little and he was gone so much that she worried that they wouldn't warm up to him easily when he was home. She really wanted them to look forward to him being home. She just made it all...perfect for all of them."

"While she did all the hard stuff behind the scenes."

"Right. Not that she regrets any of that. I think a lot of it was subconscious, honestly," Lindsey said. "And I think that's why she was drawn to you. You could give the girls all of those good times they were missing."

"And me being fun meant that the girls would warm up to *me* and would make it easier for me to be around once the baby is here."

"Yep."

He sighed. "So I do need to pull back, quit being intense about being more involved."

Lindsey clearly didn't agree with that. She tipped her head. "As my best friend in the world, you know what *I* wish for her?"

"What?"

"That she would get to be Chad once in a while. That she could just enjoy. That she wouldn't have to think of all that other stuff."

Logan studied Lindsey. "She's never done that?"

"Never. Because there's no one that knows as well as she does all the things that need to happen behind the scenes and on the side of the fun. Not even me. My boys aren't involved in dance. And they aren't into ghosts and stuff. You know what I'm saying?"

There was something about the way Lindsey said it that made Logan feel a bubble of hope. "You mean there hasn't been anyone who knows all of that stuff as well as she does...until now."

She gave him a bright smile. "Exactly."

"You're on my side." He said it almost as if to confirm it.

"I am." Lindsey turned and started down the steps, but she paused partway down and turned back. "Of course, I'll have to kill you if you mess this up."

He gave her a single nod. "Of course."

Then she gave him another smile and headed for her car, leaving Logan alone with the Doucet girls.

And a whole new plan.

11

"So he stayed and took care of you for two days, told you he wants to marry you, told you he's in love with you and the girls, and you're still not going to let him come to the dance competition this weekend?"

Dana looked across the support group circle to Gabe. "I don't know what he told you, but—"

"He didn't tell me any of this," Gabe said. "This is the first I'm hearing of it. I knew you and Grace were sick and he changed his shifts around with Josh, but that's all I knew."

Dana frowned. "Well, I can't let him come. The other moms, and dads, are still annoyed and it's easier if he's not in the middle of all of that."

Interestingly, Logan hadn't said a word about the competition. She'd finally mentioned last night that they wouldn't be home until late on Sunday night, kind of hinting that he wouldn't be with them for the weekend. He'd nodded and said he'd be at her house when they got there.

"But you and the girls and Logan talked about how all that really matters is that *you* all know your situation and how everyone feels, right?" Bea asked. "Chloe and Grace are fine with everything?"

Dana nodded. "They still think we're going to have a wedding coming up, but they are fine knowing that Logan is there for them no matter what their last name is and that they will still be big sisters and all of that."

She'd meant it when she said the only people who really needed any explanations about their situation were the girls and their friends and family. She really didn't care what Tiffany and others like her thought. But something still niggled in the back of her mind. It mattered to Logan. Not because he didn't know their situation, but because he liked the idea of everyone knowing they belonged together. That was sweet. But calming the gossips wasn't a reason to get married.

Still, the thought of leaving it all as is bothered her because of what he'd said in her kitchen the other night. He didn't feel legit.

"Are you going to have a wedding?" Lindsey asked.

Dana looked at her in surprise. Lindsey hadn't asked her anything about Logan at all. She hadn't asked how things were going, if he was still at her house after practically moving in for the two days she and Grace had been sick, if he was still pissed about the dance team. Nothing. She'd dropped off supplies but hadn't stayed. Of course, Dana had been passed out in bed and wouldn't have been much of a conversationalist. But she was surprised that her friend was asking her questions in front of the group rather than privately.

"I don't know," Dana told her. "I know it's controversial for people to have babies together and not get married, but I think the important thing is that he's around to bond with the baby and help out. Getting married is...more than that."

Lindsey nodded. "But he seems to be ready for more."

He did, kind of. But he hadn't asked her about more since that night in her kitchen. "He's brand new to all of this. He's still learning. We're still figuring out how to do this together."

"Your girls love him."

Dana widened her eyes. Lindsey was arguing with her on this? "Of course they do. They're girls. All girls love Logan."

Lindsey rolled her eyes. Dana gaped at her. Lindsey had *rolled her eyes* at her? "Your girls love Logan because he's awesome with them and because he loves them."

Dana frowned. "I know."

"And he's great with *you*."

"What are you talking about?"

"I mean, he doesn't really let you boss him around and just take charge. And he thinks you're awesome. And he sees stuff like when you're trying to protect him from things he doesn't need protection from. He doesn't let you push him away."

Except he had. He hadn't insisted on going to the competition. He hadn't *insisted* on getting married. He hadn't insisted that he loved her. Dana swallowed hard. That was what was bothering her the most. "Ever since I told him that he was making things messy, and threw up on him, he hasn't said anything about coming to the competition. Or about us getting married. He's been just doing the fun stuff he was doing before. He hasn't made any waves or...insisted on anything."

"Isn't that what you wanted?" Gabe asked. He sounded annoyed.

Dana looked at him. "I thought I did," she admitted. "I thought I wanted things to be easy and have him just do the basic stuff that would make things...easier on me. But..." She hesitated. But this was her support group. Okay, one of them was the brother to the man who was making her question everything. But she needed advice. This was where she came for that. She wet her lips. "I've gotten to know him," she said. "And I've realized that whether by charm or persistence or a crazy combination of both, when he *really* wants something, he goes after it. And usually gets it. He's...passionate. And verbal about his feelings. No one wonders how Logan feels or thinks about things, right?"

She looked around the circle and noted all of the nodding. Then she focused on Gabe again. "Well, I don't know how he feels about me."

Gabe opened his mouth but she held up a hand.

"And I would. If he *really* felt something for me, I would know it. Everyone would. When he found out we were having a baby, he immediately threw a party. He brought you and your mom and Addison and the kids to my house the very first night. He dove into the world of ghosts for Grace and dance for Chloe. Hell, even if he has a favorite *song* everyone knows it. He wants the world to know that he loves my girls. He...isn't shy about his feelings."

Gabe didn't try to speak again. But he nodded his agreement.

She drew a shaky breath. It was all true and she'd been thinking about it for days, but it was more official now that it was out loud. She knew Logan cared about her. She knew he'd be there for her. He'd not only proven that, but he did what he said he'd do. She'd seen that over and over. And she knew he'd love the baby. If he could fall for two little girls who weren't his biologically and that he'd really only known for a couple of months, then he would be head over heels for his own from day one.

"So, I mean, things with the baby are going to be great. Logan's going to be an amazing father. And that's the most important thing. But..." She swallowed hard and shrugged. "I guess I was just thinking that it might be...nice...if he loved me too since, well, *I'm* in love with *him*."

Gabe's eyes widened and Dana heard Addison sniff, but it was Lindsey that spoke.

"Dana," she said gently. "I don't think it's true that he doesn't love you."

"He's never said it. And he says *everything* he's thinking."

Lindsey smiled. "Maybe. Or maybe he says everything he's thinking when he knows exactly what to say."

"What do you mean?"

"All of the situations you mentioned before—with his friends and his family and the girls—he knows exactly where he stands. Your little girls were *so* ready to be loved. And they wear their hearts on their sleeves. Ghosts and dance and green slime and barrettes...those are all obvious things they need that he can provide. Things he could dive into. What Chloe and Grace need from him is obvious. But you...you don't really need him at all. He doesn't know *how* to love you. But I think it's obvious that he dove right into what's important to you. Your passion isn't ghosts or dance...it's Chloe and Grace. And he went all-in there."

Dana felt her heart clench. "I didn't..." She swallowed. "I don't know how I need to be loved either." Because no one had ever been there, full-time, through it all, to love her up close and personal. She'd always known that Chad loved her. But theirs wasn't an everyday, face-to-face thing.

Lindsey reached out and took her hand. "I know that you think Logan is all about saying whatever he's thinking and feeling."

Dana heard Gabe actually chuckle at that.

"But," Lindsey went on. "Maybe he's trying to show you the way *you* show...everyone."

"What do you mean?"

"You *show* us how you feel about us. You *do* stuff for us. You take care of us. You give us stuff. And you support us."

Dana stared at her. "I do that?"

Lindsey laughed. "You do."

"Absolutely," Bea said.

Dana thought about all of the care packages and videos she'd sent Chad. How she'd planned for everything to go a certain way when he was home. How she *did* things to make things easier on him. "I guess I do."

"You definitely do."

She looked up at the deeper voice and met Gabe's eyes. "Yeah?"

"Yeah. So if he's trying to *do* things for you, maybe you need to *say* things for him."

Dana felt a little twirl of excitement go through her. Yeah, maybe she did. But she couldn't just *tell* him how she felt. This was Logan, after all. It had to be bigger and louder and better than anything else.

Surely she could come up with something like that.

Maybe.

———

The guys had come through. Dana let herself into the house an hour later.

"Hey, girls!" she called.

"Mommy!" Grace came running with Chloe right behind her. "Caroline came to see us!"

Dana dropped her purse on the table inside the door, smiling at her girls' enthusiasm. "She did?" The only Caroline they knew was Logan's mom. "How come?"

"She brought us stuff!" Grace said.

"She brought *me* stuff," Chloe corrected.

Grace crossed her arms. "I can have some too. She said so."

"But they're for *me* and the team."

"What is for you and the team?" Dana asked.

"The *stuff*!" Grace grabbed her hand and started tugging her down the hallway to the kitchen.

Kylie, the sitter for the night since Logan was working, looked up from where she was doing homework at the kitchen table. Clearly Chloe had been doing her math and Grace had been coloring. "Hi, Dana."

"Hi. How is everything?"

"Great." She closed her book and recapped her pen. "We got Chloe's homework done, their rooms are picked up, and everything is ready for tomorrow. Though," she added, sliding her book into her backpack, "I can't claim credit for that." She shot Dana a smile.

There was a huge tray of cookies sitting on the center island and Dana moved closer, noting that they were decorated like dance shoes. Some were shoes like Chloe and her team wore—black with hot-pink laces—while others were pretty pink ballet slippers, some were tap shoes, and some were even flamenco shoes. They were adorable. Dana picked one up to examine it closer and had to chuckle. They were made out of Nutter Butters. "What's ready for tomorrow?" Dana asked.

"Everything," Kylie said. "Caroline brought the cookies over and Logan got everything packed and a lot of it loaded in your car."

Dana frowned, forgetting the Nutter Butters for a moment. "*Logan* got everything packed? What's everything?"

"Everything, Mom," Chloe said. "He helped us pack our clothes and we've got treats and all my costumes and shoes and stuff. The only thing he didn't put in the car are the cookies because they'd melt and the stuff for the cooler. But it's all ready to go."

Dana set the cookie back down. "Were you supposed to tell me that you needed a bunch of cookies for the team?" she asked Chloe.

Chloe gave her a cute little grimace. "Yeah. I forgot."

"So Caroline did it."

"Yeah. And she said she loved it," Chloe assured her.

"And Logan got everything packed?" Dana asked.

"He even got me gummy ghosts!" Grace told her, bouncing on her toes.

Dana gave her youngest a smile. Of course he had.

"Yep, he did everything." Kylie rose from the chair, slinging her backpack over one shoulder. "And he said that it would make you nervous, so he used this checklist and said to give it to you so you knew what was packed and where it all was." She handed Dana five pages of paper.

The top said *Checklist* and each page was for a different bag. There was a bag for Grace, a bag for Chloe, another bag for Chloe with all of her dance stuff, and a bag for Dana. Her eyes widened as she read down the list of things he'd packed for her. One line read *unsexy underwear (don't need the sexy ones if I'm not around)* and another read *Laughing Lavender body spray (because you always smell amazing but the Sunshine Shenanigans is my favorite and I don't want anyone else smelling that)*. She laughed, even as she shook her head. He'd packed for her. Even her body spray. And with some real thought put into it. He'd managed to be sexy and sweet even as he was packing her underwear. And he'd included her curling iron and even little things like Band-Aids, antacids, and her prenatal vitamins. She was impressed.

The fifth page was a list of snacks and extra supplies like *scissors (just in case)*, *super glue (you never know)*, and the CDs that he'd made for each girl with their pump-up music on them.

"So..." Feeling a little flummoxed, Dana looked up. "I guess I don't need to pack tonight."

Kylie grinned at her. "Nope. And the girls are fed and homework is done. I guess you have the rest of the night off."

Dana thought about that as she paid Kylie and walked her to the door. At the support group they'd told her that she showed her love by *doing* things. And now, on the receiving end of someone doing something for her—something big that would have taken her a lot of time and energy—she had to admit that it did make her feel taken care of. She liked that. She liked knowing that the people she cared about understood that she was loving them when she organized and planned and *did*.

But this someone wasn't just anyone. This was Logan. And he'd not only shown an impressive knowledge of what needed to be done and planned for the weekend, but he'd...done it. Without fanfare. Without telling her. Without bringing in a whole army to do it. He'd enlisted his mom's help, but that was right up Caroline's alley. The rest of this, though, wasn't Logan's usual. He was the guy who threw parties and was loud and boisterous about everything.

Tonight, he'd packed pajamas and antacids.

She really didn't have anything to do. She'd caught up on her work at the office since she was going to be out tomorrow. She'd planned the evening for packing and organizing so she really did have free time now.

Back in the kitchen, the girls were sampling Caroline's cookies. "These are really cute," Dana said.

Chloe grinned around her bite. "I know! I thought she would just do regular round cookies. But these are so cool!"

"And look! Black teeth!" Grace bared her teeth, showing the black frosting coating them.

Dana laughed. "Cool." And made a note to not let the girls eat those cookies before they performed.

"And Logan gave me a special CD," Chloe said. She wiped her hands on her shorts and hopped from the stool to the floor. She ran to the table and grabbed a square plastic CD case. She held it up. "Everyone gets one, but he made mine special. He *talks* on the beginning of it. And look!" She pointed to the label Logan had stuck on the front. "It says You Rock! Get it?" Chloe asked with a grin. "Rock? Because the music is rock music."

Dana nodded. "Yep, I get it. That's really creative."

And suddenly she had an idea. She had free time. She didn't have to plan or pack or *do* anything. Maybe she and the girls could just...have some fun.

"You girls want to help me with something tonight?" she asked.

"Sure!" Grace told her.

"Like what?" Chloe asked.

"What if we got...or *made*...some stuff to go with those CDs for everyone?" she asked.

ERIN NICHOLAS

"What would we make?" But Chloe was definitely interested.

"What about something with glitter?" Dana asked. She was thinking back to the leprechaun poop that Logan had made for Chloe's class party. "And we could say 'Show everyone your SPARKLE this weekend'. We could make...dance slime! We can make it bright pink like your dresses and add glitter to it and it will be like good luck slime."

Chloe's eyes were wide. "Really? That sounds really cool!"

"I want to help!" Grace announced.

"Okay, let's do it." Dana grabbed her laptop from the foyer and brought it back to the table. They looked up recipes for slime and stumbled upon a video for making homemade stress balls with balloons and slime. "We could get clear balloons and fill them with glittery pink slime," Dana said. "And the girls could have them backstage and use them to not get nervous before you go on."

"Yes," Chloe breathed, looking at the final product on the screen. "Let's do that."

"I want one too!" Grace said, bouncing on Dana's lap.

"Me too," Dana told her.

They headed to the hobby store and were home and mixing slime within the hour. Dana had also grabbed some little jars and bubble wands for the homemade bubble solution she'd decided to add to the gift.

After the stress balls and jars of bubbles were finished and sitting in a box, ready to be packed up the next day, Dana sat at the table, filling out the tags.

At the bottom she wrote, *Love, Chloe, Grace, Dana.* And she only hesitated a moment before adding *and Logan.*

12

———————

"**O**kay, time to go. We've met our quota of jackasses tonight."

"Hey, man, what's your problem?"

Logan sighed. "You. And your stupid friends."

"We're here for Tank's birthday," the drunk, who had just led his friends in a raucous version of "Happy Birthday," said.

"No, shit," Logan said drily.

"That's why we're *here*, man," the drunk said. "We came here last year for his birthday and he said it was the best bar in New Orleans."

"That's because this *is* the best bar in New Orleans," Logan told him, taking his arm and steering him toward the door. "And that's, in part, because we don't let guys in who've had too many daiquiris on Bourbon. Daiquiris make douchebags." That was true. The too-fruity drinks that could be purchased in pretty much every establishment on Bourbon Street were for tourists, particularly bachelorette parties and I'm-50 birthday parties and girls' weekend trips. "Men should not drink daiquiris," Logan told him, nudging him through the French doors and out onto the sidewalk. "At least, they shouldn't drink them before coming in here. When you want a real drink, and think you can handle it without turning into a douche, come back and order a Pimm's Cup or a Sazerac or even just a shot, okay?"

The guy suddenly looked crestfallen. "But we love your bar, man."

"Then don't be a dick when you're inside it," Logan told him.

"Fuck," the guy muttered sadly. "Okay." His friends joined him on the sidewalk.

Logan watched them walk away, fortunately without giving him any more shit. He returned to the bar.

"You know I serve daiquiris at Pete's, right?" Josh asked as Logan joined him behind the bar.

"Yeah, yeah. So you know better than anyone that they're stupid tourist drinks that come from a mix, taste like Kool-Aid, and serve only to get people so fucked up they don't care that the crappy pizza is overpriced."

Josh gave a low whistle. "What the hell is wrong with you tonight?"

"Nothing." Which wasn't even a little bit true. Chloe was performing her solo dance tonight, and the team was competing tomorrow in regionals and had a good shot at nationals. And he was here with these jackasses. He sighed as a guy waved him down from the other end of the bar. "What's up?" he asked.

"This is the wrong bill," the guy said.

Logan took it from him and frowned down at it. What the hell? He never got tabs wrong. How the fuck hard was it to keep track of a few beers and a cocktail or two? "Dammit." He turned to redo the guy's ticket, and his elbow caught a tray of glasses on the edge of the bar. The entire thing crashed to the floor, the sound of glass breaking against the stone, ear-shattering. But not nearly as loud as Logan's bellowed, "Son of a bitch, hell, damn, fuck!"

The entire place went quiet and he looked up to find the room staring at him.

"What?" he snapped. "I'm having a bad night."

Everyone went back to eating and drinking, but the volume of conversation and laughter was definitely muted.

Josh moved in with a broom and dustpan. "Historic moment," he said, sweeping up the broken glass.

"What?"

"You losing your shit. You're usually the laid-back, easygoing, fun guy, right?"

"I'm. Having. A. Bad. Night," Logan said through gritted teeth.

"Why don't you just go to Baton Rouge?" Josh asked, dumping the glass pieces into the garbage.

"You know about Baton Rouge?"

Josh put a hand on his hip. "You've been talking about it for a month."

"I have?"

"And the butterfly barrettes and the tights and the fucking Taylor Swift song they're performing to. Dude, if you weren't my boss, I would have been giving you shit about all of that a long time ago." Josh shook his head. "Butterfly barrettes and tights, man."

Logan ran a hand through his hair. "Well...that's my life now."

Josh nodded. "Yeah. I know. Except that you're *here* and they're in Baton Rouge."

"Yeah."

"You need to go."

His heart thumped against his ribs. "Dana doesn't want me there."

"Bullshit."

Logan swung to his right. Caleb and James, another of the firefighters from Engine 29, were at the bar.

"Bullshit?" Logan asked.

"Dana wants you there. You're just a lot of trouble," Caleb told him.

Logan couldn't really argue with that. "Yeah. But," he said, "I could sit up in the back, where no one would see me."

"You would do that?" Josh asked, clearly disbelieving.

"Sure. I can...stay out of things."

Josh, Caleb, James, and even the guy at the end of the bar who didn't really know Logan, all laughed at that.

Logan scowled. "I can. If I have to. But I want to be there."

"Yeah, well, you should definitely go," Caleb said. "But then you need to propose to Dana."

Logan blew out a breath. "Yeah. I've already done that. She doesn't want to get married."

Josh handed Caleb and James each a beer.

"You've already proposed?" Caleb asked.

"Yeah."

"How did you do it?" Josh asked.

"What do you mean?" Logan asked. "I said, 'Marry me.'" Actually, most recently, he'd said something like *just fucking marry me*. He grimaced.

"That's not a proposal," James said, lifting his beer.

"The fuck if it's not," Logan said. "What do you think a proposal is?"

"A proposal is a big deal," Caleb said. "It's not just 'hey, let's get hitched since I knocked you up.'"

"Or 'marry me so I can be a step dad to your daughters and go to all the dance recitals'," Josh said with an eye roll.

"I didn't—" But Logan frowned. Okay, he'd basically done that. "Dana's not big on making things into a production."

"But *you* are," Caleb said, pointing his beer bottle at Logan. "You're all about big productions."

"I—"

"For sure," Josh said right over the top of Logan's protest. "Everything is a big deal with you."

He wasn't sure *that* was true.

"You need to *propose* to the woman," Caleb said. "Like for real. Something big and something fun and something *you*."

Just then, his phone pinged with a text. He pulled it from his pocket, hoping like hell it was Dana begging him to come to Baton Rouge.

It was from Amy. *These are awesome! The girls love them. Thanks!* The text included a photo. Frowning, Logan slid his fingers over the screen to enlarge it. It was a gift bag. Propped next to the CD he'd made was a jar of clear liquid with a bubble wand next to it and...he squinted, then enlarged the photo again. There was something that looked like a balloon with pink stuff inside. The note lying next to everything said, *You ROCK! Let everyone see your SPARKLE this weekend, while you BLOW the competition away!*

And they were signed, *love, Chloe, Grace, Dana, and Logan.*

He felt his heart turn over in his chest. Dana had made gifts for the dance team. And she'd included him.

Yeah, he needed to propose to her. Right now. He looked up at the guys. "I need to go to Baton Rouge."

"You're going to need glitter." Owen slid up on the stool next to James. "And body glitter and craft glitter are *not* the same thing."

Josh laughed. "He needs glitter to propose?"

"Oh, you're proposing?" Owen asked.

"What did you think he was doing that you suggested the glitter?" Josh asked.

"Doesn't really matter," Owen replied. "Glitter is always a good idea."

"You're right," Logan agreed. "And it turns out, I have a lot of glitter in my life now."

———

An hour and forty-eight minutes later, Logan slipped through the door to the balcony in the darkened auditorium where Chloe would be performing. He'd checked the schedule on the door and he hadn't missed her. He could hardly believe how nervous and excited he was.

He peered over the balcony railing and spotted Dana's head. She was six rows back, right in the middle. His chest ached looking even at the top of her head. God, he loved her. He wanted her. And now that his friends had convinced him that a big, showy proposal was the way to go, he could hardly wait to lay it on her.

He'd stopped by the hotel where everyone was staying, flirted his way into Dana's room, and had done it up right. He'd thought about rose petals and candles, but decided he had to do this right for *them*. So he had four balloon bouquets that said a variety of things from *Thinking of You* to *Congratulations*, a huge stuffed plush crawfish, a jar of Ellie's sweet tea, and he'd spelled out Marry Me on the bedspread with Rice Krispies treats.

If she said no to all of that...

Well, he'd have to keep trying.

Grace was sitting next to her, her little legs kicking as she watched something on Dana's phone. He assumed it was *Zombie Zuzu,* one of her favorite cartoons. The love for her also squeezed his heart. Yeah, Dana had to say yes. He'd do anything. He'd... well, fuck, there wasn't much he could do that she couldn't do for herself, but he'd just...love the hell out of her. That he could absolutely handle. She'd come around. Eventually. Probably.

The little girl who was on stage finished her routine and smiled at the judges, then exited the stage. The judges bent over their scorecards, scribbling. Logan took a seat and leaned back, trying to get comfortable.

But he wasn't comfortable. Not up in the balcony in the shadows. Not when his girls were down there.

He wondered if Chloe was nervous. And if she'd giggled at the addition of Justin Timberlake's "Can't Stop This Feeling" to her pump-up song CD. He hadn't put it on anyone else's because no one on the team had requested it, but he'd put it on Chloe's because he'd sung it—and danced to it—for her in the kitchen one night. Then he'd showed her the video that had just regular people dancing in all kinds of places. And it was JT. And Logan rocked that song. Even though everyone was cool when they were singing and dancing to JT. At least, that's what he'd told her.

And was Grace bored? Sure, she had *Zombie Zuzu*, but that wasn't really her favorite. He thought maybe he should get her into old episodes of *Scooby Doo*. Though the ghosts were never real in that show and she'd probably roll her eyes.

And, of course, he wondered how Dana was. Was she nervous about Chloe too? Was she wondering about him? How did she feel about *Scooby Doo*? Was she—

"Excuse me, everyone."

Logan's head snapped up and he looked to the stage. He'd been lost in thought and hadn't seen Dana get up and go to the stage. But that was the woman he was in love with, standing center stage, in the spotlight, holding a microphone.

All of which was so out of character, it took him a second to process it.

When he did, he sat forward, his heart thumping hard in his chest. He didn't know why, but something was up if Dana was calling attention to herself like this.

"Hi," she said, as the crowd quieted and gave her their attention. "My name is Dana Doucet and my daughter is performing here tonight. And she'll be out here in just a minute." She glanced toward the wings and smiled.

Logan assumed Chloe was standing there, waiting to go on.

"But I was hoping you wouldn't mind if I take just a few minutes of your time first."

There was a little bit of whispering in response, but no one asked her to get off the stage.

She smiled. "This won't take long," she said. "But I have a very important question to ask someone who's here in the audience tonight."

Logan felt surprise ripple through him. He leaned in as if to get closer to her.

Dana gripped the microphone with both hands, and Logan knew that she was trembling. She didn't do spotlights. So this was...big. Whatever it was. But he was starting to feel a bit of anticipation in his gut.

"Logan, I know you're here," she said.

That ball of anticipation grew.

"Of course you're here. That's where you always are when it comes to us. Your girls."

The ball of anticipation blossomed into hope and moved up to his chest.

"And I know that it's probably killing you a little bit to not be down here front and center, or backstage getting everything together. But you're here anyway. In the back in the shadows. Because you're not really here as a dance dad tonight. You're just here as...a dad."

Her voice was a little wobbly at the end, and Logan felt his throat tighten. And he had to actually blink hard against the sudden stinging in his eyes.

"And that's exactly how it should be," Dana went on. "It's what you're good at. You do make things fun and light and easy. But you also solve problems. And you make us feel secure. And you make us feel protected. And loved. But there's something else that you're really good at—" She paused and swallowed hard. "Something that you're the best at," she added quietly. "You see me. You see me in a way no one else does. And when you see me that way —as capable and loving and good and amazing—you make me see it too. And if you never do another dish or another homework project or change a single diaper, you have already done so much for me, you've become so important to me, that I can't imagine not having you in my life. Not because you're helpful, but because...you love me." She took a deep breath. "And I love you. I'm *in* love with you."

A ripple of noise went through the audience as people reacted.

"So..." She grinned and motioned to the audience.

Well, to Grace.

Logan couldn't breathe. He couldn't blink. He couldn't swallow.

The most beautiful woman in the entire world, a woman who didn't need him at all, who could handle *his* life with one hand tied behind her back and blindfolded, had just told him she loved him. On stage, in front of an auditorium of people, with a microphone.

Logan watched, stunned, as Grace ran up the aisle, holding a big white square in her hands, to join her mom on stage. Chloe came out of the wings and she took the other end of the white square and they held it up together

It said *Can we have your last name? Please?*

In huge, pink, glittery letters.

Logan wasn't able to blink the tears away this time. He dashed them off his lashes with the back of his hand. Then vaulted out of his seat.

"Yes! Hell yes!" he shouted down.

His girls spotted him in the balcony and they laughed. Grace started bouncing up and down. "Yay! Logan's my dad now!"

Chloe just shook her head at Grace, but she was grinning.

Dana was crying. But smiling.

He ran down the stairs from the balcony, and by the time he got to the main auditorium, they were coming up the center aisle toward him. They met in the middle. He took Dana's face in his hands, staring into her eyes. "You proposed to me," he said in awe.

Her eyes were still watery. "I did. Big and unexpected and fun...just like you."

"I love you," he said, running his thumbs over her cheeks. "I love you so damned much."

She nodded. "Will you marry me?"

"Tomorrow if you'll let me." Then he kissed her. Hot and hard but not nearly as deeply as he wanted to because he suddenly had a six-year-old and a ten-year-old wrapped around his legs.

Laughing, he let Dana go, but not without giving her a we'll-pick-this-up-later look. Then he scooped the girls up in both arms and hugged them tightly.

"Miss Grace Elizabeth Doucet Trahan," he said, giving her a smacking kiss on her cheek. "And Miss Chloe Diane Doucet Trahan." He kissed her on the top of her head. "I love you both so much."

"We can keep *all* of our names?" Grace asked, her eyes wide.

He nodded and met Dana's eyes again. "Last names help people know who you belong to right?" he asked. "You definitely need to keep all of those names."

Dana's tears fell again with that, but he couldn't reach for her. His arms were full.

Still, he knew that she knew he'd be reaching for her later on tonight...and he was never going to let her go.

He finally set the girls down. "Hey, Chloe," he told her. "You need to get on up there and dance, don't you?" He nodded toward the stage.

She gave him a big grin. "Yes!"

"And I'll be sitting right down here." He pointed at the seats on the main floor.

"Okay!" She turned away and started for the steps to the stage.

"And hey!" he called after her.

She turned back.

He gave her a wink and a grin. "Your hair looks amazing."

———

O*ne year later*
      Dana paced back across the nursery floor. "You know, baby girl, this is getting ridiculous."

But Maisey Trahan wasn't listening to her mother at all. As usual at three a.m. Every night.

"You're seven months old," Dana told her as Maisey continued to fuss. "You're going to have to either figure out how to sleep through the night, or you're going to have to tolerate me in here every once in a while." She patted the baby's back. "I mean, you like me just fine when you're hungry, right? And the swing we got you for the yard? Totally my idea. He thought you were too young." She turned and started back across the floor. "Also, I'm not going to make you dance. He'll want you to, but if you'd rather play soccer or something, I'm in." She patted and bounced and paced. "But I'm sorry to say that he will keep on insisting on those headbands and barrettes." Dana ran her hand over her daughter's head, smiling at the baby's relative baldness, even at seven months. The baldness that was making her daddy a little crazy.

But Maisey wasn't mad about not having a lot of hair. Nor was she mad about future dance classes. She was flat-out mad because it wasn't Logan in here with her.

"My turn yet?"

Dana turned.

Logan was in the doorway, his shoulder propped against the frame. He wore only pajama bottoms and they sat low on his hips, and Dana felt a stirring of heat even as she held their fussing baby girl.

She sighed. "One of these nights she's going to let me settle her down." It was the same every time. They took turns getting up in the middle of the night with the baby, but since she'd been born, Logan was the only one she wanted at that time of night.

He grinned. "Maybe." He pushed away from the door and

stepped into the room. "She likes you just fine at three in the afternoon."

Dana surrendered Maisy into his arms. "Yeah. What is it about this middle of the night thing that she'll only settle for you?"

He put Maisy up against his shoulder, patting her back and cooing to her. She immediately started to quiet. He looked at Dana. "I always do my best work when the sun's down, babe."

She laughed. He didn't even mean that sexually. He definitely was a night owl. The fact that his family business was a tavern had worked out perfectly for him.

"Well," she said, tipping her head and studying her amazing husband with the little girl who had stolen another piece of her heart, "I sure hope the next one is a mama's boy."

Chloe and Grace loved her, of course, but Logan was very popular with *all* of the Doucet Trahan girls. A little boy who thought she hung the moon would be okay.

"You just let me know when you're ready to work on that," Logan said, giving her a hot look.

She laughed. She'd kind of planned on telling him the news tonight when he came into the nursery anyway, and now it seemed like the perfect time. "Well, we all have about eight and a half months to get ready for that." She started for the nursery door, wondering how long that would take to sink in.

"Babe?" Logan asked.

She turned back. "Yeah?"

"You want to try to get pregnant again in eight and a half months?"

But she could tell that he already knew what she'd meant. "No."

"No?" His eyes widened and then his grin widened. "You're pregnant again? Already?"

She shrugged. "Well, what did you expect when you hooked up with the most fertile woman in Louisiana?"

Then she blew him a kiss, gave her now-perfectly-content baby girl a loving look, and headed back to bed. She needed her sleep. After all, she had to decorate one hundred Nutter Butters in the morning. As tombstones and ghosts. And no, it wasn't Halloween. They were just for an everyday snack-time. In Grace's classroom.

Dana smiled as she made her way downstairs on her nightly detour through the dark house. She couldn't wait to see what kind of Nutter Butters and what color of slime Maisey was into. And if they'd have another dancer, or a pianist, or basketball player. She put her hand over her stomach. Or maybe all of the above, she thought, as she moved the globe from one end table to the other.

––––––

Thank you so much for reading Logan and Dana's story! I hope you loved Taking It Easy!

There is so much more coming from the
Boys of the Big Easy!

Coming up next, you can grab the Christmas novella, **Eggnog Makes Her Easy!**

Lindsey is expecting to spend Christmas with her sons alone while her husband Matt is serving his country overseas. But Santa has a surprise for her at the Christmas party...and he's going to make the most of her love for eggnog and mistletoe!

And don't miss the FREE prequel novella, **Easy Going**, and book one, Going Down Easy!
Find it all at
ErinNicholas.com

Book three, **Nice and Easy**, is coming early 2019!

———

**Read on for an excerpt from
Easy Going, the FREE series prequel!**

EXCERPT FROM EASY GOING

A sexy, New Orleans bartender.
A little jazz. A few beignets.
And ONE very hot weekend.

Just one.

Supposedly.

———

"Delicious" – Goodreads review ★ ★ ★ ★ ★

"Oh my stars, that was hot!" –Goodreads review ★ ★ ★ ★ ★

"Super sexy, but sweet, too...as well as a bit surprising." –
Goodreads review ★ ★ ★ ★ ★

———

Excerpt

"What can I get you?" Then he glanced at Addison. "And please don't say a hurricane." He gave her a wink.

She smiled. "You don't know how to make a hurricane?"

He chuckled. "You can't get your liquor license in New Orleans without proving you know how to make a hurricane." The drink had been invented at one of the most famous bars in the Quarter, Pat O'Brien's, and they served them by the gallons over there. But they didn't make the best ones. Several places served them and a few even did it pretty well. Pierre Maspero's, for instance. But no one could touch the recipe Ellie Landry used at her tiny dive bar just outside the bayou town of Autre, Louisiana.

So Gabe didn't even try.

"If you want a hurricane, I'll take you to the best place for them in Louisiana," he said. Though why he'd said "take you" instead of "send you," he wasn't sure. "Just like if you want gumbo, I won't serve it to you, because if you're gonna eat gumbo, you're gonna do it right and that means havin' my grandma's. Now," he said, taking out a glass and filling it part-way with lemonade. "If you want a Pimm's cup that will make you wonder how you ever drank anything else, or seafood pot pie that you'll dream about, or brown butter pecan pie that you'll want to roll around in, then you've come to the right place."

Addison looked at Elena with wide eyes. "Brown butter pecan pie?"

Elena laughed. "Yeah. And it's that good. It's how Gabe and Logan get all the ladies."

Addison looked back at Gabe. She lifted a brow. "Which one are you?"

"Gabe." He pointed behind her. "That's my brother Logan."

Addison glanced over to where Logan was setting plates of food down in front of customers. She looked back. "You both need pie to get ladies?"

"No one said *need*," he told her with a grin.

"What do you know about pralines?"

"I can make you a praline milkshake that will make you want to propose to me," he told her honestly.

"Huh. What's in that?"

Playful. That was exactly his impression of her from the texts, and he couldn't begin to describe how amazing it was to find out she was the same in person. "Whiskey, caramel, ice cream and—"

"Say no more," she said. "I want that."

"You got a ring in your pocket?" he asked.

She laughed. "Maybe we New York girls are harder to impress than the girls you've been feeding whiskey to."

Grab Easy Going right now!

CPSIA information can be obtained
at www.ICGtesting.com
Printed in the USA
LVHW030413180322
713694LV00005B/925

9 780999 890738